PRAISE FOR THE CELTIC WOLVES NOVELS

Summer Moon

“No sophomore slump here! DeLima clearly demonstrates the outstanding storytelling ability that is making her an author to watch . . . A rich and multilayered story with an action-packed edge!”
—*RT Book Reviews* (top pick)

“Rich mythology, gripping characters and captivating storytelling . . . *Summer Moon* is proof that Jan DeLima’s writing debut was no fluke—there’s a new werewolf queen in town!”
—*Rabid Reads*

“A fun shifter story that you won’t want to put down!”
—*Open Book Society*

Celtic Moon

“A haunting tale, a page-turner woven with skill and care. DeLima is a delicious new voice.”
—Yasmine Galenorn, *New York Times* bestselling author of *Flight from Death*

“DeLima’s debut is a romantic, suspenseful and rich story about survival and loyalty to those who matter most.” —*Booklist*

“*Celtic Moon* has a great werewolf world . . . A fun start to a new paranormal series.” —USATODAY.com

“A welcome addition to the paranormal romance world arrives with this terrific debut novel.” —*RT Book Reviews*

“Original and compelling . . . a shifter story that stands out from the crowd!”
—*GraveTells*

“An engrossing new series . . . Fans of the ... series by Ilona Andrews or ... t to check this out.” ...*tics*

Ace Books by Jan DeLima

CELTIC MOON
SUMMER MOON
AUTUMN MOON

Autumn Moon

JAN DELIMA

ACE BOOKS, NEW YORK

An imprint of Penguin Random House LLC
375 Hudson Street, New York, New York 10014

AUTUMN MOON

An Ace Book / published by arrangement with the author

For more information, visit penguin.com.

ISBN: 978-0-425-26622-9

PUBLISHING HISTORY
Ace mass-market edition / October 2015

PRINTED IN THE UNITED STATES OF AMERICA

10 9 8 7 6 5 4 3 2 1

Cover illustration by Gordon Crabb; back cover photograph: abstract in forest © Kesipun/Shutterstock.
Cover design by Diana Kolsky.
Interior text design by Kelly Lipovich.
Interior art by Jan DeLima.

For my family

Acknowledgments

As always, I must thank my family, especially my husband and sons, who are affected the most by my writing schedule and support me regardless. Thanks also to Michelle Vega, my editor, for her gentle guidance and insight, and to Grace Morgan, my agent, who has been with me from the beginning of this publishing journey. Also, a special thanks to the art department for my truly exquisite covers, and to everyone involved in bringing my stories to the world. I am beyond grateful!

She hid
A tenth of the gift
So that not all did
The whole garden enclose.

—Taliesin
From *The Mabinogi*
Patrick K. Ford translation

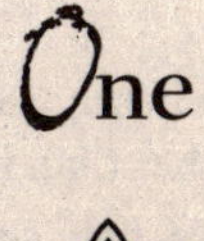

Rhuddin Village, Maine
Present Day

It crept from the forest under a blanket of morning mist. Elen felt its approach like a brush of poison ivy across her skin, smooth to the touch until its toxins seeped in. Clutching the north-facing gate, she stood her ground within the protected walls of her garden. Even so, morning glory vines withered as if kissed by frost.

An unnecessary warning, for she knew who mastered this boastful display. The mist thickened into fog, rolled and shifted and soon took form. Wings emerged to lift a serpentine body off the ground. It was a white dragon made of clouds, conjured by magic, vapors and a powerful sorcerer. If the dragon were made of blood, scales and fire, it would be no more ominous.

Pendaran was flirting.

The apparition flew directly at her, over the grain fields and through her orchards—so close she could almost feel its breath. And as it arched toward the sky in that final moment before impact, soaring mere inches from her head, she lifted her arm and brushed the underbelly of the beast, refusing to cower.

Moisture clung to her hand; water and wind, no more—and nothing insidious other than its conjuror. But it seeped into her bones nonetheless, cold and empty as a winter night without stars. A chuckle echoed from afar, deep, sensuous *and pleased*. The dragon circled twice above her garden and then dissipated—but not without a parting gift.

A letter descended, weaving a path in the charged air to land by her feet. Her name, penned in black ink, bled into the moistened parchment.

Moments passed, and Elen continued to wait, making sure the apparition didn't return. The sky turned hues of lavender and pink as the dawn chased shadows and warmed the earth. But the letter remained as a precarious reminder of the dangerous game she played.

"I need a cup of coffee," Elen muttered to herself for no reason other than to break the silence of a too-quiet morning. Even the forest creatures had fled to the safety of their burrows. The start of this day required something more potent than her usual herbal tea.

In answer, a winter wren flitted from the protective branches of the hawthorn tree to land on the fence entangled with blackened vines. When Elen continued to ignore the letter, the wren issued a sharp impatient twerp.

"It's a summons to Cymru," Elen said without needing to open the envelope. She knew what message it contained, and why Pendaran, the leader of the Guardians and the most dangerous of them all, had chosen that particular form of delivery. Even in modern times, Wales heralded a dragon on its flag, because the beasts of ancient lore had once thrived in their homeland of Cymru. The last one had died in the year AD 331, a few months before Elen was born.

A shimmering disturbance ruffled the air around the auburn-and-white-striped bird.

Elen sighed, in no mood for a lecture but prepared for one as Ms. Hafwen revealed her true form. A woman the size of the wren, with coloring much the same, offered an indignant glare. Ms. Hafwen was a pixie. Elen had not expected an otherworldly creature to be so earthly plain, but as her tutor often stated, beauty came in many forms, and hers was knowledge.

Disappearing into the wilted vines, the pixie emerged wearing a silken navy dress cut low in the back to accommodate translucent dragonfly wings. She had clothing stashed in all corners of the cottage and gardens. Ms. Hafwen put as much value in preparedness as she did in knowledge. Only a trusted few people were allowed to see her true form; the others only saw a winter wren.

"Well," Ms. Hafwen clipped, "open the wretched thing already." Her voice shouldn't carry as it did, but like the song of a wren, *everything* was amplified. "I need you alert for your next lesson, and not muddled with doubts about what that letter contains. Let us deal with it now and move on."

"Fine." As a grown woman, having someone issue her demands had required an adjustment, but the education she'd gained over the summer outweighed any inconveniences to her pride, not to mention her privacy. Elen bent and scooped up the letter. Still, knowing what needed to be done hardly made the process any more agreeable. With dread knotting her stomach, she broke the wax seal. Pendaran's penmanship was bold and efficient, like the man.

Elen,

Be ready this evening when the sun sets on your horizon. Wear the dress I sent you. It is time we had our first dance.

Pendaran

Heart thumping against her chest, Elen crumpled the letter into a ball. She wanted to tear the damn thing but kept her anger in check—to some degree. "He issues a summons under the pretense of a date."

"And what did you expect?" With a soft hum, Ms. Hafwen lifted off her perch and flew back and forth; her version of pacing. "He has been courting you for months, and now he's grown tired of correspondence alone. I am not surprised."

Indeed, Elen had four months' worth of parcels piled in her orchard barn. She didn't allow them within the protected walls of her garden. They had begun arriving after the first of May, when Pendaran had witnessed her abilities firsthand. Following the advice of someone who knew him well, she'd written him polite acknowledgments, as one would a strange uncle who's suddenly shown interest in a banished niece. She'd wanted to return the gifts, but it had been agreed upon by her family that the least insulting response was a better solution to bide more time—until Pendaran made a more intrusive move.

Well, that move had been made. A dragon conjured by clouds demanded more than a generic thank-you card. It required her presence as requested, and if she refused . . .

Elen briefly closed her eyes. If she refused, the war her brothers had been preparing for, along with other rebels who rejected the Guardians' sadistic leadership, would begin again.

"You are not ready for this, Elen."

"No," she wholeheartedly agreed. "I'm not." Bitterness thickened her throat. She was a doctor not a soldier, and she despised violence. But the consequences of not acting might result in the deaths of people she loved, along with weaker members of their race who couldn't call their wolves—like her. And that, she mustn't allow. Not if she could help it, because unlike anyone else of their kind, she could call something much more powerful. Nature begged for her command. And she was learning how to answer its call.

"I'm stronger than I once was." Elen cast her gaze toward the horizon, gaining confidence with her proclamation. Cool nights had painted the forest in rich hues of amber and red as summer's final days came to a brilliant end. Autumn was her favorite time of year, and she inhaled the scent of crisp apples, pumpkins ready to be cut from their vines, and the promise of a bountiful harvest.

It made her smile, and smiles were such precious things, but not nearly as precious as family. "I'm going to Rhuddin Hall." Elen lived a short walk from her brother's home—less, if she took the trail through the woods. "I need to warn Dylan."

Like all women, she kept some secrets close to her heart, but not ones that endangered her brother's territory and the people he protected. Dylan was the alpha and leader of Rhuddin Village—their *Penteulu*, when addressed in their old tongue. He must be informed about this latest development.

"Heal the vines before you go," Ms. Hafwen ordered.

"They will die soon regardless." Elen's garden had a week, if that, before true frost arrived and earth's winter slumber began.

"But that must be nature's doing."

Understanding her tutor's concern, Elen stayed to

complete the task. Nature needed to run its own course, unhindered by enchantment, dark or light. If one interfered, the other must right the imbalance. It was the first lesson Ms. Hafwen had taught her. The second had been how to nurture growth from within, and not steal it from another source. The latter still posed a challenge.

Elen reached for the entangled strands. The vine's energy rose to greet her, sweet as its flower that opened each morning; it was weakened but not dead. As natural as breathing, she stroked it with her senses, like blowing on embers, allowing what was already there to ignite and grow. New leaves emerged as buds unraveled in brilliant cones of blue.

"Now ease its growth slowly," Ms. Hafwen chimed in with a sharp warning. This was when things usually went astray. "Taming nature is like taming a horse. It is temperamental and stubborn, but if steered with a firm yet fair hand, it will honor you with obedience."

"I'm trying," Elen ground out. Control had always been her weakness. Even now, the energy wanted her to stay and feed it. More vines grew, buds began to burst, and that was when Elen received the first bite.

A pixie slap felt a whole lot like a hornet's sting. Truly, one would never know the difference until they'd been stung several times. That had been her third lesson.

Another sting.

"That doesn't help," Elen snapped, and when the third sting bit into her hand—she stung back. It happened instinctively. A random thought to gather a small surge of energy and send it toward the hovering pixie.

Ms. Hafwen tumbled through the air before righting herself. She drifted a moment, and then settled once again on the nearest fence picket, appearing stunned.

Instantly remorseful, Elen rushed over, wincing when

she broke contact with the vine. Even in that brief moment of separation she'd felt its shock—and its yearning for her to return. "I'm sorry, I didn't mean—"

"Bee's knees!" Ms. Hafwen exclaimed. "It is about time." Shaking her wings, the pixie laughed. Not that Elen had ever heard such a sound, but if butterflies were to fly through strings of a harp, it might offer a pale comparison.

She didn't know whether to groan or smile with relief, and ended up doing a bit of both. "You really should stop referencing that dictionary of modern slang. Many of those terms aren't used in regular conversation."

The gateway between Faery and earth had been closed for several centuries, and much had changed during that time. A curious creature, Ms. Hafwen collected a full library, transcribed to her size, to learn modern customs and names. Her interpretations were interesting, if not entertaining.

"I will use the ones I like, and whenever I so choose." Her tone refused argument.

Not that Elen intended to give one. "Did I hurt you?"

"No, but you could have." Ms. Hafwen rarely offered praise, and her slight nod of approval had the same impact as a full applause. "You harnessed the exact amount of energy from the vine to repel me without causing true damage."

"Can the same technique be applied to medicine?" Elen was a healer, and using this power for good was her true objective. The weaker members of their race, the ones who couldn't shift and heal, were the reason she'd learned the medicinal uses of plants, and eventually human healing techniques. It had proven a valuable skill over the years, even if they only came to her when no other option was available. Her connection to nature frightened the villagers. Not that she blamed them. How could she, when it frightened her more?

"You must learn to protect yourself before helping

others." Ms. Hafwen gave an impatient wave. "Selflessness is useless if you're not here to provide aid." She paused in consideration. "I do believe you are ready for more intricate lessons. A gathering circle perhaps. I shall prepare the lesson while you speak with your brother." Then she dismissed Elen with a wave and flew toward her tiny stone cottage, located in the shade garden, where she'd ordered it built upon her arrival six months prior. "Be nice to your Cormack when you visit Rhuddin Hall."

"He isn't *my* Cormack," Elen called after her. "And I'm not the one who isn't being nice." Her brother had offered Cormack a place in his guard. Worse, the man had actually accepted. Cormack had once been her dearest friend, but in the week he'd been home he hadn't spared her a visit, or even a word in passing.

Their estrangement was her fault, but regretting mistakes wouldn't change them, and she had already apologized in pathetic proportions. If Cormack wanted to see her, he knew where she lived. Besides, she had enough to deal with at the moment—because while her friend wanted nothing to do with her, her enemy wanted to dance.

Two

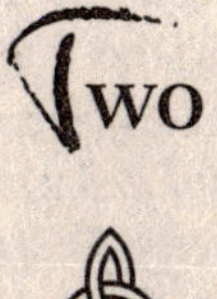

CORMACK WAS TIRED OF THE INCESSANT STARES. HE HAD lived among these people for more than four hundred years as a wolf without notice, but now that he walked as a man they suddenly *saw* him—and for some bloody reason they couldn't seem to look away. It didn't help that his current post at the front gate offered an open view for their inspection. A group of villagers who worked in Rhuddin Hall had gathered along the stone balustrade, looking down on him with unabashed curiosity.

He ignored them all, easy enough to do—except when two of them actually approached through the kitchen gardens with determination in their feminine strides, holding a basket of what smelled like warm bread. They were sisters, Sulwen and Lydia; he knew their names, but he was in no mood for their giggles and flirtations, when they had never offered him even a parting glance before now. Enid, their mother, managed the kitchens of Rhuddin Hall.

Sarah, now the head of Dylan's guard and Cormack's direct supervisor, waved him toward the inner gatehouse, her office of sorts. The enclosed room protected the controls of the retracting iron gates and was large enough for a desk, two chairs, and a landline to the main house and outer posts. When he entered the small space, she tilted her head toward the sisters. "Give them some slack. No one could've guessed you'd turn out to be so pretty. The novelty will wear off soon."

"Not soon enough," he muttered. Had his expression warranted a warning? It must have, he realized, and he made a conscious effort to relax the muscles of his face.

Cormack had studied and trained for several months to master this new human form, and still had much to learn, but at least he was no longer a bumbling oaf. He'd lived for centuries as a wolf, but only six months as a man. Moreover, he'd had the mind of a human while trapped in a body he couldn't change. He understood eight human languages, but knowing them and speaking them with an unfamiliar tongue had been a challenge—a challenge he'd conquered before returning home.

More important, he'd learned how to wield a sword, still the most efficient weapon used by his kind. Their immortality had two weaknesses: one's head and heart must remain attached. Other less vital bits healed during a shift—*if* one had the ability to call their other half, which he now did. Thanks to Elen.

However, there were nuances of humanity that continued to elude him. Like facial expressions, and discerning when to hide them. Wolves had no use for such trivial deceptions. They took what they wanted and expressed what they felt.

Sarah chuckled over his response. Tall and lithe like many women of their kind, she was lethal in both wolf and human forms. And loyal. She had earned her position, and the respect of the other guards. Even so, her responsibilities demanded severity. She kept her red hair shorn to her scalp to deny her enemy an accessory to grab and leverage against her in combat. As usual, she wore leather pants with zippers up the sides for easy removal if a shift became necessary. Her sword rested on her left side, held by a studded scabbard.

"Well, you're saved from this ambush, at least," she said, then raised her voice loud enough for Lydia and Sulwen to hear. "Dylan wants to see you in his office. I'll watch your post until you return."

Cormack gave a nod of gratitude and strode in the opposite direction of the sisters. He remembered when Rhuddin Hall had been a rectangular structure that resembled many of America's earlier defensive forts. Over the years, additions had been added, with turrets on all four corners and walkways along the roof. It was now a fortress to defend the alpha's family who lived within its stone walls.

Choosing the side entrance away from the kitchens, he paused to acknowledge Porter. The man sat behind a wall of computers with various live feeds of Rhuddin Village and the forests beyond displayed on the screens. "Dylan asked to see me." Humans, Cormack had learned, needed addressing with words, even on matters they already knew. He supposed it showed acknowledgement, but in his opinion they talked too much, and if they kept their mouths shut, things would be much easier.

"He's waiting for you." Porter managed technology within the territory, but his primary role was to guard the alpha's family, a position that outranked even Sarah's; porters were second only to the alpha. This one kept his head shaved to flaunt a Celtic cross on his bare cranium, a tribute to his Irish mother. Porter had always been tolerant of Cormack's presence, even as a wolf, perhaps because the man couldn't shift, though many stories were told of his viciousness in battle. His true name was Finnbarr, just one of many secrets Cormack knew of the people who lived in Dylan's territory.

As a wolf, Cormack had been invisible to everyone but Elen.

The door to Dylan's office was open; he knocked to announce his presence and then waited—yet another human custom he'd trained himself to perform. Dylan sat behind a large wooden desk carved in the shape of a crescent moon, resting on three howling wolves.

Not a leader to waste time, he waved for Cormack to take a seat. "Damn, I don't know if I'll ever get used to seeing you as a man." Neither did he avoid awkward subjects. "You have the look of your family."

Cormack's throat thickened. Memories of his sisters hung heavy in the air. *I will not betray you as my family did,* he wanted to say but held his tongue.

Dylan gave a solemn sigh. "I see shame in your eyes and I won't have it." He refused to let the matter pass without addressing it. "There's much history between your family and mine. Some good. Some not. Our actions were fueled from here." He made a fist over his chest. "Mine as much as theirs. I don't condone what your sisters did. But I understand why. It's the Guardians who own that blame, not you, not me—and not your family. We will let it rest and remember them with the respect they deserve."

Siân and Taran had paid for their betrayals with their lives in the same conflict that had forced Elen to take a Guardian's ability to shift and give it to Cormack. Siân had succumbed under torture in a neighboring territory, while Taran had given the location of Dylan's family, *including Elen,* to protect her daughter. Melissa, Cormack's niece, was the only family he had left. Everyone else—siblings, uncles, aunts, cousins, *even his parents*—had met violent deaths by Guardian hands.

Cormack blinked away the burning sensation in his eyes. Emotions, especially ones concerning regret and loss, were a human disadvantage he had yet to control. He focused on a subject he could address without weakness. "Have the Guardians made contact?"

Avoiding the question, Dylan veered the topic back to his obvious agenda—reviewing Cormack's performance. "Sarah's informed me that you've proven capable of your position."

"I wouldn't have taken the post if I wasn't."

A glint entered Dylan's dark gaze, one that indicated approval. "Why did you accept? I know Luc offered you a post in Avon." Pride filled his voice when referring to his younger brother. Luc resided in Avon with Rosa, his wife. Only a four-hour drive from Maine, Luc and Rosa's land was located on an island surrounded by rivers in the White Mountains territory of New Hampshire.

It was where Cormack had been for the last few months preparing for his return. "I belong here." Rhuddin Village was his home. More important, it was Elen's.

"No other reason?" Dylan pressed.

Only one that matters. Cormack began to suspect the true motivation behind this interrogation. However, he too had learned how to evade, and since Elen wasn't the person sitting before him, he offered another reason. Not the entire truth, but earnest nonetheless. "You took me in as a *Bleidd*." "Wolf" in their mother tongue, but the Guardians used the term with disdain for those of their kind born in wolf form who couldn't shift. He should have been killed at birth, but his family had refused the Guardians' order and was hunted as a result. "You were the only leader who offered us sanctuary. Now that I can shift, I will protect others of our kind who can't—just as you did for me."

Silence filled the room, but not an uncomfortable one. Dylan frowned as if pondering the best course of action to resolve a troubling situation. "I don't take my brother's guards without a valid purpose," he eventually said. "I have a personal request, but I would have some answers from you first."

Cormack had accepted his offer without much thought, because he'd been ready to return. But this family's loyalty to one another was greater than most, and with neighboring territories, their united bond posed a dangerous threat to the Guardians, especially now that their enemies were aware of the untamed power this land offered.

And of the beautiful woman who graced its forest. She was the greatest treasure of all. And sensing this request somehow involved her, Cormack said, "Ask and I will answer."

"I believe you care for my sister. Am I mistaken?"

Feeling the muscles tense in his forehead, Cormack made a conscious effort to hide his expression. "You're not mistaken."

"Elen, as you know, is stubborn concerning her independence." Frustration bled from Dylan's voice as he broached the topic of its source. "And too damn kindhearted for her own good."

Cormack grunted in agreement. "Yes." An understatement, but the truth.

"You were . . ." Dylan paused. "Friends."

Cormack despised that word when it referred to his relationship with Elen. "We were companions, nothing—" He snapped his mouth shut. He'd been about to say *nothing more*, but to insinuate such a thing would be an insult not only to Elen but to his own honor.

Taking swift advantage of his blunder, Dylan leaned

forward. "Now that you can, you would have more than friendship, were she to offer."

Cormack felt trapped—and manipulated into revealing more than he planned. Not even Elen knew his true heart. But it was not only his alpha who held his gaze, but a man concerned for his sister. Wolves, when it came to claiming their intentions, didn't play games with words.

And his beast raged to be heard. "Yes, I would have more, but I will settle for companionship if that's all she offers." His tone had been too sharp, he realized, when Dylan's gaze narrowed. "I would *never* harm Elen. Or take anything she isn't willing to give."

"Ease your wolf, Cormack." An order, but the scent of the forest filled the office, called by Dylan to help him concede without shame. "You wouldn't be here now if I thought you would harm her. Don't forget I was there the night my sister ripped a Guardian's power from his body and gave it to you."

Elen had done it to save Joshua, Dylan's teenage son, and the separation of wolf and man hadn't gone well. The results had left the Guardian a keening mass of distorted flesh.

"She called for you," Dylan reminded him, as if the memory could be forgotten. "When even Guardians fled in terror, it was you who went to her without regard to your own life."

How could I not? "She was hurting." Elen never kept the power she received, and she'd needed a source to accept it. He had offered himself as that source.

"The villagers are frightened of her." Dylan made a motion with his hand that expressed his disappointment. "More now with you walking about. You are undeniable proof of her power." His dark gaze searched Cormack's.

What did he expect to find? Regret? Or doubt? When it came to Elen, he had none. "They are fools."

Dylan nodded in agreement. "So you're not afraid of her?"

"No," Cormack scoffed.

"Then please explain to me why you've been avoiding her. I don't pry without reason, so I'll have the truth from you now before I decide whether you're the right person for the task I require."

Cormack looked away, struggling for an explanation. In the end, he chose blunt honesty. "I needed to learn how to wipe my own ass." His ineptness during those first few weeks as a man hadn't been something he wanted Elen to witness. "Literally."

"Ah." Dylan reclined in his chair, easing the tension in the room. "And knowing my sister, she would have wanted to help." He chuckled then, no doubt from the image his words evoked. "Literally."

"She's a healer." Cormack found no humor in his situation. "Helping others is what she does."

"You've been home for a week. What's stopping you now?"

I don't know how to approach her. As a wolf, yes—but not as a man. Pathetic, he knew, but having a nice little chat with a group of Guardians seemed more achievable than facing Elen in her current mood. All his experiences in life hadn't prepared him for a pissed-off woman. It left him on unstable ground. "I'm giving her time to adjust."

Dylan winced. "Gods no . . . don't do that! Just trust me on this . . . Women don't think that way. Go to her. *Now.* And talk. They like it when you talk. And be prepared to grovel."

Cormack held back his surprise. "You would advise me on how to approach your sister?"

"Elen insists on remaining at her cottage." Irritation flicked across his face. "I don't want her there alone. She trusted you once, and you proved worthy of that trust. For over three centuries, you were her shadow. I need you to be so again. Are you willing to protect her?"

Willing? Cormack took a moment before answering to clear his expression and calm his beast. The true intensity of his feelings wasn't something Dylan should witness, but the man wanted assurances, and he would have them. "I will protect her until the day I can no longer draw air into my lungs."

"I'm counting on it." Apprehension riddled his cryptic response, as if he'd been forced to make a concession due to a greater concern. "I'm assigning you as Elen's personal guard."

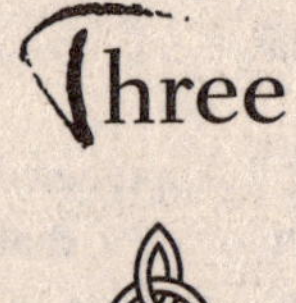

Three

ELEN FROZE IN THE DOORWAY OF DYLAN'S OFFICE, HAVING overheard a murmur of male voices as she approached, unable to distinguish the conversation until she rounded the corner. But the last damning bit registered all too clearly: *I'm assigning you as Elen's personal guard.* Blood pounded about her temples as she stared at the back of Cormack's head and realized who'd been assigned.

"Absolutely not!" She barely breathed through her outrage. Even worse, she regretted her words as soon as they left her mouth, because a tiny part of her—okay, not so tiny—wanted him back in her life. But she wanted him there by choice. *Not* by assignment.

Conversation ceased. Her brother, wise to her wishes, immediately cleared his expression. Cormack, not so wise, looked appropriately guilty.

And so absurdly beautiful, she despised him all the more.

No, "despise" was the wrong sentiment, for she could never feel that way toward him, but his rejection had hurt. And he *had* rejected her at a time when she'd needed his understanding the most.

Now he regarded her with hooded eyes the deepest color of blue, as if all the delphiniums in her garden had propagated to form the richest shade and gifted it upon him. His hair had grown past the unruly stage and hung about his shoulders in a mass of auburn waves. Even now, her hands itched to explore its texture.

His build, large as a wolf, and just as large as a man, had been honed over the last few months. Wide shoulders tapered down to a trim waist. She could only imagine what waited under his serviceable navy sweater and worn jeans.

"You will either accept a guard at your cottage," Dylan said, drawing her attention away from pointless musings, "or you will move into Rhuddin Hall." The worry in his voice softened the order but also warned that his mind was set. "Those are your two options."

A terse reply hovered on her tongue, but she held it back. As the leader of this territory, his orders required respect; as her brother who'd sacrificed much to keep her safe, he would always have hers. Moreover, her wish for privacy was a petty thing when dragons delivered invitations to dance. "I need to speak with you alone." The matter of Cormack must wait, for they had more pressing concerns. She walked around the desk to stand in front of Dylan. "It's urgent."

"Does this urgent matter involve your welfare?" *His* voice came at her from behind, deep, masculine, and curious—as if he had the right to insinuate himself back into her life without even a hint of remorse.

"Please leave, Cormack." Elen had only heard him speak one other time. It affected her now as much as it did then.

She couldn't concentrate with him in the room. "This doesn't concern you."

"I disagree." The obstinate man didn't budge from his chair. "As your personal guard, everything in your life concerns me."

She could only stare. He'd changed in more ways than fur to flesh. The wolf she remembered would have respected her wishes.

"Stay if you must," she said in a flippant tone, as if this new attitude didn't disturb her in the least. When, in actuality, her heart beat in a rhythm so frantic she feared he might hear it. Gathering her composure, she handed the letter to her brother and waited while he read.

Tight-lipped, Dylan placed the parchment on his desk. "Who delivered it?"

"You should be asking me *what* delivered it." Elen gave a brief accounting of the conjuring of clouds.

He remained deep in thought for several moments. "You're not leaving Rhuddin Village to face him alone, if that's what you're planning in that head of yours."

"If that were the case, I'd already be gone." Not that the idea hadn't crossed her mind, but running would only make her family appear weak, a greater risk when dealing with Pendaran. No, this threat must be faced directly at home—preferably hers.

A low growl filled the room, lifting the hairs at her nape, more because it had come from Cormack and not her brother. He held the crumpled letter in his fist. Obviously he'd learned how to read. Among other things, she was sure.

"What the fuck is this?" He brandished the wrinkled parchment in accusation. "That putrid ass mentioned a dress. Has he been contacting you?"

His outburst surprised her enough that it never occurred to her not to answer. "Pendaran has sent me a few gifts."

"Gifts?" Apparently he'd also learned how to swear. Quite proficiently, in fact, as more vulgar words followed. "What kind of gifts?"

"Nothing of significance." Truly, the jewels, brooches, paintings, garden statues, and silk gown held no value to her when given with ill intent. The collection of pebbles she kept on her windowsill, given to her by Melissa, Cormack's niece, was far more precious.

Cormack turned to Dylan. "And you allowed this?"

Her brother sneered at the insult. "Do you think I haven't considered every other alternative that doesn't involve ceding my territory to our enemies?"

A trail of mottled red began to crawl from Cormack's neck to his face. He was angry, Elen realized. Livid, actually. "If you've sanctioned communication from their leader, is that not yielding?"

"Spoken like a wolf," Dylan returned with more appreciation than annoyance. "But you must learn to embrace your humanity if you're to protect others who have." He went on to state the stark reality of their precarious position. "The Guardians have attacked us twice now; once here, and once in Avon. As you know, there are other leaders willing to stand with us against them, but not enough. You saw how many followed Pendaran's orders in Avon."

Cormack's lips peeled back at the memory. "Cowards," he spat.

"Some, but not all. Power is seductive to our kind." Green bled into her brother's dark gaze. He held tight control of his wolf, but lines bracketed his face with strain. "I have five hundred and seven people living in Rhuddin Village under my protection, but only eighteen of them can shift. Nineteen," he amended, "now that you've returned. Luc and Rosa have eleven shifters among two hundred and twelve, and I included them in that tally."

All true, of course, but hearing their numbers stated in such a way only strengthened Elen's resolve for the approaching evening. Rhuddin Village and Avon were mostly inhabited by members of their race born without the ability to shift. They lived for centuries, healed faster than humans, but were vulnerable in a battle against shifters who healed instantly during the change. The Guardians, led by Pendaran himself, viewed them as undeniable proof that their bloodlines were weakening due to overbreeding with humans. A ludicrous notion born of fear and prejudice. But poisoned minds weren't easily swayed. And like her brothers, she would do what she must to keep their people safe.

As if he hadn't heard, or didn't care, Cormack shoved the balled parchment in her face. "You're not going." He spoke low, but his eyes raged.

"Agreed," Dylan confirmed. "It's time to end this farce. Elen, make a list of what you need from your cottage. You're moving into Rhuddin Hall."

"No," she said. "I won't bring danger directly into your home, not with Sophie and Joshua here." *Not again.* He'd almost lost them six months earlier because of her, and she refused to risk their lives when she was fully capable of defending herself. "My cottage is close enough. I won't leave our territory, but I must face him from my own environment."

Like sun on wet earth, Dylan's frustration rolled off his shoulders in waves. "Elen—"

"No," she repeated, shaking her head with conviction. On this matter, she wouldn't bend. "You treat me as if I need protection." She flicked her hand toward Cormack. "Assigning me guards without my consent." She could rip the very life force from any living thing, plant or creature, if she so chose. "As if I'm weak—"

"Your compassion is your weakness," Dylan asserted with annoying insight. "Correspondence is one thing, but this is a different situation. If you are harmed . . . if you are taken . . . if I, as a leader, allow that to happen without retaliation—what will the consequences be?" His voice rose, unbending in its authority. "Answer me, Elen!"

She closed her eyes, knowing the answer, and hating that he was right. "The war will begin in earnest." Because neither of her brothers, Dylan nor Luc, would submit to Guardian rule, since it would only bring more deaths to the weaker members of their race. Or enslavement. Worse, she couldn't bear the thought of another battle because of her. Not when it was her family who suffered most.

"Elen needs her cottage," Cormack said. He spoke low, but his calm intrusion gained both Elen and Dylan's full attention—hers for more personal reasons. "You would encase her in a fortress of cemented rock," he explained, waving his hand around the office with its whitewashed stone walls, "when her greatest weapon is her garden and the forest that surrounds her home. Nature is her sword. How would you react if asked to face an enemy without yours?"

Elen leaned into the polished wood of the desk to steady her balance. His understanding rendered her speechless. He *knew* her. Of course he knew her, but now he had a voice that gave him the ability to articulate that knowledge. And he'd done it in a way her brother would appreciate.

And he wasn't quite finished. "Avon put her at the same disadvantage." Cormack lifted his arms in demonstration of his fairly new form. "The battle before, the one that took place in these very woods . . ." His voice trailed off. *The one,* he might have said were he less considerate, *where she'd ripped the power from a Guardian and given it to him.* He said instead, "You see before you what she can do in her own environment."

Seeking confirmation, Dylan pinned her with an assessing glare. "If this is your reason for wanting to stay, I would hear it from you." He thought like a warrior, and all this talk of weapons and defenses swayed his decision more than any of her former arguments.

If she weren't so grateful, she may have been put out. Either way, she didn't deny its accuracy. "He's right."

Dylan pushed back from his desk and shoved open his office window. A crisp breeze ruffled the drapes and carried the scent of pine and earth. Ivy grew along the outer wall and spilled over the sill, a blanket of green edged by red as autumn's cool nights painted its glossy leaves.

Knowing her brother needed reassurances, Elen crossed the few paces to stand beside him. She reached out to stroke the twisted stems with her right hand and gently placed her left over his. This ivy was strong and old, and so was its power as it rose to greet her. Touch was a direct conduit for her gift, and she allowed just a taste of what she held to flow along her arm and into his skin.

As always, she felt the transfer. It began as a tingle, like the awakening of blood-deprived limbs, but soon burned like red embers against tender flesh. The energy of his beast recoiled at her invasion. Pure in soul and savvy in spirit, it knew when to run.

Where most men would have shrunk from her grasp, Dylan only sucked in his breath. "Enough," he said. "You've made your point."

Slowly, she eased the flow before removing her hand. The vine gave one last surge at her withdrawal. Five months earlier it would have made her knees buckle at the cost of its life. She weaved slightly, but as Ms. Hafwen had taught her, she mentally closed off her sense receptors until the energy receded without harm to either her or the ivy.

Pleased with her own improvement, Elen scarcely contained a smile. "I don't know why the Gods chose me for this gift, but the time has come for me to use it."

He scowled, unimpressed with her claim but observant of her progress. "You're learning to control it."

"Yes." She dared not discuss how in current company, because only Ms. Hafwen chose who knew of her existence. Breaking the trust of the Fae yielded nasty repercussions. "If Pendaran wants to make contact, he'll find a way. Avon is proof of that." When he'd summoned all unmated females with power, including a child. Even Elen hadn't been able to resist his call. But, as Cormack had rightly known, she'd been weakened then.

No longer.

"If you remain at your cottage," Dylan said after a long pause, "you'll be keeping a guard with you."

A concession, but not a full one.

However, she knew when to push and when to negotiate. "Fine, but whoever stays with me must do so by choice—and not by your order." When he went to argue she held up her hand. "No," she pressed her concern. "Anyone who accompanies me becomes a potential casuality. I've no use for a guard unless they're willing and aware."

"Elen," Cormack interrupted, "I am both." His familiarity caught her off guard, as did her name on his lips. "I know what you're capable of better than anyone. And I'm willing to stand by your side in whatever capacity you need."

Oh, that was *so* unfair. How many times had she imagined him professing those very words over the summer, only for more intimate reasons other than this? *Don't go there!* Elen mentally shook those dangerous threads from her thoughts. She mustn't presume what he may or may not want from her, for the sake of her sanity, not to mention her heart.

Thankfully Dylan saved her from making a response. "That's settled, then. Cormack, you'll go with her now. I'll inform Sarah of what's happening. Report directly to me. Elen has a secure landline in her kitchen. Use that for communication. Porter will watch the boundaries while Sarah prepares the villagers. I'm posting Gabriel and John between Rhuddin Hall and the cottage. I'll update you on further plans once I discuss the situation with my wife."

"Understood," Cormack said.

Her brother's gaze landed back on her, black like their Roman father's had been before his death, and just as stern. "If Pendaran finds a way through our guards, under no circumstances are you to go with him. No matter what he offers or who he threatens—you *will* resist him. Do you understand?"

Hearing him plan for the possibility made her stomach churn, and rightly so. "Of course." Because she knew the consequences were she to fail.

Four

THE LATE-MORNING SUN SET THE FOREST ABLAZE WITH the rich colors of autumn. An emerald carpet of moss lined the packed clay of the trail, while oak trees formed a ceiling of glimmering copper and gold. A paradise, if there ever was one. Cormack allowed himself a brief moment to appreciate the view, well aware that his senses were muted in his human form, that the pine was less pungent and the rustle of woodland creatures reduced to whispers of scurrying feet. And that Elen marched ahead of him in a flurry of silent scorn.

He was home, or nearly there, since her cottage was around the next turn. And the rightness of it defied all challenges to come. If she continued to ignore him, he would correct her soon enough. Their enemies would arrive by evening; of this he had no doubt. But for now he watched her from his new perspective, standing a head above instead of waist-high and looking up.

His gut tightened as memories flooded his thoughts, made more poignant by the danger that threatened them. How many times had they walked together along this trail to her cottage? Hundreds maybe? Even thousands? He remembered when this path had been the only passage to her home, named Emerald Trail for its endless carpets of moss. But then his observation had been through the eyes of a wolf, keen in ability but useless for what he desired most.

From either viewpoint, there was no sight in this world more beautiful than Elen in her forest. This place *belonged* to her. Dylan may be its defender, but she was its master. Her fair hair danced in the wind, as if the element of Air couldn't resist touching a flowing part of her. Slender but sturdy, she kept her shoulders back and her face forward—or any direction away from him.

He scanned the area for anything amiss, but the only disturbance he found came from her. Now that they were alone, her obvious resentment thickened the air like poison. Was she even aware that trees wept as she passed? Of course she was—or might have been, if fury hadn't muddled her judgment. Leaves still green, not ready to fall, wilted on their branches in her wake, trickling down like weak rain.

"You're angry with me," he voiced aloud as humans found necessary. Dylan had advised him to talk, so he would to breach this dangerous silence.

"I'm not," she clipped without lessening her pace. She wore a simple top over a printed skirt that wrapped around her waist, held together by meager strings that formed a bow by her side. One tug would unravel it.

Did she not know how such things tempted a man? "Now you're lying."

She whipped around so suddenly he almost plowed into her. "I'm hurt," she corrected, "not angry. There's a difference."

Maybe there was one, but he couldn't make out the distinction just then. Not when storm clouds held less turbulence than her gaze. "I never meant to hurt you."

A delicate frown marred her features as she studied him for a long while. "What are you about, Cormack? You wanted nothing to do with me for six months, and now . . ." She waved her hand about in a frantic gesture as if trying to grasp his reasoning from air. "And now you volunteer as my personal guard. I don't understand you."

"What's there to understand? I've always protected you." From the day she'd served him dinner on a porcelain plate and not thrown scraps on the floor, he'd been hers. She'd given a wolf dignity at the price of his trapped human heart.

"Not since last spring, you haven't." She folded her arms under her chest, and the delicate mounds rose with her breaths and heated accusations. "You want me to act as if you never left. Well, I can't. I can't go back to the way it was."

Yes, he much preferred this perspective. "Neither can I."

When her lips pressed together, he realized he'd said something wrong. Her gaze held more sadness than the entirety of a barren ocean. They called to him, those eyes, as they always had. A color not uncommon to their race, they were the blue of winter horizons, so light they sometimes appeared gray, but rare because of the kindness within. And they were finally seeing him as he'd always wanted to be seen—as a man.

"Because of what I did to you?" she asked on a broken whisper. "I'm sorry. Had I known—"

"Don't!" Cormack wanted to drag her into his arms but resisted the urge. Less than a pace away, her scent rose to tease his sanity, a mixture of moonflowers that bloomed in her garden and the sweetness that was her.

"Don't what?" She leaned forward and almost drove all thoughts of resistance from his mind.

His body was weak, *and impatient*, considering her nearness after all these years of waiting; it awakened an inconvenient response. He may be new to this business, but even he understood it wasn't a good time for that. Regardless, he could correct a misunderstanding without making her aware of his uncomfortable predicament. "Don't regret what you've given me. You *freed* me from a half existence. I'm not sorry. I'll never be sorry."

Her gaze returned to meet his, filled with uncertainty. "Then why?" She lifted her hands in a helpless gesture. "Why haven't you told me this sooner? Why have you stayed away? Why have you avoided me?" The questions flowed like rivers in spring. "I thought we were friends."

Her last insult saved him from babbling like an idiot. She wasn't ready to hear what desires haunted his soul. Like boiling blood through his veins, he wanted her with a fierceness that would frighten her. "I needed to learn how to be human."

"But I would have helped you."

"I know." He cringed at the thought. "But there are some things a man needs to learn on his own. Private things."

"But we're Celts." She scoffed as if he'd made a tasteless joke. "Since when do you value privacy?"

Since I've been given a chance to have you. Needing to put an end to her questions, he provided a reason she couldn't refute. "Yes, I am a Celt, which is why I deserve to have my will respected."

And, more importantly, his pride.

That first week in an unfamiliar body was not a story for her ears, or the months that followed. Accounts of him dripping soup down his chin or fumbling with buttons and shoelaces.

Forming his first words and bumbling the sounds. Or slicing his leg while learning how to swing a sword. Having his face crisscrossed with cuts like an adolescent teen after shaving.

Or enthusiastic body parts that arose every morning without fail. And, yes, their race was known to openly love without shame, and not to judge, as it should be, but Celts also respected each individual's journey and preference.

And his was, and always would be, Elen. He'd waited centuries for her. Was it too much to ask that she wait a few months for him to be worthy of her?

"I'm a doctor," she added when her first argument failed. "And I was a healer long before that title came about. I can assure you there's nothing I haven't seen."

He hadn't needed the reminder. His loneliest times had been during her excursions to learn various medicinal techniques. She'd studied at monasteries, temples, conferences, hospitals and universities. And he hadn't been able to travel with her without attracting dangerous attention.

"Let it go, Elen . . . *please*." When she winced, he realized he'd spoken too harshly. Was an apology in order? He believed it was, but if he offered one, would it put an end to her questions—or welcome more? He wanted her to see him as a worthy mate, and not an invalid to be nursed. But her heart was too pure to understand, so he kept silent; a safer option that saved him from sticking his tongue farther into the mud.

"Fine," she eventually said. "You obviously didn't want my help six months ago, and I won't force it on you now." She turned and continued walking.

Cormack ran a hand through his hair. This business of talking was a complicated thing. He'd hurt her again, he knew. If not an apology, he probably should say something at least. "Thank you."

He didn't receive a reply.

* * *

TEARS GATHERED IN HER EYES, AND ELEN QUICKENED her pace before they betrayed her. She'd experienced her share of pain, but none this useless; it was an ache that held no physical substance but felt as if rocks pressed against her heart nonetheless. Worse, it hurt in a way that none of her medical training could fix.

And all because his evasive attitude reminded her of a certain wager. She suspected exactly what *private things* he didn't want to discuss, at least not with her.

Avon's residents found enjoyment gambling over irregular circumstances, and Cormack's had certainly been that. Regrettably, she'd learned about the obnoxious wager involving him, or rather his pursuers; more specifically, which one of them would be the first to introduce him to the carnal functions of his new body.

When Elen had left, a woman named Tesni had been a favorite to win. If only she could stop picturing them together, she might have the depth of character to rid herself of this mental torture. But jealousy was a selfish emotion, and like all things infectious, once it festered, it wanted to stay.

A wilted leaf brushed her cheek on its way to the ground, prompting her to change her focus away from self-serving motives. After wiping her eyes, she let the wind dry whatever dampness remained. She must calm her emotions before causing more damage, and she included her relationship with Cormack in that assessment. He still cared, or else he wouldn't be here now, and she found comfort in that.

If only he didn't look so damn self-assured, she might be able to find more. He formed an intimidating figure as he marched beside her with graceful strides. His sword swung from his side, the belted scabbard hanging low off his hip, with his eyes sharp and searching for potential threats.

He'd left her as a gentle friend but returned to her as a warrior. And why did that make her stomach flutter as if a thousand butterflies danced to his song?

A question for a later time, she decided for her own peace of mind. And after inhaling a deep breath for composure, she tactfully changed the subject. "Are you hungry?" It was still late morning, so she offered, "I can whip us up some coffee and muffins."

He sighed as if relief was a weighable substance and she'd just removed a boulder from his chest. "I would like that."

"Apple muffins?" she asked. "Or pumpkin?" The trail opened to her grain fields, and she hurried on, anxious to cook for someone other than herself again. Ms. Hafwen didn't count because she was too particular toward sweets and only ate crumbs she deemed worthy.

He thought about it for a moment. "The pumpkin ones with the white crunchy stuff on top."

"Pumpkin strudel?"

"Strudel," he said, testing the word on his tongue. "Make extra."

His smile was infectious. "I can do that." As they made their way through rows of apple trees with low branches heavy with ripened fruit, she had a ridiculous urge to giggle. It seemed she had little control over her emotions around him; one moment she wanted to cry, and the next she acted as if she'd never been with a man.

Which, of course, she had. But not one who held her heart so firmly in his grasp.

"What's so funny?" He kicked a fallen apple out of her path.

"Nothing."

"Tell me."

"Truly, it's nothing." Only the fact that hearing him talk back would take some getting used to, but she didn't think he would appreciate her humor on the subject, not so soon after their last bout. "I've never had to answer your questions before." She snuck a peek at his profile. "Or received answers to mine. I like it."

A sheepish grin turned his lips. "I'm glad."

She stubbed her toe on a jutting rock because of that grin. His mouth was made for pleasure. Thankfully, she caught herself before falling on her face in more ways than one and made it to her cottage without any further embarrassments.

Unlatching the wrought iron gate that led to her front portico, she announced, "We're home." The sentiment spilled out naturally because she'd said it countless times over the years. However, she'd never once heard him repeat it back as he did just then.

"We're home." He inhaled a deep breath as if to savor its scent.

The butterflies in her stomach began to dance again.

THE SCENT OF SPICED PUMPKIN AND COFFEE FILLED THE kitchen as Cormack watched Elen clean the mixing bowls and place them on the counter to dry. She had no way of knowing how many times he'd longed to sit at her table as a man, to share conversation and to use utensils as her equal. His throat thickened, and he looked out the window to get a grasp on his emotions. A winter wren sat perched on a cherry tree branch, its head cocked, watching him closely with a one-eyed glare through the glass pane. It issued a sharp cry when Elen placed two coffee mugs on the knotted-pine surface between them.

"I need to run outside to the garden," she informed him.

"How long will you be?" It was common for her to gather fresh herbs while she cooked, but it was also harvest time and she might be longer.

"Only a second." She slipped on her garden clogs by the

back door, sending him a smile that felt like a punch to the gut. "I'll be right back. I promise."

It was the smile that had given him the strength to live his cursed existence, and to wake each morning knowing she would give him another, and then another. If he spoke, it would reveal more than she was ready to know, so he only nodded as she left.

And he'd thought arguing with Elen was difficult? When a smile had turned his tongue into a bloody knot?

While she was gone, he took note of the changes in the cottage. His chair was missing, for one; she'd had a captain's chair custom made to fit his size as a wolf. And plants no longer grew inside but had been contained to her garden. She was learning to control her gift, as Dylan had mentioned earlier. A new couch filled the gathering room, large and overstuffed and inviting comfort. A stack of garden books rested on top of a trunk that contained knitted blankets within. In the center of the cottage, a stone hearth provided heat on cold winter nights.

Yes, he thought, *I am home.*

AS CHIHUAHUAS WERE TO THE CANINE FAMILY, Ms. Hafwen was to pixies, and her voice chirped in a similar crescendo when annoyed. She called from the shade garden, her usual spot for lectures because of its privacy. A miniature stone cottage rested below a hedge of hydrangeas, framed by blooms that had darkened to a dusk-colored rose. As Elen approached, the pixie flew to the top of the single turret, which brought her almost chest level.

Hands on hips, the pixie clipped, "This is not the time for you to be courting your Cormack."

"He's not my Cormack," Elen defended. "And I'm not courting him."

"Bring a man to your hearth and then feed him"—she made an impatient motion with her wings, not one to tolerate deception, especially if the giver wasn't aware—"that *is* courting."

"My brother assigned him as my personal guard. It was either that or move into Rhuddin Hall."

"Wolves," she muttered, but her annoyance dissolved with the explanation. "Too domineering to see their arses under their tails. It is both annoying and endearing. Well, there are worse challenges. We will just have to work with your Cormack. I have a lesson prepared, and it's important for you to master this one before the sun sets."

"I understand." Bitterness settled in Elen's stomach because what she really wanted to do was spend the day with him. Okay, perhaps she *wanted* to court him, but circumstances posed limitations that she couldn't ignore. "I'll meet you in the orchard barn in fifteen minutes."

The timer chimed just as Elen returned. Grabbing a pot holder, she pulled the tin from the oven. The muffins had risen perfectly. Cormack stood by the kitchen window, crowding the cozy space with his size. His nearness made her skin feel tight and jittery at the same time.

"This is new." He lifted a mason jar filled with pebbles she kept on the sill, and held it up to the light.

"They're from Melissa." She wanted to wrap her arms around his waist, knowing what he lost in the same battle that freed his human half, but his stiffened stance didn't welcome pity, or consolation. Plus the intimacy of such a gesture seemed awkward in their new relationship. "She began giving them to me after . . ." After Elen had healed her, but Cormack needn't be reminded of what his niece had suffered that night. "I made a big deal out of the first one," she explained instead. "Now every time Melissa sees me in town, she finds a way to bring me another."

Cormack had lost two sisters in that battle and almost lost his niece as well. Only four years old at the time, Melissa had been beaten to near death by a Guardian to obtain information from her mother. Taran, Cormack's sister, had died protecting her child.

The Guardian was now dead, thanks to Sophie.

Darkness and light in their most brutal balance.

"And you keep them?" His voice was soft but strained as he gently placed the jar back on the sill.

"Of course." Her earlier thoughts on the subject flowed without hesitation. "Rocks given with a pure heart are far more precious than any jewel given with ill intent."

His lips turned slightly. "To you, perhaps." There was no insult in his remark but rather something more possessive. "Thank you for saving her. I doubt my brother-in-law ever told you that."

No, he hadn't. Like all the villagers, Melissa's father kept his distance from her. Regardless, gratitude wasn't necessary when she used her gift for the purpose for which it was given.

Suddenly off balance, Elen busied herself placing muffins on a serving tray and pouring two fresh cups of coffee. A change of subject was in order, she decided, before she babbled something too personal. "Can you carry the mugs back over?"

The hint of his former smile turned into a full grin. "I can." Two simple words that held such impact, because now he could do many things he couldn't before.

And Elen was trying very hard not to think of those other possibilities.

Spiced steam rose as she set the tray on the table. Knives, napkins and a tub of fresh butter followed.

Pulling out a chair, Elen sat, scooped a good chunk of butter out of the crock, and began to spread it on a split muffin.

Cormack immediately removed it from her hands. "Let me do that."

His incapacities as a wolf had been a source of distress for him, she understood then more than ever, so she handed him her muffin to finish as well. "Mine too, please."

His gaze lifted to hers; there was gratitude there, and something else, a glint she'd never seen in his eyes as a wolf. Yes, she was trying really hard not to think of other possibilities—and she was failing miserably. He spread an even amount and handed it back to her. She ate one to his three. He was going for a fourth when he informed her, "Sarah's dropping my gear by in the next hour, so don't be alarmed if you see her truck pull up."

It wasn't normal for her to receive company. "Thanks for letting me know." Since she'd ripped a Guardian of his power, even the shifters had become skittish around her. They were partial to their wolves.

Unfortunately, it only reminded her of why their fears were justified. "Did I hurt you that night?" Avoiding personal subjects proved impossible. Even if it made him uncomfortable, their history was too intense to pretend they were strangers restricted to politeness. He stiffened. *That night* needed no clarification between them. "I already told you I have no regrets."

Which was his way of not affirming her suspicion. "And

the Guardian?" She gripped her mug for courage, afraid of his answer but needing to know. "Did any part of his personality influence you?"

"No." He reached out and pulled her hands from the mug to hold them within his. It was the first time she'd ever touched his skin. Did he not know how intimate that gesture was? Or how it affected her? When everyone feared her touch? "I'm a stubborn bastard. No man's power can dominate mine."

She rolled her eyes at the arrogant statement, not unlike many her brothers had issued over the years. Cormack's scent had changed after she'd given him a Guardian's ability to shift, which had fueled her concern, but it still held his signature, a meld of forest and night.

"Look at me, Elen." He waited until she did. "Don't waste your worries on me, when I know what it cost you."

She threaded her fingers through his, taking note of the calluses from his training. His fingers were long and well formed, and they relaxed to let her explore. The Guardian's was the only life she'd ever taken with her gift. Worse, she didn't know what frightened her more: That she felt no guilt? Or that she would do it again to have Cormack sitting here with her like this?

The sound of Sarah's truck broke the moment. He squeezed her hands gently before pulling away to open the door, accepting a black duffel bag from the female guard. Sarah offered Elen a respectful wave as she filled Cormack in on defenses for the coming evening.

Once Sarah left, he walked down the hall that led to the second floor, pausing at the bottom of the stairs. A flush crawled up his neck. "I'll just put my bag in the spare bedroom."

She swallowed, understanding his hesitation. He'd always

slept with her. Platonically, of course, but for obvious reasons, that dynamic had changed like boiling water over ice, and it shattered her quiet world with booming cracks.

"That's fine," she managed to reply in a somewhat neutral tone. "You know where everything is." To ease the tension, she stood, placing her empty mug in the sink. "I have chores to do in the garden and barn. I'll be outside while you settle in."

"Wait for me. I'll come with you."

"That isn't necessary."

"It is," he pressed, not backing down this time.

Well, Ms. Hafwen would just have to deal, because Elen wasn't good at lying, especially to the people who knew her, and there was no one who knew her better than Cormack. "Suit yourself. I'm going to the barn first. I haven't fed the animals yet, and there's something there I need to get."

Once he returned, they walked through the orchard in comfortable silence. Not quite noon, the sun had yet to begin its downward climb, and her garden danced with life. A honeysuckle ran along the outer fence and hummingbirds flitted about consuming nectar for their flight south.

"You painted the barn." Cormack craned his neck to inspect the change.

"My nephew did." Joshua had helped her with several chores over the summer. She suspected Sophie, her sister by marriage, had something to do with that. Elen accepted the help because she enjoyed his company. That, and family was too precious to refuse.

Her barn was now blue to match her cottage shutters and garden arbors; it housed four laying hens and a milking cow named Pumpkin. Turning the latch, she swung the door wide and inhaled the scent of fresh hay strewn the day before after a thorough mucking out of the stalls. The girls eyed her with greedy expectation, waiting for their midday treat. "No corn muffins today, ladies. Sorry." But she did take a moment to replace their water and feed, since her morning routine had been foiled by a letter.

"What of your clinic?" Cormack asked. "Do you not spend your days there any longer?"

A bitter laugh fell from her mouth. "When I'm there, no one comes, so I've stopped wasting my days waiting." It was the non-shifters who needed her assistance, and they'd always been skittish around her. And now with the proof of her power walking about in all his sinful grinning glory, they all but ran from her. Some still came as a last resort, but usually in the dark hours of the night, and almost always for concoctions unrelated to their health. "There's a call button by the door. Porter programmed it to send an alert here if I'm needed." She patted the small bulge of a cell phone clipped to the waistline of her skirt. An alarm also rang within the cottage. "For a while I thought to open the clinic to humans, but . . ."

"That's too much of a risk," Cormack finished for her.

"Yes." For all appearances, Rhuddin Village was like any other town, but certain amenities demanded too much contact with the outside world, so they kept the clinic disguised underground. Humans, usually hikers gone astray, were sent to a hospital on the other side of their mountain region.

"I'm sorry," he said.

Having sat through many of her frustrated rants over the years, Cormack understood her. It was upsetting to have a skill and the means and not be able to use it. But she'd buried those demons when she'd accepted Ms. Hafwen's help. Happy with her choice, she no longer craved the company of people who shunned her and was ready to begin a new chapter in her life.

"Don't be sorry," she said. Her brother had the clinic built in the event of a war among their kind. "When it sits empty, I know that no one's suffering and that the war has yet to come."

"For now."

Six

"YES, FOR NOW." ELEN SHARED HIS GRUESOME OPINION. The likelihood of another conflict had been the second reason for this visit to her barn. The garment box she came to retrieve sat on a shelf in an abandoned stall, trimmed in gold embossment. She snagged it off the shelf and returned to where Cormack waited. With the sun at his back, he filled the doorway as a shadowed figure silhouetted by light. And as she drew closer his expression became more discernible—and clearly displeased.

"It's the dress Pendaran sent me," she admitted before he asked.

He glared at the box as if it held snakes within, or the destruction of the world. "Please tell me you're not thinking of wearing it."

She couldn't, because she was. "He's powerful, Cormack. I want to prepare for any outcome. If he finds a way through our defenses, I'd rather not challenge him on something as pointless as wearing a dress." No, she reserved her energy for more important battles. "It's not woven with poison or enchanted with curses." She'd checked for the former and Ms. Hafwen the latter.

"Why would he need to," he growled, "when the message you'll send by wearing it is vile enough."

A rolling series of twerps announced the approach of a winter wren, the piercing sound more amplified in their closed space. Cormack jumped at the unexpected noise, then frowned when Ms. Hafwen swooped over his head and landed on Elen's shoulder. She had the impact of a falcon hunting its prey; a miniature harpy, if there ever was one.

Elen straightened her spine and lifted her chin; if she was to stand before him with a bird on her shoulder, she might as well do it with confidence. When otherworldly tingles touched her cheek, she was relieved; Cormack was to be one of the trusted few to know her tutor's true form. She felt slight tugs of her hair as Ms. Hafwen shifted and then stood in all her dragonfly-winged glory.

"A pixie," he whispered in reverence.

Of course *he* would know what form of Fae she was, when even Elen had mistaken her for a faery upon their first meeting. "Ms. Hafwen, this is Cormack." She tilted her head slightly so as not to squish her tutor. "Cormack, Ms. Hafwen."

A look of panic crossed his features, or perhaps indecision. Abruptly, he unsheathed his sword, placed it point down and hilt forward—and then kneeled.

WASN'T THERE A VOW HE WAS SUPPOSED TO SAY? SIÂN, his eldest sister, had recited it often enough. Cormack kept his gaze lowered to the hay-strewn floor and tried to remember the blessed thing. Something about trust, honor and kept secrets . . .

"I will honor your trust by keeping the secret of your existence safe from . . ." He paused, scrounging his brain. *Safe from what? Mortals? Guardians? Humans?* He went with, "Harm." He hoped it was close enough.

The pixie twittered. "Was that supposed to be some sort of fealty?" Like a wren, her voice carried strong and sharp. Was she connected to her animal, he wondered, as they were to the instincts of their wolves? Comparable traits made him believe so, and for a tiny creature to emit such a mighty sound gave witness to the many marvels of nature. "Lucky for you, young man, I am not royalty. You will keep our secret safe from *all*, but *harm* was a noble attempt. I choose who knows of my existence, do you understand?"

He understood that the Fae enacted vengeance in creative ways, if the stories were to be believed. And that she must be ancient to consider him young, since he was more than four hundred years old. "I won't betray you."

"Do *not* disappoint me! Now, you may stand in my presence, or sit, or do whatever suits your comfort." Ms. Hafwen added, "Within respectable reason, of course. I am not a monarch. There are quite enough of them already in the Faery High Courts. I am, however, an advisor at both the Summer and Winter Courts, and now Elen's tutor."

He chose to stand, sheathing his sword after straightening to his full height. "I've never seen your kind."

"Well, now you have. So there's no need for you to look all gobsmacked over it." The pixie rearranged herself within the curtain of Elen's hair, poking out a regal head with dark curls tucked under a golden coronet.

Gobsmacked? He wasn't sure what that meant but cleared his expression just to be safe. The crown challenged her claim about not being royalty. For all he knew, court advisors held prestigious positions among the Fae, and by her bearing alone, he suspected they did. "My sister told me stories, but I never thought they were real."

Siân could have filled a library with tales about the Otherworld, or *Annwfn* in the language of their ancestors. There were many names for the Land of Faery, where the fair folk lived and the Fae reigned over seasonal courts. A place where winged creatures sipped nectar from flowers—and others craved a darker sustenance. The Irish Celts called it Tír na nÓg.

His sisters should have been here to witness this. The futile wish strengthened his resolve. He'd survived the loss of his family, but if something were to happen to Elen . . .

Never. It was a thought too painful to finish, let alone endure its reality.

"Another disbeliever," the pixie scolded. "And from a man who carries the blood of wolves in his veins. Well, that's no surprise, I suppose, not with all the preposterous tales the humans have woven about our kind. We are real, but the last gateway between this world and the Land of Faery was destroyed a long time ago. A new one has formed, but it is still very young. Travel will be limited for many years to come . . ." She paused and then amended, "Many centuries to come in your moon phase. Time passes at a gentler pace at home."

"What Court do you prefer?" Learning of worlds other than this one gave him something to focus on. Plus, curiosity overrode better judgment. "Winter or Summer?"

"Winter, of course. My animal is a winter wren, after all." She inhaled, and the delicate sound traveled like a whistle on the wind. "I can smell it coming. Can you? When the snow falls, I will stay in my animal form until spring."

Practical, he thought, doubting that dragonfly wings

carried well in cold temperatures. "Is your home as beautiful as the stories say?"

"It is," Ms. Hafwen said, "but there are certain things I've grown to appreciate here as well. Our kind should never have meddled with the lives of humans, but I understand their temptation now and will admit I have become less critical."

A delicate snort came from Elen.

"You speak of Ceridwen," Cormack dared to broach. The Celtic Goddess was the creator of the first Guardians, and the reason they, and their offspring, had the blood of wolves in their veins. He was a third generation descendant; his grandfather had been an Original Guardian, beheaded for mating with a human.

Elen hissed at his blasphemy, "Cormack—"

"He has a right to ask," Ms. Hafwen interceded. "As do you all. Yes, curious wolf, I speak of Ceri the Crone. She has made her own mistakes, to be sure, but not the worst. At least she is remorseful for hers. She has sent me here to help right one of many wrongs."

"I hope you're referring to Pendaran."

"You may be surprised to hear this," Ms. Hafwen informed him, "but his mind was not always corrupt, nor was the rest of his brethren. They were quite honorable in the beginning. Ceri had a son with a mortal, as you know."

"I'm aware of Taliesin's story," he said.

"If you are referring to that fable the humans have spun, then you know little." Ms. Hafwen either sneezed or made an indignant sniff, he wasn't sure which, but if someone were to thump a flute, it might make a comparable sound. "Ceri was betrayed by her apprentice; that part is true enough. And there was a chase, you can be sure of that, but it was far more earthly than magical. It lasted decades in your time, and as these things are bound to do, resulted in a child who resembled his father. They are not one and the same, as your story is told."

"According to my mother"—Elen offered her own bit of knowledge—"Taliesin was found in a basket on the banks of a river. She said he was barely born."

"Merin was there," Ms. Hafwen confirmed. "She would know the truth of it."

Hearing Elen speak of her mother made him wonder if they'd been in contact since the battle at Avon, where Merin had betrayed Pendaran to save her children. It was a painful subject for Elen, and for good reason, so he reserved his concern for a private time.

For now he had a pixie eager to impart her knowledge, and with the threat of the Guardians lurking, he was keen to know more about their beginnings. "Will you tell us what really happened?"

"Young man, you warm this teacher's heart with all your questions, but I can share only some of this sad story. Ceridwen, for reasons that are not mine to divulge, was unable to bring Taliesin into our world and was forced to leave him here. In her grief, she destroyed our oldest gateway, but not before assigning guardians for her son. Forty-eight warriors to be exact. She gifted each of them with the knowledge of transformation sealed by the blood of wolves."

"A dangerous binding." Elen's tone extended sympathy without judgment.

"Indeed," Ms. Hafwen agreed. "I have often wondered if Ceri's anguish seeped into that initial joining. Fear can make a mother do desperate things, and that binding was as powerful as it was dark. In return, they all vowed to raise and guard Taliesin where she could not. They called themselves *Gwarchodwyr*, 'Guardian' in your mother tongue, and they were noble warriors until power that was not meant to be theirs tainted their human souls."

Cormack had better words to describe their taint. He took more pleasure than he should by pointing out, "Only nine of those Original Guardians remain." They formed a self-proclaimed governing body and titled themselves the Council of Ceridwen, led by Pendaran in all his putrid flesh and fur. And they hunted, enslaved or killed any descendant born over the last two thousand years who they deemed as unworthy.

Having been born a Bleidd, he was considered the most unworthy of them all.

"Where beings seek power, there will be divisive ways." Ms. Hafwen's voice carried the melancholy song of a wren. "I cannot judge, for the Fae are not immune from its lure. The quest for power sullies even our gilded courts." A hand no larger than a dried pea made a dismissive gesture. "But we've wasted enough time discussing the past, when it's our future that deserves our attention in the present. All that has come must not come again. So be off with you now. I have prepared a lesson for Elen, and she needs to master it before the setting of the sun. Since you're such a curious wolf, I'm confident you can find the sheets to make your own bed."

"I can." Cormack realized he'd just been sufficiently shooed by a pixie. "But if you don't mind, I'd like to stay and keep watch."

His gaze lifted to Elen's and held. Did she have any idea the picture she formed? Standing in a humble barn as hens pecked the floorboards around her feet? Like Ceridwen in that legendary fable; embellished or not, if the Goddess had looked like this in the barn at the end of her chase, it was no surprise a child was conceived.

Like a rare jewel that glimmered more because of her unassuming surroundings, Elen's hair hung about her shoulders in wild waves with an enchanted creature entangled within. She'd grown more assured over the summer; her gaze still soft, still welcoming—but with less fear now, and more notably, less regret over a gift that was meant to be hers.

Mine, whispered his beast as it rose to make its claim. Bound by the blood of wolves; there was no denying that. In fact, he felt the binding more than others, having lived in the form of his beast for most of his cursed life. He winced as an uncontrolled snarl fell from his lips.

"I do mind," Ms. Hafwen clipped with finality. "Especially with you about to go all growly on us. You will only serve as a distraction, so you must leave."

"A run might do you some good," Elen offered as a gentler rebuke. "I'll be safe with Ms. Hafwen while you're gone."

Pain shot down his spine as his darker half demanded release, forcing an acceptance of the inevitable. "I will check on you in an hour."

"Cormack," Elen called just as he turned to leave. "Have you heard news of Taliesin's whereabouts from Avon? Sophie's worried where he might have gone, as am I."

He shook his head. "You were there with us the last time he was seen. He left the day after the battle on Avon's bridge." Cormack didn't blame the poor bastard for wanting to disappear, but he had left Elen's family to deal with the aftermath of the Guardians' last assault. In consideration of current company, he kept his opinion to himself. "As far as I know, he hasn't contacted anyone since."

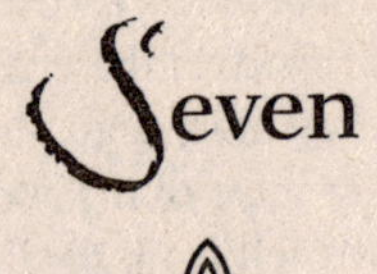

Seven

NEWPORT, RHODE ISLAND
AYRES ESTATE

THE OCEAN RAGED, CRASHING AGAINST THE GRAY ROCKS of the Rhode Island shoreline, as Taliesin drew closer to the brink of the cliff. The woman who stood on the banks below raised her face to the salted spray and tendrils of her golden hair whipped about her serene profile. She wore casual modern clothes, forced to blend with humans since his last fuckup in Avon. Her jeans tapered into knee-high boots, and a black sweater hugged an undeniable feminine form.

She was on a different shore, in a different country, but Merin belonged near water.

Even here, her melancholy seeped into his bones with more virulence than the frigid Atlantic winds. It didn't stop him from admiring a Celtic warrior in her element, even if he was the cause of her sadness. A narrow path had been worn into the cliff's edge, and he followed it to the banks below.

"You are certain that Pendaran isn't aware of this place?" Merin questioned as he approached.

"You're safe for the moment." That was because Pendaran was currently engrossed in pursuits of Elen, but sharing his recent vision would only stir Merin to act, and risk changing the outcome of this evening's events.

"Then it will do," she said as any nomad would, "until we move again. The others will arrive in the morning."

Like her children, Merin protected non-shifting members of her household from the Council. They were called *Hen Was*, the offspring of the first Guardians, born in their human form and forced to become slaves when they couldn't summon their wolves. Unlike a Bleidd-born wolf, they'd been allowed to live and serve. The *Hen Was* in Merin's ménage had been with her for more than a thousand years. Torn between two worlds, they lived as long as the rest of this afflicted hybrid race. But unable to shift and heal, they wore the scars of their experiences. Humans shunned their mutilations, and Guardians preyed on their disadvantage. When Merin's betrayal had become known, all twenty-six of them had followed her into hiding.

Not that he faulted their loyalty. As one of the few Guardians who'd offered him compassion in his youth, there wasn't much he wouldn't do for her. Any moments of normalcy, however brief, he owed to Merin. Reopening his New England estate was a minor infraction to the conventions that tangled his cursed reality.

As a Seer, he was hobbled by visions of a future he couldn't change without hurting the very people he tried to help. If he meddled with the freewill of humans, the results were never good, as his last interference proved under summer's first moon.

It was a personal hell. To know, to care and to wait helpless in the shadows of his visions while others bore the weight of his existence. Even Guardians and their offspring were bound by that divine code, a treaty cast from the heavens; their souls were human and their fates as precious and precarious as mortals.

And just as easily damned.

"Why did you do it?" Taliesin needed to know. He could predict futures but not thoughts, and Merin's had always been strong in both respects. "You could have killed Pendaran, but you let him live because I asked you to. Why?"

A soft sigh fell from her lips. "Can we not forget that encounter?"

"No." He didn't have the luxury of forgetting.

"You offered your own life, Taliesin." Her distressed tone provided an odd comfort. "To stop the violence, you were willing to die."

"So?" After days without sleep, when images of savagery—past, present and future—flooded his mind with ruthless potency, he was still willing. Like his ill-assigned protectors, he wasn't completely immortal to this world. Or so he bloody well hoped. He'd yet to have his head or vital organs removed to test the theory, however. "Would it matter to you if I did?"

"You insult me with such a question," she hissed as concern turned to anger. "And yourself for asking it." Her voice carried the weight of burdens that belonged to him. "I promised to keep you safe, and to foster you as if you were my own blood. What do you think would happen if I allowed you to die for us?"

"You believed my mother would retaliate?"

"Of course!" She turned her sharp gaze on him with undeniable certainty. "I would."

Ah, it was no wonder why Ceridwen favored this woman, as did he. "Well, I'm fine, as you can see."

"Our lives are a gift," she continued, ignoring his attempt to ease her conscience. "Our wolves, our longevity . . . it was all given to us to protect you. A gift can just as easily be taken away. Then everything I've done, all those years I've allowed my children to believe I rejected them, all those years I followed Pendaran's orders . . . it would all be for naught."

She paused on a broken breath, a rare show of weakness from a warrior who never faltered from her chosen path. "I shunned my sons and tortured my daughter. And now, when I look at them, I only see hatred in their eyes." She made a quick sweep of her cheeks, shaking her head. "No, my sacrifice has been too great to have it all end with you. And if that's selfish, then so be it. I've earned the right to a bit of selfishness."

He hadn't thought his list of regrets could grow any longer. Leave it to Merin to prove him wrong. "Even if you had killed Pendaran, there are other Council members all too eager to take his seat," he pointed out. "And your children will forgive you." Merin wasn't aware of this, but that forgiveness had already begun, now that they knew her actions had been a ruse to keep them away from Pendaran and his Council, along with the many descendants who could shift and followed the Guardians' creed. "And Elen will learn who ordered that torture."

There'd been a time when the Guardians, bloodthirsty pricks that they were, had used fear and pain to trigger the change, until all attempts had proved unsuccessful. Even for Elen.

Merin's head tilted with interest, too sharp to miss his unfiltered comment. "What do you know that you're not telling me?"

"I've told you enough," he clipped, angry with himself.

"Have you spoken with Pendaran? A meeting has nothing to do with your Sight," she pressed. "At the very least, you can share that."

"No." When she frowned, he elaborated, "I haven't met with him."

"Sin," she chastised. "You told him you would. To put him off will only make him focus more on my children."

She rarely used his nickname, and for a moment it caught him off guard. "You speak of his last words on Avon's bridge. If you'll remember I never agreed. And I stopped following his orders a long time ago."

"Pendaran views you as a son."

He sneered, "You think I don't know that?" He despised what Pendaran had become, but Taliesin still remembered a different man, before darkness seduced his honor and sorcery became his obsession. Pendaran's attempts to heal a forsaken race had only cursed it more.

"He will listen to you," she pressed.

"I can't get involved." *Especially now.* Taliesin ran his hands over his face and voiced the reality of his uselessness. "It came as an order from my mother. And I do listen to hers."

"You listen when it suits you," Merin returned, but remained quiet in thought for several moments. "The time has come, hasn't it?" When he would refute her claim, she held up her hand. "No, I'll not listen to your vague denials.

I knew this would happen when I let Pendaran live, but you gave me no other choice with your stupid stunt. Now that he's witnessed her gift, he'll pursue Elen for her power. He will want to control it through her."

A sudden vision pierced his senses; not of Elen, but of Merin. Flashes of her sitting at Rhuddin Hall's great room rolled out in his mind's eye. She was with Sophie and Dylan, and others. Joshua, her grandson, caused her to laugh. He'd seen Merin laugh before—a fake performance, he now realized. Like cake being offered to a diabetic man, the scene was as tempting as it was self-destructive. He could be a part of that family, share in their laughter—if he were willing to poison their lives.

"What will you do?" A rhetorical question he'd grown accustom to asking, since he'd just *Seen* where her plans led.

"I must go to Elen. Once everyone arrives safely, I will travel alone to Rhuddin Village. The others will stay here to open the house while I'm gone."

"Please tell Sophie I'm fine and among the living, but share nothing else. Not even where you're staying."

"You've never given me a message to deliver before." Merin frowned, making her displeasure known. "You care for my son's human wife."

"She reminds me of you," Taliesin said, "only she's nicer to me."

"Give her time." The slight turn of her lips contradicted her words. "She hasn't known you for as long as I have." Then she did something that shocked him speechless; she reached out her hand and placed it on his arm. Merin's mate had been killed before the birth of her final son, and a part of her had died with him. Offered touch was a rarity. "You know I jest."

He managed to say, “Do I?”

“Don’t leave us, Taliesin. We need you to live.”

Spoken for survival. Because his death would end them all. What he would give to have one woman want him for love. Too much, he thought bitterly, which was the reason he would forever remain alone.

Eight

ELEN'S CURRENT LESSON INVOLVED A GATHERING CIRCLE, but the only thing she'd gathered so far was her tutor's frustration. As instructed, she'd drawn the circle by dragging a shovel in the soft earth of her recently tilled cucumber patch. It seemed rather basic to provide the concentration Ms. Hafwen claimed it would. No salt filled the shallow channel, as Mae, her former teacher in these things, dictated there should be. Just crude markings and an aggravated pixie.

"If I could have gray hair, you would give it to me." Ms. Hafwen hovered with her hands pressed to her temples. "This is a simple joining and shouldn't be as difficult as you're making it."

"But Mae taught me—"

"Stop!" A disparaging sound resonated like the wail of a tortured bird. "I don't want to hear any more about that woman's teachings."

"Mae would have a fit if she ever heard you say that." Her childhood teacher wasn't a woman who took insults well. Mae, who currently resided in Avon as their healer, was a master of potions, and those who offended her usually received an interesting comeuppance in return.

"Maelorwen hasn't earned the right to know me, and I doubt she ever will." Ms. Hafwen settled on a nearby sunflower, with her wings fanning at a pace to soothe and not fly. "I need you to follow my teachings now. This lesson is a gathering circle, *not* a protection circle. It is for you to concentrate on, nothing more."

Like training wheels on a bicycle, Elen supposed, feeling like a child learning balance on unfamiliar ground.

"I told you when we first met that you'd been given a powerful gift." Ms. Hafwen paused to shoo a hovering bee seeking pollen. "And that you needed to do more with it than run rivers of moss and force transformations."

"I remember." Excitement and trepidation fluttered within her stomach, sensing this lesson was going to be different from her former ones.

"That time is now. Energy is elemental," the pixie explained. "Your gift is linked to the element of Earth, which is why you have clung to your garden and the forest around you. But you can do much more, Elen. You can command the other elements if you but ask. They are all connected to nature."

"How do I ask?" More important: "How do I control them if they answer?"

"With respect." A simple answer filled with warning. "Until you master this skill, it's best to practice on a confined space. *Call* the air that services your plants," she repeated from her earlier instructions. "Use your senses. *Feel* it, like you do your garden. Then invite it to join the ground you have designated within your circle."

"I'm trying." Elen had been standing in the center of the earth-scribed ring for more than an hour now.

"I know you are, but it's imperative that you succeed when you try."

"I'm aware of that." And she was, all too well. The soil under her feet was the easiest to connect with, warm from the afternoon sun and rich with nutrients from composted plants; it was a renewal of life that vibrated up the soles of her bare feet.

"Good," Ms. Hafwen chimed. "That's good. Doubt is your greatest enemy. You must believe you can do this. If you want the elements to respond, you need only to invite them with conviction."

Elen inhaled a deep breath and released it slowly, banishing all dangerous uncertainties from her mind. She could do this. No, she *would* do this. Opening her senses, she savored the taste of autumn on the back of her tongue. A sudden breeze ruffled her hair and brushed across her skin. It coaxed a sigh of pleasure. "It feels . . . I don't know . . . *sensual*."

"That would be the element of Air." Her tone was matter-of-fact, offering insight with understanding. Ms. Hafwen was Fae and didn't fault natural occurrences of life, including pleasure. If it was misused with ill purpose, or non-consent, then she would. But that was not the case in this situation. "It is the carrier of nature's procreation. Never forget the purpose of each element, because it will respond in kind. Air breeds, Earth feeds, Water cleanses and Fire resolves."

Yes. Elen identified the differences. Air was lighter, quicker, and more spirited than Earth. Water was too far away, but she sensed its cool presence in the lakes and streams that veined off their great mountain and into the forest. Fire wasn't ready to meet her just yet, but the others . . . Oh yes, the others were more than ready to play.

Especially Air.

It teased by circling her with tender caresses, and she teased back by whispering acknowledgments in return. In her mind's eye, she envisioned all the life Air helped to sow. Was it not Earth's messenger? And, as Ms. Hafwen had pointed out, the carrier of procreation? She pictured it flowing as wind, caressing flowers, wheat and trees as it traveled and spreading seeds and pollen on fertile grounds.

Sensing its building momentum, she held out her arms, palms up. And to her delight, a small disturbance formed in the center of her right hand; it was a vortex, albeit a tiny one no larger than her tutor, and it tickled as it danced across her skin. "I did it." She laughed, losing her concentration, and the disturbance dissipated into a gentle breeze. "Oh no . . . It's gone."

"Is it?" Ms. Hafwen asked in an unusually quiet tone. "Are you sure?"

Elen paused, feeling its lingering force, but it was a different energy than what plants provided. It seemed contented to wait, and to rest for future storms. "I don't know," she admitted.

"Touch the circle." The pixie flew a good distance away before issuing that command, and then further still to settle within the protective branches of the hawthorn tree. "Don't break it," she warned with a piercing cry that carried to where Elen stood. "Just tap it, and then step back."

Curious, she walked to the edge of the circle and touched her toe on the inner rim.

And a maelstrom erupted, encasing her in the eye of a vortex the width of the circle and the height of her barn, if not taller. Air and Earth enclosed her in their furious joining, forming a moving wall of turned soil and wind.

"Holy shit!" Joshua's voice filtered through the contained tempest she'd created. "That is *so* cool!"

Panicked, Elen swept her foot over the ground to break the circle, and the vortex dissipated, but not as gently as the first one she'd conjured. Dust and gravel whipped about her garden and traveled through her orchard, causing a weaving tumult of trees and projectile apples. The shutters on her cottage banged and groaned but held firm until the worst of it calmed.

"What are you doing here?" Elen asked her nephew, blinking grit from her eyes.

Joshua held up a covered plate. "I brought Ms. Hafwen a present." Tall like his father, the teenager had to duck under her garden arbor to avoid hitting his head. He wore jeans and a T-shirt, while the sword Dylan had given him hung from a belted scabbard and rested against his thigh.

"The closing needs work." Ms. Hafwen flew to Joshua's shoulder, a prime perch to glare at Elen from. "Unless it's a hurricane you're wanting to produce, you need to unravel the joining before setting it free. But you did well, Elen. I am pleased. You accomplished what I wanted you to. From this point on, Air will respond to your call. Remember that in times of need. Now," she chirruped when she turned to Joshua, "my dear boy, what have you brought me?"

Joshua, Sophie, and now Cormack, were the only ones who knew of Ms. Hafwen's true identity. But Elen suspected Joshua was her favorite.

Less gangly now that he'd stopped growing, he had his mother's brown hair but resembled Dylan in every other way. He'd aged in the short time Elen had known him, but there was still a youthful mischief about him, a blessing in light of what he'd survived. Having been in the battle that took place in these woods, he'd watched Guardians kill his grandmother and kidnap his mother.

And he'd seen Elen mutilate one right before his eyes.

Did it matter that she'd ripped out the Guardian's power to save Joshua's life? Yes, she knew that it did, but once violence was seen, it could never be unseen, at least for those who still bore a conscience. And that knowledge had a way of aging the innocent.

His black gaze now bore the weight of that experience. But he still lived, and learned, and offered sheepish grins as he held up the plate with a pixie attached. "Apple crisp, anyone?" The little cheat knew Ms. Hafwen had a weakness for baked sugar and fruit. "Enid left it on the counter, and I didn't want it to go to waste."

"Of course you did not." Ms. Hafwen was all aflutter, trying to peel the foil away from his blatant bribe.

"How did you get here?" Elen asked.

He gave a flippant shrug. "I walked."

She shook her head, knowing full well he'd understood the implication of her question. "I meant how did you get around the guards?" Even now, Cormack was in the woods that surrounded her cottage, meeting with Gabriel and Sarah.

"I have my skills." Joshua made a sliding motion with his free hand, demonstrating how smooth he thought his skills were.

It might have earned the welcome he sought, if worry hadn't tightened her chest. "Do your parents know you're here?" She knew they didn't but asked the question anyway.

"I overheard them talking," he hedged. "Porter's busy securing the outer gates. Sarah, Gabe and Cormack are outside your orchard and the rest of the guards are regrouping at the bend of Yellow Moss stream. Mom went with Enid to warn everyone in town—"

"So no one saw you leave," Elen finished. Sophie, no doubt, had told him to stay put. "Your mother will worry if she comes back and you're not there."

Their territory was massive; it included a village in the valley of a mountain region, along with several lakes, notable rivers and countless streams all joined within a wildlife refuge that protected the territory from modern development. The enormity of their land posed an almost insurmountable challenge for defenses, especially when hunted by creatures who thrived in such a concealed, and vast, environment.

"She'll be pissed," he said with a determined tone, so like his father it was eerie. Stubborn as wolves, the two of them were, and just as courageous. "But I'm old enough now to be drafted for human wars, and it's not right for you to face yours alone."

Elen wasn't sure what might burst her heart more: love or fear?

"I'm not alone," she pointed out while turning toward the horizon. The afternoon sun had yet to sink below the canopy of trees, but they only had an hour, if that, before it fully set. "And you know this isn't a human battle we're dealing with."

"Are you saying human wars aren't dangerous?" he challenged.

"You know I'm not." Just as she knew when an argument was futile—and when to call for reinforcements. She unclipped her cell phone from her waist and hit Sophie's number. Dylan didn't trust the modern devices, even though Porter secured their connection, but Sophie always answered hers.

She picked up on the first ring. "What's happening? Are you okay?"

"I'm fine," Elen said, "but Joshua's here."

A curse that would make Cormack proud came across their connection. "I'm on my way."

Nine

When Cormack returned to Elen's cottage, he found it filled with her family. Dylan remained quiet at the kitchen window, looking out toward the fields, while Sophie paced in front of the stove. A solid woman with protective instincts as fierce as wolves, Dylan's mate formed a menacing presence with a serpent whip wrapped around her waist and a glare to match.

"My son has decided to stay here with his aunt," Sophie explained when Cormack entered the room.

This was not the quarrel he wanted to intrude upon, but he understood a man's need for independence. "Joshua is of an age to make that decision. And from what I've heard from other guards, he's proven more than capable."

"You sound like my husband." Sophie's tone held a mixture of anxiety and acceptance that her child was now an adult who didn't need her permission. "And you're right. All of you." She nodded as if it were a soothing gesture to calm her fear, proof that this human was no coward. "I don't like the idea of her facing Pendaran alone either. Whatever comes—we'll face it together."

"As you can see," Dylan said without humor or argument, "the plans have changed. Porter and Sarah have been informed and will alert the others. Porter's staying at Rhuddin Hall, and Sarah is positioned on Emerald Trail. They'll contact us if they see anything."

"The forest around the cottage is clear," Cormack reported. "But the sun is about to set." He searched the gathering room beyond the kitchen. A fire flickered in the stone hearth, but otherwise it was empty. "Where's Elen?"

"In her bedroom." Silent until then, Joshua tilted his head toward the hallway that led to the upper rooms. He clearly wasn't pleased by his parents' protective company. Gods willing, he would live long enough to one day cherish it.

Cormack took the stairs two at a time and bumped his head on the eaves as he turned the corner, unaccustomed to navigating at this height. The upper chambers originally consisted of three bedrooms, but the center room had been replaced some time ago with a fully functioning bathroom. Like many cottages in this area, pine boards covered the ceiling and floors, a common resource from the northern woods.

"It's me," he announced as he entered the master chamber, annoyed that he felt the necessity. Decent sized, the room fit a large bed and several cabinets to organize Elen's clothes. His territorial instincts rose with his beast. He'd slept with her in that bed more nights than he could remember, covered by quilted blankets while listening to the even sounds of her breathing. Obviously they'd been platonic nights, but he considered this room his as much as hers. The fact that his bags remained in the spare room felt wrong.

"In here," she called from her closet as a pair of flat shoes and shiny pants flew onto the floor behind her.

He approached, and her scent greeted him as he walked through a haze of moist sweetness. "You showered?" *For that putrid ass?* "Why?"

"Because I was covered in dust from my lesson."

Then he saw her. And within the breadth of seconds his annoyance transformed to lust. He halted by the end of the bed and could do nothing but stare, unable to move as resentment roiled in his gut.

Unaware, Elen bent to gather her strewn items as butter-colored material flowed around her graceful form. The garment reminded him of frilly frosting, sweet, layered and edible to the core.

"You've heard, I assume," she said without looking in his direction—too comfortable with his company to sense danger. Six months of separation had not lessened their familiarity, even if it had only been the bond of friendship.

"They shouldn't be here," she continued. Her voice was thick with concern, as he knew it would be. "Joshua is as stubborn as his parents." She cast him a quick glance over her shoulder—an exposed shoulder, he noticed, in that concoction of cloth designed to display her body in all its womanly perfection. When her eyes met his, her features fell, misinterpreting what she saw. "Pendaran's here."

"Not yet," he clipped. "And you're not wearing that." Tempted to shred the thing, he fisted his hands by his side. "Take it off."

"What?" She closed the closet door and her skirts fanned about her to settle into each and every one of her divine curves.

"That . . ." He paused, forcing a calming breath into his

burning lungs. "That *thing* you're wearing doesn't protect you. Remove it."

"You're overreacting," she argued, unaware of her precarious position. "It's dated, but I can move freely in it, and I'm fully covered."

Which only proved how misaligned this current culture was.

He didn't care a frog's fuck about it being dated. It was provocative, and she intended to wear it in the company of their enemy—that's all he cared about. Clothing that teased offered far more temptation than full nudity, and that *thing* she wore was designed for such a purpose.

"Take it off," he repeated for the third—*and last*—time. "Now."

"No." Her spine straightened with determination, which only served to swell her breasts above the low neckline of the garment she wouldn't be wearing for much longer. "It will insult Pendaran, and he's been known to kill for less. I want to get through this evening without starting another war."

Her eyes widened when he closed the space between them. Slowly, he fisted the material of the skirt and pulled it up to bunch around her waist. Other than the brief moment when he'd held her hands, he'd never touched tender parts of her skin, and his hand itched to dive under the layers of fabric. The vanity mirror on the opposite wall provided a glimpse of her from behind. Lace undergarments covered her firm bottom, easily ripped off in seconds.

"Cormack," she hissed, "what are you doing?" The items she held fell to the ground as she braced her hands against his chest, clutching rather than pushing away.

If only she'd pushed him away.

A growl rumbled up his throat. "I'm proving a point." He

shoved his leg between her thighs. "This dress won't protect you. And these . . ." He shifted the silken material of her skirts to one arm, hooked his thumb through the thin lace covering her ass and snapped, "What are these?"

"Panties." It came out as a breathless whisper as she squirmed against him. "And you've seen me in them before."

Oh yes, he'd seen her in her undergarments many times, but seeing and feeling were two different animals entirely. And the skin at her hip . . .

He inhaled a ragged breath to control his sanity.

The skin at her hip was warm and soft—and every fiber in his being lured him to flatten his palm and just feel. For almost an eternity, he'd longed to touch her. But Pendaran could just as easily be in this position by evening's end, and the potential violation hung between them like rotten air.

Lowering his mouth to the soft flesh under her ear, he growled, "I could bend you over and be inside you in less than a second."

He expected anger—*wanted* it, even. That had been his purpose, had it not? She needed anger in her blood if she was to face their enemy. What he did not predict was her sudden—and staggering—reaction.

Her chest rose and fell on panted breaths as her body yielded with invitation. But then something changed as she leaned back and glared at him with accusation. "You'd have to be aroused to accomplish that."

She thinks I'm not? Obviously, her bunched skirts buffered the damning evidence. It took several moments to gather his wits, and guilt for his behavior followed. Pendaran would arrive soon, and he couldn't allow her to greet him like this. He set her down and let her skirts fall to the floor, but continued to hold her arms while she found her balance.

"If a man," he began, but then amended his prejudice,

"if a person wants to violate another, they don't need to be aroused."

She stiffened, jarred by his crudity. "You insult me if you think I don't know that."

Shit, he wasn't handling this right. A frustrated sigh fell from his mouth as he tried to find the right words to explain his reaction. "I've seen things . . . secret things that you haven't. You've always had a voice to share what you've observed. As a wolf who couldn't speak, no one hid their perversions from me. And I've witnessed atrocities that . . ."

He couldn't go there. He couldn't endure the thought of something hideous happening to her.

"You forget who you're talking to," she said in a voice heavy with experience. Having been tortured as a child to call her wolf, she would understand some of it, but not all. "Those atrocities you mention will only get worse if war ensues. Wearing this dress is the least of my worries, but enough of one that I am planning to have pants on underneath just in case I need to dump it and hide."

A sudden yawn overtook her.

"Those flimsy things?" He glared at the fallen items on the floor. "They'll protect you no better than the ridiculous lace that barely covers your ass."

"Don't underestimate the power of spandex," she teased, but he knew it was an attempt to lighten the mood he'd created. "They'll protect me as well, or as little, as any clothing. And they can't be seen under the dress. The matching top is in my purse. Also, I believe Pendaran wants to control my gift"—her voice caught in another yawn—"not my body."

"Rape is about control." But she was right; it wasn't only her body that could be violated. The sudden enlightenment tightened his gut. Cormack had been too clouded by his own desire to consider Pendaran's true objective. His apprehension increased when her eyes began to flutter close. "What's wrong? Why are you acting tired?"

She snapped them open, and then shook her head as if to remove remnants of sleep. "I don't know."

"Talk to me," he ordered. "What are you feeling?"

Her eyes dilated. Like obsidian pools, the pupils obscured the winter blue outline with an unnatural defocusing. "Pendaran," she slurred like she'd had too much wine. "He's here. Not in flesh, or in fur, but in spirit. Tell Ms. Hafwen . . . she's researching something in her library . . . her cottage is . . ."—another yawn—"under the hydrangeas."

"Elen, wake up." He grabbed her shoulders and shook, but then flinched when her head fell backward too quickly. Cradling her neck, he shouted in her face, "Wake up!"

Footsteps sounded on the stairs. Sophie turned the corner first, clutching the serpent whip at her waist. The scent of apple blossoms and old power filled the room. The ancient weapon had been a gift from Taliesin, and the wearer often received warnings from the Otherworld. "Pendaran is spirit traveling," she panted. "And he's here."

Elen made a garbled noise that resembled, "What have you done to me?" and then slumped in his arms, unconscious.

Ten

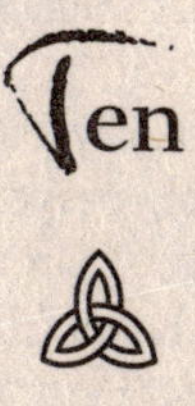

She sensed him before she saw him. He hovered as a spectral image, colorless like a faded photograph, but composed even while separated from his earthly body to travel in a space of death. Not that he would have been aware, because children were trained not to be seen, but she'd observed him in her youth—then much later at Avon. A slender man with green eyes clouded by his misdeeds, his hair had always been dark, but in this realm it appeared like a gray void above a pale face.

"We meet again, my dear, but under better circumstances." Exuding self-satisfaction, Pendaran's voice came to her like a distant echo through fog.

"What have you done to me?" Elen was still in her room but separated from her body. She could see Cormack's tortured face as he hugged her lifeless form to his chest, and Sophie running to the stairs—to get Ms. Hafwen, she hoped.

Pendaran asked, "Who is Ms. Hafwen?"

"A friend." She realized too late that thoughts and voice were intertwined in this realm, and she replaced hers with visions of her garden. She pictured her sage, with its velvet skin and pungent sent, and hyssop, with its lavender blooms adored by bees, and heart-shaped foliage that made a lovely tea when dried.

And her comfrey, so hardy it thrived alongside her native yarrow, both with healing properties but in different ways.

"Enough," he ordered. "Do not waste my time with a bloody catalog of your garden." He turned toward the room, viewing the same scene. "I am pleased to see you wearing my gift, but the company you keep leaves much to be desired."

She had a sudden thought. "You've done this to spy on my family?"

"I have been informed there's some truth in the rumors I've been hearing, but it required a firsthand evaluation, and now I have one. The human wears the Serpent. The lad has the look of your kin and the command of a wolf. And the Bleidd is now a man. Merin's progeny has grown powerful away from Cymru."

His precise assessment heightened her panic. "We shouldn't be here." Souls who wandered too long on the other side sometimes never returned. "I'm going back."

"Not just yet." His tone resonated like glass, smooth and easily shattered. "We've yet to have our first dance. I did not come without notice. You received my invitation. If naught else, I am a gentleman. I will ask that you reciprocate in kind, and we will have a pleasant evening. If not . . ." He paused, letting that thought hang and his threat molder. "Well, let us hope it doesn't come to that."

Utter fear gnawed at her conscience, exacting truths as

sure as any mortal facing their demise. "I don't want to dance with you." She made an attempt to leave, to focus on her loved ones and sink back to where she belonged.

"You will dance if I ask you to," he taunted. "And you will leave when I am ready to dismiss you." He held her spirit firm with whatever he'd used to conjure her there. "Let us go for a meander, shall we? It is time we become better acquainted."

It was posed as a question, but she had no choice or control over the path he brought her down. They traveled around the outskirts of Rhuddin Hall, over the villagers' homes, through the forest and up the great mountain. It was an assessment of their territory. A familiar building soon came into focus, built into the ground and concealed by trees. She tried to keep her spectral thoughts discreet. Her clinic, closed and quiet, appeared as devoid as she felt.

Pendaran paused to investigate. "This hospital is your space." He projected his voice with his thoughts. "I can sense your energy here almost as strong as in your garden. Why do you waste your time fixing the weak?"

"Because you waste your time hurting them," she challenged in return.

"Ah, so that is how it will be." Disappointment spread from his image like a murky cloud. "What I do is for the greater good of our race, and it is not a waste of time. Take your gauntlet, for example."

Curiosity proved difficult to contain. "What gauntlet?"

"The one Merin supervised on your seventh year when you still hadn't called your wolf. Surely, you remember. You weren't all that young."

Only one memory came to mind from that year. "Are you referring to my torture?"

"Torture?" A ghostly laugh resonated in the empty space.

"Really, Elen . . . is that what you remember? You are prone to dramatics, I see. You will have to work on that flaw if we are to spend time together."

"I remember my mother holding me down while shoving rods into my spine."

His shadowy hand sent an absent wave. "Children undergo treatments all the time to strengthen them in their societies."

"Please spare me your philosophies." The thought came unbidden, and before it had a chance to fully unravel, a wave of malevolence strangled whatever substance she retained in this place.

His echo followed, soft but cruel. "I appreciate tenacity, but not disrespect. You will hear my views whether you care to or not, because you are ignorant and have much to learn. Do you understand?"

"All too well." And for the first time in a long while, her heart wept for her mother. How many times had Merin endured Pendaran's perverted opinions to keep them safe?

"Perverted? My dear," he said, his tone teasing more than chastising, "you have not seen me perverted. But let us resume before your insolence becomes a waste of my time."

Her goal was not to insult and she tried to quiet her thoughts.

Mollified, he continued, "For instance, those mouth brackets modern humans put on their children to straighten their teeth. Are they not metal vises that cause pain for years? What purpose do they serve other than vanity, and to help them attract better mates?" He shook his head as if he actually cared. "But you have studied human medicine, have you not? Let me think of an analogy you might understand."

Eagerness abounded from his direction. Whether it came from his imparted wisdom, or the prospect of punishing her for not appreciating it properly, she wasn't sure. She only knew that either possibility posed an agreeable outlook in his mind.

"I have one," he declared, overly satisfied with his own brilliance. It shimmered in the space between them like diseased fireflies. "Some humans are born with curvatures of their spines, is this not true? And they are required to wear a brace with only one hour's relief a day. While others sleep with devices that send currents to contract their muscles while they grow. Are these not tortures done to make them stronger? Would you deny their pain only to keep them weak and malformed?" He challenged, "What is the difference between their intentions and mine?"

She thought of Cormack and the other Bleidd hunted throughout their lives. And the *Hen Was* forced to be slaves. "The difference is a conscience."

"You profess that as if it's a good thing." A frown blotted his pale reflection. "And does not man's history prove otherwise? I would say my standards are purer, and unbridled by the frivolous weakness of emotion."

How was she to debate with a sociopath? And why was she even trying? "You are vile." Even as the thought formed, she knew her attempts at peace were doomed. This place bared her soul and her opinion was impossible to hide.

"Sometimes," he admitted. "If only our kind had the yearly migration of your ruby-throated hummingbirds, then my hand would not be forced." A wistful sigh echoed like wind in a wasteland with nothing to hinder its travels. "Alas, nature would have done it for me. Even now, they are feeding in your garden, preparing for their great flight south. The weak die naturally during the course of their journey, so only the strong return each year to breed. They are one of nature's most divine solutions, if you ask me."

He flicked his hand, and several tiny winged hummers appeared, faded and crazed, circling in disjointed separation.

"Return them," she pleaded, "or they will die for no purpose."

Arrogant and uncaring, he continued to lecture, "Our gauntlets were given to help trigger the change, but I do believe yours may have generated something more interesting. You can thank me for that. Your mother agreed to perform your procedure only after she'd learned I had plans to implement it myself. You should be grateful for my interest, because look where it has brought you."

One by one, he pulled the wild spirits of the hummingbirds from her garden. Without momentum, she suspected their tiny earthbound bodies fell to the ground to die of starvation, unable to feed in the hasty intervals they needed to survive.

"And you wonder why the Goddess has rejected you," she accused, abandoning all pretense of civility.

A dark wave of rage encircled her soul, vindictive and insidious. "You dare preach to me of Ceridwen." Old language echoed from his frenzied ire. "Ignorant *Drwgddyddwg*, I am not the abandoned one."

Meaning "Evil Bringer." A sad irony, to be sure, that it was the Guardians, and perhaps Pendaran himself, who had coined the insult for non-shifters like herself. "It is you who is evil, not me."

The element of Air brushed against her, even here, like a warm breeze on a winter night, letting her know that the elements were not hindered by conventions as limiting as life and death. They existed universally. But it withdrew once it sensed her anguish. Air was a spirited element, and it didn't respond to negative emotions.

The notion made her change tactics. And as loathsome

as it was, she reached out her senses in this void with playful intent. Pendaran's essence drew her as much as it revolted her; like the darkness to her light, one did not exist without the other. It welcomed her approach.

She felt his surprise, followed by interest, and then his ultimate withdrawal.

But it was too late. His control weakened the moment she claimed her side of the connection. Gaining strength, her vision spread down the long journey Pendaran had taken to find her, over an ocean and through the rugged mountains and lush valleys of her homeland. Cymru had been touched by modern development, just as the rest of the world. But it still called to her, as it always had. She didn't know if he continued to share her thoughts, nor did she care. She was home.

Pendaran's empty shell lay within an overly groomed forest. Now whole after the battle of Avon, his arms were folded crosswise over his infamous sword. Merin had removed his hand on Avon's bridge, but limbs were able to regenerate during a shift. Not completely infallible, they did require strengthening for days, sometimes weeks; like atrophied muscles, they needed exercise to rebuild. Their race was born of human flesh, after all, and even the first Guardians retained some of that fragility. And vital organs, like brains and hearts, continued to be their ultimate weakness.

Hochmead Manor loomed in the distance, Pendaran's stronghold since the days of dragons, when an older castle had stood in its place; and a hill-fort before then. He was the very image of an ancient Viking, only laid to rest on ground instead of sea, preparing for his journey to Valhalla.

Too bad she and Fire had yet to meet to make the ceremony complete. And even as the concept formed, Elen knew her connection to Pendaran had been the catalyst of its inspiration. The darkness he embraced was like molten wine, heady and potent in the veins. She even tried to regret it but found she could not.

Nonetheless, the weapon gave her an idea. And the anticipation was as tempting as dancing under the stars on summer's first night. Mae, her former teacher, would understand its lure. Named Cadarn for strength, the sword had been forged under the Druids' Great Oak. Branches of the sacred tree, and the ivy that grew around it, encased the weapon in woven scabbard of Celtic knots.

And vines, especially old and powerful ones, loved her. If it still lived—*or not*—she could make it grow, but the latter would kindle a darker version of its former essence.

"What are you doing?" Pendaran tried to sever their connection but it remained now as her trap to control. Or perhaps balance was more accurate, for she still felt his resistance.

"Hush and be quiet. You're under my influence now." In her mind's eye, she called to the forest of her childhood. She knew this place, and it knew her. "What happens if our earthbound bodies die while our spirits are separated?"

"You lack the nerve and the skill to fulfill such a threat."

"When we last met in Avon, I might have agreed. But not today."

Air will respond to your call. Her tutor's words whispered through her thoughts. *Remember that in times of need.*

Was this not such a time? And with her recent lesson fresh in her mind, Elen called upon the playful element and offered a joining. She asked Air to be her messenger, and to caress the vines of Cadarn's scabbard. The element brushed against her like a cat seeking comfort—or marking its territory. It twirled around her spirit, interlacing with her energy, and then it soared.

"Who is this tutor who imprinted your mind with Otherworld knowledge?" Doubt replaced his former arrogance. "Is it this Ms. Hafwen you mentioned earlier? Answer me!"

Refusing to respond, Elen concentrated on her task. The woven oak and ivy were dormant, *not* dead. A bud formed, and then another, and soon they stretched into fresh branches and fervent vines and began to grow into a tangled mass about Pendaran's lifeless form below.

His spirit recoiled, as all predators do when their prey proves more dominant than docile. An incantation wove in the space that bound them together, as old and powerful as the knotted boughs she'd rekindled with life. She welcomed the unraveling. Soon their connection weakened, then severed completely, and his body below arched with his returned spirit. She watched from above as he coughed and clawed at the vines.

And wrath knew no better host than the sorcerer who craned his face to the sky. "This is not over, Elen. Our dance has just begun. We will meet again. And I will have the answers I seek."

For an instant, the separation engulfed her in emptiness, and then panic. Air tugged her spirit toward a familiar path. By retracing her journey, her disorientation calmed. She focused on her family, on their desperation and their love. It was an undeniable draw, and the catalyst she needed to return.

Eleven

ELEN DREW HER FIRST BREATH WITHIN THE WARMTH OF Cormack's arms. Her throat burned, and the atmosphere tasted thick with salted tears—and she'd never felt more alive. Sore and exhausted but blessedly whole. A sob fell from his mouth as he buried his face in her hair. And when she opened her eyes, a pixie landed on the end of her nose.

"There you are," Ms. Hafwen chirped, "*finally*. Your brother was about to have a gasket." The misused slang suggested it wasn't only Dylan who'd been in danger of blowing a gasket. "I know what you did," she proclaimed on a warbled sounding exhale. And then the most extraordinary thing happened. If the pixie hadn't been a nose length away, the whole event may have gone unnoticed, and Elen may have never seen her tutor's slightly pointed teeth revealed in a way that almost resembled a smile. "I am beyond proud of you, Elen. Beyond proud."

Dylan leaned over, his dark gaze haunted. "Say something so I know you're okay."

She cleared her throat, and then winced. "I'm okay."

He closed his eyes briefly. "You scared the shit out of us."

But it was Cormack who cupped her face and rested his forehead against hers, forcing Ms. Hafwen to flutter off. "Is he gone?"

"For now, but I angered him." She turned her head toward her tutor, who hovered above his shoulder. "Pendaran knows I have otherworldly help. He's not sure what, but he knows your name. I didn't mean—"

"Hush your fears," Ms. Hafwen soothed, her wings a blur as she lingered in place. "He knows nothing of significance, or I wouldn't be here now."

"I insulted him." Elen swallowed. "I tried not to . . . but I couldn't help it." Her throat felt dry and her voice came out like a parched murmur, but there was too much they needed to know. "My thoughts were open for him to read, and I may have started the very thing I wanted to avoid. We need to prepare."

"Sleep now and we will plan later." Ms. Hafwen lifted to circle around the room, issuing a series of chirps to gain attention. "A body drains without its spirit," she announced, "and Elen must rest. Everyone downstairs. Yes, Dylan ap Merin, Penteulu of Rhuddin Village, that means you too." The formal address earned her a wolf's glare. "Pendaran will be in no shape to retaliate for a least a week, if not longer. It was his energy that summoned Elen's spirit, and he will suffer three times more for its use." More than one satisfied smirk followed that comment. "I believe there's some apple crisp left. Sophie can make us tea"—she paused to hover in front of Dylan's face—"while you listen to my rules, even though I suspect your mate already broke them, and you knew about me before today."

"If I'm not mistaken," Dylan countered with respectful authority, "as the protector of this land, you should have introduced yourself once stone was cast for a permanent dwelling. I've seen the miniature castle in my sister's garden. If it has a name, you are required to tell me. Does it have a name?"

A scattering of tweets followed, and they sounded suspiciously like a laugh. "Well, I will admit that you are the first to trump me with my own customs. But it is refreshing to know that at least one of you remembers the old ways. My dwelling is a cottage, not a castle, and it is named Brynmor."

"If I forgive your infraction," Dylan offered, "can you forgive my mate's? Sophie is new to our ways and only told me out of concern. We will protect your existence from all."

"It is a fair resolution," Ms. Hafwen said with an airborne sway that mimicked a gesture of harmony. "And I accept."

Too exhausted to argue on Sophie's behalf, Elen could only watch the scene unfold. But she made a mental note to speak to her brother about some of those customs, because she suspected Ms. Hafwen may have taken advantage of her lack of knowledge of the old ways.

When Cormack began to lay her back against the pillows, Elen stilled him by tightening her hold, not caring if he thought her too clingy. She needed him. "I would like you to stay."

"Are you sure?" But he was already positioning himself to sit next to her.

She managed a weak smile. "I'm sure."

"I'll feel better if one of us stays in the room to watch over her." Sophie leaned over and gently squeezed Elen's hand. "We'll be downstairs if you need us."

Not even the pixie argued.

Snuggling into Cormack's warmth, Elen's eyes closed of

their own volition, too heavy to keep open now that she felt safe. She'd rest while the room cleared, but only for a moment. Once they were alone, she had some things she wanted to ask him about those few minutes before Pendaran's arrival.

HE MUST HAVE PISSED OFF THE GODS SOMEHOW, Cormack decided, to be cursed for centuries, and now that he was free to pursue his love, evil wanted her too. Holding a glass of water to Elen's mouth, he managed to coax a few swallows before she drifted off to sleep once again.

Sophie observed them from a winged-back chair that he'd brought in from the guest room and placed at the foot of the bed. "Ms. Hafwen says this is normal." Her tone was hushed and heavy with concern. "But she's been like this for almost two days."

"Should we wake her again?" To ease his own anxiety, he watched Elen's chest rise and fall with even breaths. Holding her lifeless body in his arms was a horror he would never forget.

"If she needs to rest, then we should let her rest. But she should also eat." Sophie stood as if wanting to leave but hesitant with indecision. "I called Rhuddin Hall earlier and had our cook prepare some meals. My son has pretty much cleaned out Elen's fridge. Will you be okay watching her alone for a while? We could use showers and a change of clothes. I want to check in with Dylan and hear the reports from the guards. If you're not up for it, I can send Joshua—"

"Go be with your mate," Cormack said before she finished. Sarah had stopped by to give them updates. So far, their territory remained clear of Guardians, but he too wanted another report. "We don't all need to be here watching her sleep.

Ms. Hafwen is confident that Pendaran will be incapacitated for at least a week." Even the pixie had returned to her stone cottage while Elen slept. "If I notice any changes, I will call."

"Thank you, Cormack." Her hand rested briefly on his shoulder. "I'll return in a few hours with food. We'll wake her then."

Setting the glass down on the nightstand, he waited until the sounds quieted and he knew the house was free of company before pulling back the blankets and crawling into bed with Elen. Finally, he got to hold her without the protective eyes of her family watching.

She murmured as he folded his arms around her and tucked her head under his chin. Sophie had removed that vile dress and replaced it with a nightshirt. With Elen's soft breaths fanning his neck, he managed to drift off to sleep.

But when he woke, she had turned and kicked off her blankets. Her left breast rested against his arm, and the dark outline of her nipple pressed against the soft material of her shirt.

His reaction was immediate. He tried to think of something else, to draw his starved gaze away, but he was weak and enthralled, and he couldn't find the will to fight his infatuation. Within seconds, his cock swelled to painful lengths.

Cormack had never understood why that particular body part had been given so many names—until he had one. Because the damn thing was uncontrollable; it deserved its lineage of titles. He'd practiced saying many of them, but "cock" was the term that came readily to mind; quick and eager like the appendage itself.

As a Bleidd, signals of desire hadn't connected from his human mind to his wolf's form—*thank the Gods!* It was a mercy of his curse that held no limits of gratitude. Now that he was in his rightful body, however, the signals connected strong and clear, and his human anatomy was more than ready to make up for four hundred pent-up years.

Cool air brushed between them as he shifted away from her. Her brow pinched in sleep, and she rolled toward him, unconsciously seeking his missing heat. The nightshirt twisted as she turned, and the neckline scooped forward—exposing her breast in all its coral-tipped glory.

He sucked in a breath. "Fuck me," fell unbidden from his mouth, a popular saying among the guards that he hadn't fully appreciated until then. How was he supposed to resist this? He had never known temptation as he did in that moment.

He wanted to touch her, to trace the circle around the puckered flesh. Was it soft? Would it tighten more if he did? He'd never caressed a woman in that way, or caressed one at all, for that matter. And Elen was not just *any* woman; she was the one he'd been waiting more than three hundred years to touch. His hand lifted of its own volition, almost reaching the darkened peak before he snagged it back.

No, this was wrong. Exploring her body while she was unconscious, and without the ability to refuse, was no better than what their enemy had done. Swearing under his breath, Cormack covered her with blankets and moved his treacherous body to the vacant chair.

WISHING HE HAD LOCKED HIS OFFICE DOOR, DYLAN closed his eyes and groaned as Sophie's fingers worked the muscles around his neck and shoulders. Between the shock with his sister, calls to allied leaders to warn of Guardian activity, and meetings with the guards and villagers, he'd earned this moment with his wife. And by the Gods, if another person interrupted them, he might just rip off their head.

"You're so tense," Sophie soothed, twisting and untwisting the stiffness of his back.

"I've been neglected by my mate for two days." He received a nip on his ear for the remark.

"You'll be neglected for another two if Elen doesn't wake up soon."

He frowned with renewed concern. "You said she's woken in intervals." Necessity had forced Dylan to return to Rhuddin Hall, but Sophie had kept him updated on his sister's condition.

"Yes, but I don't think she's aware. I had to walk her to the restroom, and then she fell asleep again immediately afterward. Cormack promised to call if he needed help."

"This is a dark business that Pendaran has brought into our midst." And Dylan didn't know how to fight this battle.

"He's a coward," she sneered, "to attack her in spirit where none of us can help."

"Pendaran doesn't understand honor," Dylan corrected. "But he's not a coward. He looks for the most efficient way to achieve his goals and uses it. He will come for Elen again, and we must prepare for all tactics. Even if he is weakened, I don't trust his reach. This fight could very well take place on grounds that we can't see."

"I wished you'd convinced her to stay here, but I'm glad she has someone with her at least. Not that Ms. Hafwen isn't someone," she amended, "but you know what I mean."

Yes, he did know—which was the reason he'd assigned Cormack as her guard. "What do you think of him?" Sophie had been in his company for two days now, and he wanted her opinion. "I almost intervened when that relationship first began, but Elen was so . . ." He sighed with frustration, hating the fear the villagers, and even the guards, had of her, and finished, "friendless."

"He's nothing like his sisters," she said with some reservation. "I think he loves her. And Elen deserves to be loved. And whatever their relationship is, or becomes, it's between them. He's been by her side this whole time, leaving only when I helped her out of that dress."

"I'm not surprised, but I'm glad to hear it." It made his decision to place him there more agreeable. Not that any others had wanted the post, but he hadn't had the heart to tell Elen that. Dylan's patience on that matter had grown thin a long time ago. His sister's tender heart was the reason he began accepting others of their kind into his territory, and their fear of her was quickly turning into disrespect. It would be addressed soon.

"I'm waking her to eat when I return," Sophie said with the mixture of authority and caregiving instincts that had drawn him to her in the beginning. "I've had Enid prepare some meals to bring over, with blueberry tarts." A rueful sigh fell from her mouth. "Maybe those will smooth Ms. Hafwen's tweaked feathers. I'm not sure how she guessed I told you, but the winged tyrant has been ordering me around for two days. I remade her tea three times yesterday because, according to her, it was too bitter."

Dylan chuckled. "Bring her some of Enid's special mead with the tarts, and she'll be your best friend before she finishes the first thimbleful. Honey, especially fermented honey, is like catnip to felines for pixies."

"Mead, huh?" Sophie laughed. "I'm not sure I want to see a drugged Ms. Hafwen, but I will bring a bottle just in case."

Trust was a new and precious development between him and his wife. He had little doubt that Elen and her pixie had put the fear of Fae-wrath into her, but Sophie chose to confide in him anyway. Concern, he was sure, helped his wife's decision. For her sake, he'd treated every situation as if he hadn't known about Ms. Hafwen's presence and had kept her secret between them.

But he was pleased. No, he amended, he was happy, the happiest he'd been in a long time—and he'd be damned if he'd let Pendaran and his followers threaten his family yet again.

The reign of the Guardians must end.

Which prompted him to confide his own news. "Isabeau has called a meeting with other leaders who have joined our cause. It will take place in her territory on Thursday."

Her hands stopped their ministrations. "You're going to Minnesota?"

"I have to."

"This isn't a good time."

"There's never a good time. After Avon's battle many of the leaders have decided to stay close to their own territories and not get involved. Isabeau has helped us twice now. I need to go."

Instead of arguing, she sought reassurance. "But it's just a meeting?"

"Yes, as far as I know. She's been contacted by Edwyn, one of the Council members. She has more information she doesn't want to share over the phone or by messenger. I have news as well. Others might too. It's time we meet to see who's still with us, and before we're in the middle of another crisis. I would bring you with me—"

"No, I need to stay here," she said before he had a chance to finish, claiming her role as the alpha's mate in his absence without hesitation.

It affected him as it would any wolf.

Tired of war talk, he swiveled in his office chair and

caught her up in his lap, capturing her mouth as she gasped in surprise. "I need you tonight," he whispered against her lips, kissing down to the sensitive skin under her ear. "We'll check on Elen, and if she's well, I want you home in our bed."

She turned her neck to give him better access, running her hands along his arms and clutching him closer. "Do we have to wait until tonight?" Her body unfolded, and then she began to release the buttons of her shirt.

A knock sounded on his office door.

Dylan snarled at the interruption. "Unless the Guardians are at our bloody gate," he barked at the intruder before they were stupid enough to open the door, "go away."

"Only one." Porter's voice came with muffled displeasure as the bearer of bad news. "But you might be wanting to talk to this one." A pause. "It's your mother."

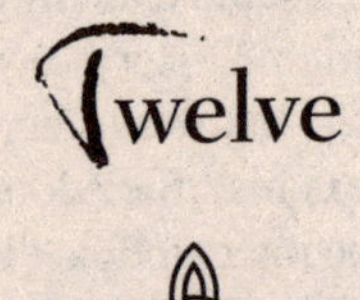

Twelve

SOMETIME LATER, AND SHE WASN'T SURE HOW MUCH later, Elen stretched in her bed, awakened by the warmth of sun on her face. Was it morning already? The rays of light came from her north-facing window, righting her disorientation; the sun was high and that placed the time around noon.

Had she been asleep since yesterday? The bed was empty. She remembered Cormack holding her for a while, and waking her to drink throughout the night. Elen sat up, and then frowned. The dress had been removed at some point and replaced by a nightshirt. Had he undressed her? No, she was soon remedied of that notion, vaguely recalling gentle orders to raise her arms and a soft scent that was Sophie's and not his, guiding her to use the restroom.

But she'd dreamt of him. Oh yes, her subconscious had replayed those minutes before Pendaran had arrived to steal her joy. Excluding her family, everyone in Rhuddin Village feared her touch. Her lovers, few that there were, had been mortals during her time at medical school. Needless to say, it had been a long while since she'd felt pleasure by a hand other than her own.

Out of respect, she'd never fulfilled her urges in Cormack's company. She'd understood the mind of a man was trapped behind the eyes of a wolf. He had no way of knowing about the neglected state of her needs. If so, he never would have lifted her skirts and proclaimed, with utter confidence, of what he could do *in less than a second.*

Even now, her nipples tightened at the memory of his hand on her bared hip, and his thigh wedged between her legs. She was deprived of all sensual comfort—utterly and completely deprived. And she craved it like air. Little did he realize that if she'd felt evidence of an erection when he'd threatened to bend her over, she could have easily climaxed in his arms.

Heavy footfalls sounded on the stairs, causing her to jump. Cormack turned the corner holding a tray of food. A smile spread across his face when he noticed her sitting. "I thought I heard you stirring up here. I brought you something."

Her heart pounded so hard she had an urge to press her hand against her chest to calm its frantic rhythm. He was shirtless and freshly showered, his damp hair drawn back like he'd given it a quick comb with his fingers. His jawline, strong and as stubbornly set as any Celt's, lacked stubble, so he must have shaved. His jeans rode low on his hips. A smattering of dark bronze hair—not much, but enough—trailed from his hardened stomach to his waistband. The width of his shoulders filled the doorway, and the more she stared, the more intense his gaze became.

Feeling heat crawl up her neck, Elen looked away. Why couldn't he have been hideous? Not that it would have mattered if he were. Desire was fueled by the heart, and since her heart ached for him, her flesh responded in kind.

Surely, she wasn't the only one who felt this longing building between them. Not after the suggestions he'd made, and the possessive behavior he'd shown. He struggled with the nature of his wolf, she knew, as all shifters did. Human minds maintained their conscience while in wolf form, but wolves had no such limitations when the forms were reversed.

Or was all this attention his way of repaying the kindness of friendship? And if she suggested a physical relationship, would the idea revolt him? Or worse, would he leave again?

So many unanswered questions, and the unknowing was torturous, but she dreaded a refusal more.

Cormack stepped into the room, lowering the tray. "What's wrong?"

"Nothing." *Everything.* And she must learn to control her emotions around him because he read her too easily. But they had greater concerns than her wanton libido and needy heart. "Is everyone all right? Are they still here? Has there been any fallback from Pendaran?"

The muscle on the side of his jaw clenched, as if he knew she'd avoided his question. He wasn't pleased, she realized, but allowed it. "All is well," he assured her softly. "Your family left this afternoon, but they've called and sent enough food to last a month, and they'll be back to check on you in the morning. No word on the Guardians, but we are preparing."

Sensing a guarded tone to his voice, she asked, "Did anything happen that I should know about?"

"Nothing that can't wait until tomorrow."

"Good," she said, not ready for another major challenge just yet. "Still, I should call Dylan and Sophie and let Ms. Hafwen know I'm awake."

"Already done. And you have been officially ordered to rest for another day. Tomorrow will come soon enough."

"I still have to go to the barn." Elen did her own chores. "The animals need to be fed."

"Done," he said again.

She relaxed back against the pillows. "Thank you, Cormack. Thank you for being . . ." She almost said *my friend*, but that term had become rudely genteel for what he meant to her. "Thank you for being here."

He paused as if to say something, but then gave a sharp nod instead.

To fill the silence, Elen scooted over to make room for the tray and patted the bed. "How long have I been asleep?"

"Two days." He handed her a piece of buttered toast. "Eat."

She almost choked on her first bite. *Two days?* Snagging the glass of orange juice off the tray, she took several sips to wash it down. "I need to shower and change."

"You need to eat first." He handed her another piece of toast with a look that suggested he might force-feed her if she didn't accept it.

After the third piece, she said, "Enough. I'll eat some more after I shower." She felt a bit woozy, but otherwise fine. Her need to use the facilities prompted her to move. Cormack stood to follow, but she held up her hand. "I can manage."

And it was then that understanding dawned. Yes, some things did deserve privacy, especially when desire and pride blurred the line between caregiver and consort. And with that awareness came a fluttering in her belly that refused to subside.

The shower cleared the remaining cobwebs of sleep, and after a thorough teeth brushing, she combed her hair and applied a layer of her moonflower moisturizer. Wrapping a towel around her torso, she opened the door to find him leaning against the opposite wall. Had he been waiting there this whole time?

His heated gaze traveled from her wet head to her pink-polished toes. "How do you feel?"

She almost gripped the doorframe for support, but suspected he would mistake it for tiredness, when her weakness was anything but. "Much better, but I'm not ready for any of Ms. Hafwen's lessons just yet. I would like to go for a walk outside and get some fresh air."

Apparently not satisfied she wasn't going to fall on her face, he said, "I'll wait here while you dress, then we'll go for a walk together."

"Okay." At the moment she had no mind to argue. Closing the door was another change in their relationship, because as a wolf he'd never been barred from her rooms. She dressed in black cotton pants, fuzzy socks and a T-shirt. Underneath, she wore pink lace underwear and a matching bra. Lingerie was her selfish pleasure, but as Ms. Hafwen often reminded her, it didn't hurt to be prepared.

SOPHIE SAT NEXT TO DYLAN AND RESISTED THE URGE TO place a comforting hand on his arm. The great room had been cleared of all villagers, while Sarah and Porter stood at both entrances. Merin sat on the opposite sofa, with a rod-straight posture and her hands folded neatly in her lap. She wore a plain black pantsuit, and if not for the slight rise and fall of her shoulders, her nervousness would have gone unnoticed.

Sophie didn't trust Dylan's mother, though she couldn't help but sympathize with her. Having made her own desperate decisions to keep Joshua safe, she would be a hypocrite not to. Her sympathy only went so far, however.

Tucker, her hound, sauntered around Porter and into the room, glaring at Merin while he sat on his haunches, leaning his torso against Sophie's legs. The dog had once belonged to Taliesin, although to say he *belonged* to anyone was debatable; Tucker chose where he stayed. He was the size of a Great Dane, with white fur and red-tipped ears, and as a hound from the Otherworld, he came and went as he pleased.

A low growl rumbled from his throat; it was an announcement of his authority, not a signal of intent to lunge. Sophie had learned the difference. This sound was much less ominous than the other. But it obviously unsettled Merin, who eyed the swords mounted on the walls.

"Shhh," Sophie soothed, running her hand down his back.

"Then it's true." Merin's gaze landed on her, so like Elen's it was eerie—but harsh instead of gentle, like a winter without sun. "It responds to your command."

She refused to cower. "Yes." *Sometimes.*

An unexpected grin turned her lips. "My son has chosen his mate well."

"I'm human," Sophie announced without shame. *Judge me how you will, I don't care.*

"My mate was human." Merin gave an absent wave. "Power does not make a warrior's heart, and there was no greater one than his. No, it is what a person is willing to sacrifice to protect their family that proves true strength." As if reminded of her purpose, she turned her attention to Dylan. "Pendaran has forgotten this, and it will be his downfall in the end. I know I am not welcomed here, but I have knowledge of the Council that you need to know if you are to survive. Will you accept my help?"

"He attacked Elen from the spirit world," Dylan challenged, his voice a distant storm waiting to unleash if given the chance. "How are you to help us with that?"

Merin sucked in a breath, and then stood. "Did she survive it?"

Sensing genuine distress, Sophie realized that others before Elen had not. "She is resting now."

"I should have killed him," Merin sneered, beginning to pace. "I want to see her."

"Not today." But after a long pause, Dylan signaled Porter to enter the room. "I will ask Elen if she's willing. If not, you will respect her wishes. Do you understand?" He waited until his mother gave a tight-lipped nod. "We have a lake house nearby. You are welcome to stay."

Merin paused and then looked away briefly, blinking something out of her eye. "Thank you," she said, turning back, her former composure in place. "I accept your offer. I have much to share, but I'll need to return to my own household within a few days."

Sophie had remained neutral throughout this tense reunion, not sure if Dylan would kick Merin out or invite her to stay, and ready to support his decision either way. But his offer of the lake house was the sign she'd been waiting for. His judgment wasn't completely closed against his mother, or the information she seemed willing to share. True or not, he intended to listen.

And as that thought unfolded, another more potent one followed, only this one didn't come from her consciousness. Sophie stiffened as a brush of power stroked down her spine, circling her waist. The scent of apple blossoms filled the air. Merin's nostrils flared, and her gaze landed on the serpent weapon Sophie wore around her waist. Like the hound, the weapon had been given to her by Taliesin. The wearer received messages from beings in the Otherworld, and she tensed every time one came. As they were never sent without purpose, she'd learned to appreciate them.

Melissa, Cormack's five-year-old niece, was saved because of one such message.

Merin is not your enemy. The serpentine voice wove about her senses. *Listen to her, and listen well.*

Dylan waited with interest in his dark gaze. "Well?" He too had come to appreciate the messages.

"It speaks to you?" Merin asked. Not with resentment but with approval, like a predator welcoming another warrior into her pack.

"Yes." Sophie didn't lie, placing her hand on her husband's arm and squeezing gently, a gesture he understood. *I will tell you after and let you decide what you want to share.* He gave a curt nod.

Standing, Sophie avoided Merin's curiosity by asking, "Would you like to join us for dinner? We still have a few hours yet, but that will give you time to settle in the lake house and return later." Protective instincts raged, but Joshua was an adult, a fact of which he constantly reminded her. If she didn't include him, he would, no doubt, include himself. "Your grandson will be there, if you would like to meet him."

As would Sophie and Dylan, fully armed of course, but forgiveness did not come in day, or even a summer.

"There is nothing—" Merin's voice broke, and she looked away again, obviously uncomfortable with showing emotion. "There is nothing I would like more."

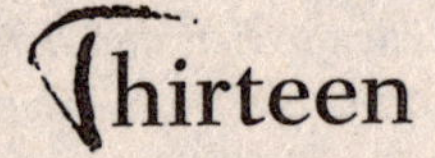

Thirteen

Hints of summer's last days lingered in the air like a parting celebration of harvest. Leaves began to fall in the first trickle of autumn's confetti. The afternoon sun sent a warm breeze through the forest, and Elen closed her eyes to savor the scents of pine and rich earth. There was always this one week of remembrance, where the days remained warm like summer even while the nights cooled.

They had taken the easier trail to Indigo Falls, one of her and Cormack's private retreats near her cottage. It was warm enough that sweat dripped down her spine. He walked next to her, holding a basket of food, while Elen carried a blanket and two towels. The picnic had been her idea. He'd frowned at the towels, but she'd taken them anyway just in case. July through September were the only months when the water temperatures were tolerable, and this may be her last chance for a swim.

After alerting the other guards of their intent, he'd been silent on their journey. She enjoyed his company and kept her questions contained, even ones concerning his behavior before Pendaran's arrival.

But it was a comfortable silence, and she didn't want to ruin it with conversations that might end this peace that had grown between them once again. This was the wolf she remembered, her confidant, and her companion for more than three hundred years.

Not surprisingly, his concern was obvious, and she felt compelled to ease it. "I feel great, so you can stop looking at me like I'm sick or about to fall asleep again." She held the towels to her chest and breathed deeply. Every day was a gift, and she would not waste this one on worries and fear. "I haven't been to Indigo Falls since you left. I needed this."

When she snuck a glance in his direction, she saw his gaze had grown dark. "Or maybe it needed you," he said quietly.

His intimate assessment made her stomach flutter, but she let his comment disappear into the growing sounds of rushing water. Indigo Falls opened around the next bend and soon came into view. White rapids churned over gray rock that reflected blue, the water falling into the pool below. A small waterfall, but private, and it had been her and Cormack's special place for many years. On hot summer days, they had come here often to swim in the waist-high waters fed by rivers off the mountain. They had dried in the sun afterward, watching clouds in the sky or birds flit about the wildflowers that grew on the banks.

Even now, bees gathered on tansy and goldenrod, as if they knew their days were almost at an end. A maple tree grew on the bank, its roots fed by the falls. Its leaves had turned a blazing burgundy orange, but had yet to fall. She whipped the blanket and let it spread under its shelter.

Removing his sword, Cormack sat next to her on the blanket. He placed his weapon on the opposite side, by his thigh, and then opened the basket to hand her a sandwich. She nibbled at it because he looked like he might revolt if she didn't. She wanted to talk to him, ask a million questions and more, but that had never been their relationship. She found herself feeling flustered in front of the one person who knew her best.

"You seem unsettled," he said in validation of her thoughts, reclining back on his elbows. "Do you want to talk about what Pendaran did?"

His legs extended beyond their blanket, and she tried not to stare at the bounty spread out beside her, but it was difficult not to, with a navy T-shirt hugging his chest and stomach and his biceps flexed to support his weight.

"No." Pendaran was the last person she wanted clouding this moment, but Cormack had broached the subject, so she would address it. "You were right, if that makes you feel any better. I should never have placated him by wearing that dress."

"I agree, but it doesn't make me feel any better. And I understand your motivation. But the way he came for you . . ." Bitterness laced his voice, frustration as well. And anger; it hovered low under the surface, ready to boil if given the proper heat. "It wouldn't have mattered what you wore, and I couldn't defend you."

"On that battlefield I can defend myself," Elen said softly. "But not here," she readily admitted to ease his self-reproach. "Not when it comes to physical violence." Her brother's assessment had been more than accurate. Her conscience was her weakness. "I'm grateful you're here."

He blinked slowly, watching her through a heavy-lidded

gaze. He began to say something, but then shook his head. "As am I."

"He's not interested in me in any romantic sense," she rambled, needing to fill the suddenly charged air that hung between them. "He has no respect for life, only power. He views differences as a weakness to be destroyed." She shared her assessment, and the conclusion she'd reached. "Where I believe the aspects that make us unique *are* what makes us interesting. Everyone is worthy of life. I can't even pretend to play his game, and should never have tried."

"But he's still interested in controlling your gift."

"Yes." She looked down. "And I angered him. But I will deal with my next challenge when it comes. For now I just want to enjoy this day."

Taking her cue, Cormack sat up only to pull an apple from the basket. He flipped open a jackknife and sliced the fruit with deft skill. A cup of peanut butter followed. Scooping a liberal amount onto a wedge, he handed it to her. "I know it's your favorite."

She accepted the offering. "You know too much about me, and I know nothing about you."

"You know everything that's important," he returned. When she pursed her lips, he sighed. "Ask me what you want to know, and I will answer."

He could have no idea what questions tempted her curiosity. If he had, he wouldn't have opened this door. But now that he had, she thought of a neutral subject before he closed it. "What do you like most about . . ." She gestured to his new form.

He wiggled his fingers. "Hands."

"You seem good with them." She cringed as soon as the words left her mouth, but he didn't catch the innuendo.

"Not at first," he admitted. "Learning to talk was tedious," he added, "and frustrating. I understood everything, but couldn't get my tongue to form the words."

Her heart clenched, wishing he had let her help him, but that argument had already been traveled. "It must have been a challenge."

"Anything worth having is a challenge."

Why did her heart pick up a beat with that statement? "Anything else in particular?" she prompted, because she was helpless to do anything but.

He rolled his eyes—so *not* the sentiment she was looking for. "Facial expressions. And emotions. It took a while to learn how to control them. Wolves have no need for deception, but humans do it without thinking. It's natural."

"Sometimes it's for kindness," she muttered. *When we don't want to hear the truth.* And she needed to stop reaching for answers she might not want to hear.

Flopping back against the blanket, she concentrated on the branches overhead, watching the sun flicker in the leaves like nature's flame.

Will you be my lover? That was the question burning for release. She had never realized that desire could be poisonous; a wanting so acute that acid churned in her belly, lodging against her heart. He made no signs of aspiring to a physical relationship beyond caregiver, except for that one incident—but that had been to prove a point.

"Will you keep a secret?" she asked instead.

"You know I will." He reclined on his side, propping his weight on his elbow to lean toward her.

"Do I?" She tilted her head, watching the emotions cross his face. He had not mastered hiding them quite yet. Irritation was there, and hurt that she would ask such a thing. He had broken this trust when he left her, so it was not an impulsive concern.

"I will keep your secrets until the day I die." His tone lowered in stark contrast to the glint raging in his cerulean eyes. "And I will fight anyone who dares harm you because of them."

She believed him, because of their history and because her heart told her to. "Ms. Hafwen has shown me that my power is connected to the element of Earth, but that all the elements are connected to nature. I'm learning how to call the others."

"That's what your lesson was about when I wasn't allowed to stay."

She nodded. "It's given me an insight into greater possibilities."

He remained silent for a long while. "Does Pendaran know of this? Is that how you escaped?"

How had their conversation returned to him? Because Cormack was her personal guard, that's how, a reminder she'd needed before doing something foolish.

"Yes." Elen didn't describe the image of him tangled in vines and screaming threats, but didn't belittle the danger either. "He knows my gift has grown and that I have Otherworld knowledge."

"You will practice more in the coming days." Cormack had never cowered from her abilities, and his encouragement only made him that much more appealing. "You need to master whatever you learn."

He was right, and now was as good a time as any to try. "I have yet to connect with Water." She stood to stretch and kick off her socks and sneakers.

"What are you doing?"

"Going for a swim." She swam nude, always had, and to

change her routine would be cowardly, if not an insult. Even so, her heart raced as she hooked her thumbs under the waistband of her pants and shrugged them off, then yanked the T-shirt over her head. Her lace bra and panties joined her pile.

A sound came from Cormack, like a whoosh of breath, or a groan. When he looked away suddenly, she frowned. The flush that crawled up his neck suggested either embarrassment or annoyance, and she wasn't sure which but suspected both.

"What's wrong?" This was a common activity they'd enjoyed hundreds of times, which she pointed out to ease the sudden tension. "You've seen me nude countless times."

Fourteen

SHE WAS TRYING TO KILL HIM. THERE WAS NO OTHER explanation—except for the obvious: Elen didn't share his need; she didn't feel the same hunger that was burning a hole in his gut like molten acid—so why not strip in front of him? And, as she pointed out, he had seen her nude countless times.

But that was before. Now he had an appendage that responded and the capability to touch and taste all that glowing skin. Did she not realize the temptation that posed? Elen was an active woman, working her own garden and walking more than she drove, and it showed.

He wanted to join her, but his cock was so damn hard it hurt. If he went in clothed, he'd look like an ass; if he joined her nude, he'd look like a *randy* ass. No choice but to stay here and suffer in silence as sweat beaded his brow.

"Go for your swim." His voice sounded like a sword grinding against stone.

"Why don't you join me?" She waded into the pool and turned to face him. Her breasts balanced on the surface of the bubbling waters. "It's not that cold."

No? Her nipples had hardened to taut peaks.

"I'll trust your word on that," he clipped. Had it just been this morning when he'd come damn close to feeling those delicate points?

"Your loss." Taking a deep breath, she floated on her back. Her hair spread out around her like a golden shroud; a water nymph to seduce his soul.

Closing his eyes, Cormack pretended to sleep and willed his cock to behave. He heard her splashing about, and then silence. He almost opened his eyes to check on her when a wall of cold water robbed him of breath.

Jumping up, he sputtered, "What the hell?"

"Sorry." Her hands tried to cover her giggle but her eyes echoed with impish glee. "I'm still learning control. I meant for it to be a small spray."

Her small spray had instead been a large wave that had soaked the banks of the falls and everything on them, him included. Even now, the pool swirled around her floating form as if building momentum for another upsurge.

"You need more practice." He tried to hold back a grin, but it was impossible with her. "And," he warned, "a payback."

The water had cured the problem with his appendage, so he stripped out of his clothes, hung them on a nearby branch along with the soaked blanket. His sword he placed near the bank. Their towels and basket had been spared, and he moved them farther away.

When he turned back, her face had cleared of all mischief. "What's wrong?" He threw her earlier words back to her. "You've seen me nude countless times."

"Doesn't count." Eyes wide, she shook her head. "You were covered in fur."

Her curiosity was natural, he knew, but he waded in quickly before his body responded. He was aware that women, and some men, were attracted to him. Many at Avon had made obvious advances, right down to whispered descriptions of what they wanted to teach him.

Elen, on the other hand, was impossible to read; she made no obvious advances or heated whispers of wicked promises. That one time before Pendaran's arrival was the first he'd ever seen her aroused, but even now he questioned if he'd misread her.

A sigh fell from his mouth. If only she would just rub her hand over his crotch like Tesni had done, and there'd be no confusions. He didn't read human subtleties well, and refused to risk losing Elen with the crudities of his inexperience. Like her, he would simply enjoy this day.

The water was cold but not unpleasant once his body adjusted. The gravel bottom stirred under his feet as he waded to the center near Elen. It felt good to be here with her, creating new memories from old, and seeing her smile. In the spring, when the pool was fed by melting snow, it could numb extremities in seconds, but these waters had been heated by summer. Ducking under the surface, he grabbed her by the ankles and flipped her.

She emerged half sputtering and half laughing. "Not fair. You've never done that before." Wiping her hair back from her face, her eyes shone with exhilaration, a far cry from the lifeless form he held mere days ago.

Grinning, he wiggled his fingers. "Hands."

Her expression turned serious. "I missed you, Cormack,"

she whispered. Wading toward him, she hugged him briefly and then stepped back. "I'm sorry if that makes you uncomfortable . . ." She shrugged as if to lighten the moment. "But I just needed you to know that I've missed our times together."

The shock of the impulsive embrace left him floundering for a response. Skin, he realized then, was its own erogenous receptor; thousands of nerve endings felt the slippery slide of her arms and pointed nipples against his chest. However brief, he burned in places he didn't know how to control.

"I missed you as well." *More than my heart can stand.* His voice was as rough as the gravel under his feet, and just as unstable. A drop of water trailed from her hair and fell to her lips. Drawn by the moment, or by a need that had been denied for too long, he leaned forward, wanting to taste that drop.

But he wasn't sure how, or if his attentions were even welcomed in a carnal capacity.

Her lips trembled under his gaze.

"You're cold." He groaned because of his selfishness. "We've stayed too long."

"I'm not," she argued in a breathless voice. Worse, she shuddered—as if freezing.

And here he'd been contemplating on how to kiss her.

"Out," he ordered, pushing her toward the edge. "You've had your walk, practice and a swim. Now it's time to get you home and warmed up."

ALL TWENTY GUARDS MET ON EMERALD MOSS TRAIL AS the sun began to set, summoned by their alpha to discuss upcoming events. All were shifters except for Porter, but he had earned his ranking by skill and viciousness on the battlefield. Cormack remained on the outskirts to keep an eye on Elen's cottage in the distance. After returning from the falls, she worked in her garden with a pixie close by, but he could be there in under a minute if necessary.

Dylan stood at the front of their gathering, his stance wide as he addressed the group. Except for the black eyes, his coloring was similar to Elen's, but where her features were soft and welcoming, his were stark and unyielding. "As you all know, Merin is here. She is willing to share insight on the Council, and she has earned my audience by her actions at Avon's battle. I believe she's cut ties with the Guardians," he affirmed, but with hesitation. "Make no mistake, Guardian or not, my mother is the most powerful warrior in our midst at this time."

"How long are you allowing her to stay?" Sarah asked.

"Two days." Dylan's gaze flicked to Cormack in silent warning. "After she leaves I'll be going to Isabeau's territory to meet with our allies. I'll be there from Thursday to Friday. While I'm gone, you will answer to Porter and my mate."

"And Pendaran?" This came from John. Lanky as a man but lethal as a wolf, the guard kept a groomed beard and cropped brown hair. His mate was Gwenfair, the local teacher in the village.

"We've prepared as best we can, but I feel this battle may take place on grounds we can't see. He doesn't think like a warrior, so we mustn't either. I've learned that he's still weakened from his last attack on my sister for at least another few days. Also, I doubt Pendaran will allow any form of impediment to be seen by others. With that said, I don't trust his personal reach, or his manipulations. Our alert status is down, but be watchful for the unexpected."

"If we have a reprieve, can I tell my wife to open our barn for visitors?" John asked in a neutral tone, but the fact that he broached the topic proved he'd been prodded by a personal source. "Her harvest party was to be tonight before it was canceled. Everything's prepared. If the waste isn't necessary, we'll tell everyone to come grab some food."

Sarah snickered. "Afraid you'll be eating chicken salad sandwiches for a week, John?"

"More like pissing pink punch for a month," he muttered.

Dylan held up his hand as more bantering followed. "Tell Gwenfair to have her harvest party. Merin will be with Sophie and me tonight, but perhaps Elen will attend in our place . . ." He looked to Cormack to answer.

"I will ask her," he said. "She's in good health today." Enough to strip and drive him to the point of making a near fool of himself, but he didn't share that in current company.

John stiffened, and then looked away.

Cormack should have remained silent, but any insult against Elen annoyed him. He knew she would enjoy the company of the villagers . . . if they would but welcome her. "What's the matter, John? Is Elen not invited?"

Immediately, Dylan pinned the guard with a displeased glare. "If I ever learn my sister is not welcome at an event in my territory, the person holding the event won't be welcome either." Quiet words given with lethal impact. "Is that clear, John?"

He sent Cormack a cutting glare for outing his discomfort. "I'll make sure Gwenfair and the women know to welcome her."

Meaning he'd be warning them to be nice.

"We'll see you there," Cormack said.

After Dylan dismissed the other guards, he motioned for Cormack to stay. They walked in silence toward the cottage, until the man gave a frustrated sigh. "If I keep the villagers on constant alert, they'll begin to feel trapped and resent

Elen more than they already do. If she's not received well, let me know. This fear they have of her has gone on long enough."

"They associate her power with that of the Guardians," Cormack said, having overheard more than one conversation on the subject when they knew he couldn't share. "But I think it's her lack of control they fear more. She's getting better, as you've noticed."

Once at the cottage, they found Elen in her garden cutting pumpkins off their vines. She wiped her hand across her forehead as they approached, leaving a streak of dirt. "Hi," she said to her brother. "I feel great, so you can remove that worried frown."

Not a man to prolong the inevitable, Dylan informed her, "Merin's here. She's staying two days, and she wants to see you. I told her that it's up to you."

Her expression fell. Cormack wanted to reach out to her but held his stance in front of her brother's sharp gaze. "It's time," she said after a moment, "but not tonight."

"How about breakfast before she leaves? I won't tell her either way." Dylan hugged her briefly. "Think about it and let me know tomorrow night."

Cormack waited until her brother left, helping her pile the pumpkins on the back porch. The scars on Elen's spine were not the true damage caused by her mother, he knew. Merin had rejected her children, shunned them to do the Council's bidding, and Elen had had almost nineteen hundred years to build her walls against that pain. It took more than a summer to tear them down. "Are you okay?"

"I am," she said with conviction. "But I'm hungry. I think we should go see what else Sophie sent over in all those bags."

He reached out and wiped the smudge of dirt off her

forehead. How many times had he wanted to do that as a wolf? "Gwenfair is having a harvest gathering, and we've been invited. Are you up for it?"

Her features lit with excitement before she squelched it. "I'll only make them uncomfortable."

"What if I want to go?" He didn't really. Cormack would much rather spend the evening alone with her. "Would you go with me?"

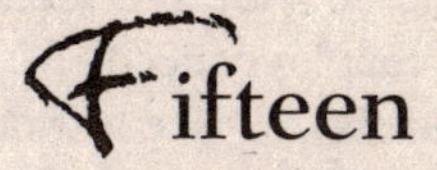

Fifteen

How had she let him talk her into this? Because he'd looked at her with those cerulean eyes and a mouth made for pleasure when asking—that's how.

Elen wore a dress she'd bought on a whim. It was sensual in a simple way; a date dress, for a woman who never dated. The material was soft, clingy and the perfect shade of purple, reminding her of lilac buds before they bloomed. It wrapped around her waist and fell to mid-thigh, and if she wasn't mistaken, Cormack had snuck more than once glance at her legs.

They traveled by car, but he drove the eight-mile stretch into town, just one more thing he'd learned to do well without her. They took the back road that led to John and Gwenfair's home, a Victorian farmhouse with gingerbread trimmings and a red barn set back from the house. A few cars lined the driveway, but many of the villagers had walked.

Forcing a smile, Elen refused to let anyone know how nerve-racking this was for her, especially Cormack—because he had wanted to come. Long tables were set up in rows inside the barn for people to sit and chat. Party lights strung from rafters added a soft glow. A modern sound system played music on a cleared section of the boarded floor where several couples danced.

It was lovely, and she felt like a fruit fly hovering over their pink punch: harmless—most of the time—but they still wanted to bat her away.

Cormack was the only shifter and guard present, because he was assigned to her, while the others kept their posts in the forest. Gwenfair approached with a welcoming smile. A petite woman compared to her husband, she had pinned her brown hair back. Flowers were entangled within the trailing curls.

"I'm glad to see you doing well, Elen." Gwenfair made a gesture toward a table of drinks. "We're relaxed here, so help yourself."

"Thank you." Elen suspected her brother's interference and likely Cormack's as well. The hosts had been warned, as had their guests, who offered nods of greeting. "I'm only going to stay a short while."

"Uncle Cormack!" Melissa, his niece, bolted from her father and jumped into his arms to be twisted in a wide giggling circle. She had red hair that curled around green eyes filled with mischief. Her father watched from a wary distance.

When Cormack set her down, she smiled at Elen. "I heard you were coming and brought something for you."

"You did?" Elen bent forward, knowing it was a pebble to add to her collection. Children didn't know to be frightened of her, but she made sure to open her hand without touching for the adults watching. "You can just drop it," she said. "Oooo, it's beautiful. I will treasure it." And she would, just as she did all the others.

The child flounced away as quickly as she had come, chasing after an older girl. There were eight children in Rhuddin Village. None of them could shift, but all were precious gifts.

"I'll get us something to drink." Cormack gestured toward the table with the pink punch. Once separated, Lydia approached him, stocky like her mother, who ran the kitchens of Rhuddin Hall. His head shook in answer to whatever her question had been.

It didn't escape Elen's notice that every unmated female snuck appreciative glances in his direction, nor did she blame them. He wore a buttoned shirt for the occasion but rolled up on his arms. It accentuated a build honed for battle, leaving no doubt he knew how to wield the sword that rested against his thigh.

Her lips turned in a secret smile, because she knew what body those clothes covered. And it was far more glorious then she, or any of them, could have imagined.

"Feel free to dance," Elen said when he returned, grateful only a small portion of discomfort leaked into her voice. The only invitations she received to dance came from a malevolent Guardian, but she refused to deny Cormack's enjoyment of the evening. "If that's what Lydia asked you."

The music slowed and couples began to gather on the hay-strewn floor in swaying embraces. Sulwen approached with determined strides, tall and willowy, and obviously hoping to succeed where her sister had failed. She blinked in surprise when Cormack held out his hand to Elen. Abruptly, she turned back toward her sister and shrugged.

"I have no interest in small talk with women who had no desire to know me before now." Cormack's hand didn't waver. "I've never danced. But it looks like they're just moving in a circle. Are you willing to risk your feet?"

"You're asking me?" Her heart beat in a rhythm much faster than the music playing.

"Who else spent time with me before this summer? Lydia and Sulwen?" he scoffed, shaking his head. "They threw me scraps from the kitchens of Rhuddin Hall when you made me a place setting at your table. Yes, Elen, I'm asking you." He lowered his hand. "But if you don't want to—"

"I want to." It hurt to hear him speak of his past mistreatment, knowing it was his reality for many centuries. Not caring of the blatant stares, she curled her arm through his. It was like holding supple rock covered in cotton. "I haven't for a very long time," she warned. Not in the real world anyway, and not with someone who made her feel dizzy and heavy all at the same time. "And the dances have changed."

She had hugged him while in Indigo Falls, and while nude, but placing her arms over his unsettled her just as much, if not more. Mimicking the less-affectionate couples, his hands rested gently on her waist, while he kept a respectful distance, not pressing into her. Still, heat rose from his body and she wanted to melt into him like chocolate in the sun. Surely he heard the rapid beating of her heart as they swayed around other couples.

He did, she discovered, when he leaned down and whispered, "Their fear will leave once they know you're learning to control your power."

Oh yes . . . He'd heard her racing response, and mistook it yet again. Unfortunately, she began to realize his true purpose for this outing, and it was both endearing and disappointing. Learning back, she asked, "You're doing this to show them I'm not dangerous, aren't you?"

His hands tightened around her waist, played with the

string that tied her dress. For an instant she sensed his frustration, wasn't sure of its source, only that he cleared his expression under her searching gaze. "It's working," he said. "They're not even looking at us anymore."

He was right. She was so consumed with him, she hadn't noticed. But people carried on their own conversations without paying any attention to her, almost like she belonged. One couple even bumped into her and didn't flinch.

The music suddenly changed, as did his expression as he watched couples break apart and start to gyrate. "I'm not even going to try that."

A laugh spilled out. "Neither am I."

They returned to her cottage shortly after, making polite excuses. The villagers were gracious enough to hide their relief, but it lingered, just not as much. Cormack parked her car in the gravel driveway that led to the front walkway, handing her the keys after he walked around to open her door.

If this had been a date, it would have been the best of her life. But it hadn't been. She reminded herself of that fact several times later that night as she tried to sleep in an empty bed. She'd grown accustomed to it over the summer, but with him back, she missed the company.

No, she amended, she missed *him*.

HE DIDN'T BELONG IN THE BLOODY GUEST ROOM STARING up at the ceiling. Cormack belonged with Elen; it was where he'd slept for almost three hundred years, but with an inconvenient appendage that refused to go down, he had no other choice.

When the hell had she bought that dress? Over the summer? It was her favorite color, so he knew she'd purchased it for herself—and that made it all the more beautiful.

Fisting his hands in the sheets, he tried to think of something else, something other than that silky material that hugged her curves, leaving little between his hands at her waist. With her face upturned mere inches under his, swaying to music, he yearned to untie the belt and unwrap her like his own personal present.

If she'd only known how badly he'd wanted to rub against her as he'd seen some other couples do, like a randy wolf in heat. He ran his hand down his stomach—because he *hurt.* He needed relief, stroking once down his hard length, but it was empty and dissatisfying.

Kicking off the sheets, he went to the bathroom, pausing outside Elen's door. It was closed, and even that grated under his skin. He knocked softly.

"Come in." She rose on her elbows.

"I'm going for a run," he told her, leaning through the door. "I'll circle the cottage and be back in a few."

"Okay." Was that disappointment in her voice? "You can stay in here afterward, if you want." His blood pounded a vicious path to his temples and other extremities. A beat passed, and then another. "As you used to."

As a wolf, she meant.

Not the invitation he wanted. "Maybe," he clipped as his beast rose in unison with his ire. But he didn't shut the door, leaving it open a crack, just in case he weakened and returned to her as the companion she wanted.

A slow drizzle cooled his blood as he passed the miniature stone cottage. A yellow glow came for the turret window, flickering like a candle. The pixie was awake, probably reading, as she'd been the last two times he'd checked on her. She was planning another lesson for Elen in the morning, or so he'd been informed. He didn't approach because he was in no mood for company or sharp voices.

He barely made it past the orchard when his beast raged for freedom. Buckling to his knees, he reached out his senses to the forest, feeding its energy to spark the shift. It hurt, but he welcomed the pain. As bones snapped like gunshots in his ears, one torture eased another.

Soon the scents sharpened, and the sounds of creatures filled the night as they scurried for their burrows, sensing a predator in their midst. He circled the cottage twice, nodding to Sarah, who guarded the entrance of Emerald Moss Trail. She gestured that all was quiet.

He didn't shift back when he returned, caving to better judgment. He needed sleep to be alert, and he wasn't going to unless he was with her. He entered through the side door he had left open, crowding back with his body until it closed. Padding up the stairs, memories flooded his thoughts. He was still home, he realized. Man or wolf, he was still home.

Nuzzling open Elen's bedroom door—*his* door—he jumped on their bed and was rewarded with a soft sigh.

Her hands curled into his fur and she rested her face in his neck as he settled next to her. The only appendage that rose was his heart, but that was nothing new. She'd owned that organ for centuries.

"I missed you," Elen whispered, her voice catching. Within minutes her breaths evened, and lulled him to follow.

Sixteen

HOCHMEAD MANOR
GWYNEDD, WALES

THE DANK AIR OF THE DUNGEON SENT A CHILL OVER Pendaran's feverish skin. The price of his last incantation had been great, but so too had been the knowledge he'd gained, and the blessed gift that grew once again in his forest. By week's end his strength would return in full, and he would have the answers he sought. Without doubt, the dissenters expected him to mount a campaign, but what would that achieve other than tedium in a delayed timeframe? Moreover, the mechanical eyes of this new world posed excessive challenges; the feeble battles they must fight were an insult to his kind.

In truth, he'd grown bored in this century—until Merin's daughter had breathed power into his soul and tangled his earthbound body with vines. He was intrigued—and how long had it been since someone produced that sentiment? Far too long. He lacked both the patience and time for an open attack. Naturally, he had a more efficient plan in mind that Elen would never expect, and the anticipation almost made him smile.

Using a plastic bin with wheels, he dragged a freshly slaughtered lamb down the winding passageway. A newspaper concealed the offering. Six flights below ground he traveled, each level separated by metal doors that blocked light and sound from his household above. He trusted no one, not even his trained *Hen Was*. The servants whispered among themselves of a dragon in this pit, but that was Maelor's bane, not his. Rumors muddled truths, so he allowed their speculations.

Not a single soul knew the Bleidd still lived, not even its mother—but she would soon enough.

Releasing the outer locks on the final door, he leaned into the battered wood, using weight more than strength for entry. Due to his weakened condition, the stench that greeted him curdled his stomach, a meld of rotting carcasses from uneaten offerings, wet dog and fetid breath. Buckling like a boy at his first battle, Pendaran retched on a decomposing pig at his feet. When the heaving ceased, he lit a single taper and placed it on a protruding stone by the door. Drippings of many candles gone by cast a hardened waterfall of wax down the wall.

"Hello, Saran," he greeted the Bleidd who huddled in the far corner, more from cold than cowardice. Gaunt from starvation, the bitch's hind legs curled under a distended belly. The wolf suffered by choice, her latest scheme for freedom—as if he would ever let her go without good cause. Her black fur clumped like a mutt with mange, yet golden eyes lifted to his, arrogant and unbroken, even after two hundred years in his keeping, the last fifty in this room. A feisty woman was trapped under all that fur. A shame, that, but he was not the wielder of this horrid curse, just the corrector.

He would have killed her long ago if not for her parents. Born of an enchantress and a powerful Guardian, Saran had been their only weakness. The Guardian was long dead, but the enchantress still lived. No greater adversary had he yet to meet. For her daughter, she would submit to his demands.

"Eat," he ordered, rolling the bin toward her. "Nourish yourself and I will let you run in the forest and swim in the stream." Saran looked away as if she hadn't heard, but a spark lit within those golden eyes, and he knew she would obey if it meant a taste of freedom. "The time has come for you to be of use to me."

Grabbing the newspaper off the disjointed lamb, he threw it on the floor by the black wolf. It heralded a picture of the human prince on the front page with his wife and yet another heir. If this county only knew their original king stood in a dank dungeon offering slaughters to wretched beasts. He pulled a smartphone from his pocket and snapped a photo. Saran growled at the flash. Some things of the modern century were useful, he admitted with bitter disdain, tucking the device back into his pocket.

Later that afternoon, he dipped his quill and penned three lines. Setting the ink with his breath, he folded the letter around a printed photograph of an emaciated Bleidd. Old ink on parchment and new ink on printable paper—was that not a symbolic mockery of what this century had wrought? He was not ready to relinquish the old but was forced to learn the new.

Even in his weakened state, he held enough power to conjure a cloud. Modern forms of delivery left a trail and were susceptible to technical error, or worse, human incompetence. His way was always more efficient.

A week perhaps, or less, and Elen would be with him in flesh to provide the answers he deserved. Saran's pit would need a thorough cleaning before she arrived.

Seventeen

WHO WOULD HAVE THOUGHT THAT WATCHING A MAN CHOP wood could be a sensual experience? But with Cormack it was. Elen sat on a bench in the shade garden, giving her a direct view of the woodshed, and of him. Her lesson with Water had gone relatively well today with only a minor flood in the forest that had already sunk into the ground and dissipated. However, Ms. Hafwen had made her promise not to connect with Fire without her present.

As always, her tutor rose with the sun and retired before it set, and she was currently engaged in her cottage with a bottle of Enid's special mead uncorked under the hydrangeas. A hiccup came from the open door, followed by a giggling twitter. Sophie, it seemed, had taken her own lesson from Joshua and offered a honey-fermented bribe in one of her parcels delivered earlier. Judging by the singing chirps between hiccups, she'd been forgiven.

Elen had called Dylan that afternoon to tell him she'd be there for breakfast with their mother, but until then she intended to enjoy a quiet evening watching Cormack stack her wood pile for winter, shirtless and slick with sweat.

Neither of them had mentioned the night before, as if they both sensed an unbalance in their relationship. He was a man now. That element alone put them on this strange precipice of possibilities, and she wasn't sure how much longer she would last without teetering that balance. She knew without a doubt—because she understood her own limitations—that she was going to fall down that cliff soon. Would he fall with her was the question that clouded her cravings. And did it matter, when she was becoming too desperate to care?

Watching him wasn't helping her endurance, so she stood to be useful. "I'm going to take a shower," she called over to him. "Then I'll heat some pasta and make us a salad."

"Sounds good," he hollered back, placing the last wood on the pile and wiping his hand across his brow. "I'll take one after you." His grin rivaled the last rays of sun as it disappeared under the horizon. "It's getting chilly. Are you up for a fire tonight?"

The butterflies in her stomach stopped dancing and began to writhe in disjointed frenzy. The idea of spending an evening with Cormack, with a fire blazing in the hearth, made her ache. Not just her body, but her heart as well, and the combination was as intoxicating to her as fermented honey was to a pixie. They had too many memories of such nights together, honed from comfort and companionship between two lonely souls. She very well might tumble down a cliff like a fool, and she no longer cared. "That would be lovely."

* * *

THE GATHERING ROOM WAS ELEN'S FAVORITE PLACE IN the cottage. None of her furniture matched, and shelves lined the walls, filled with worn and well-loved novels of every genre. Her living plants remained outside in the garden, where they belonged, having been contained over the summer. Herbs hung from the rafters in bunched bundles as they dried, adding an earthy scent of lavender, rosemary and sage.

It was her cluttered and eclectic haven. A central stone fireplace separated the sitting area from the kitchen and provided heat and comfort. She often prepared remedies in the cast-iron kettle that hung from the chute over the flames. There was something about kindled fire, wood smoke and iron that set the potions better than any modern stove.

Even now, thanks to Cormack, a fire crackled in the hearth, taking the night chill out of the air. They had spent many hours in this room together, snuggled by the fire while she read to him. Her sofa was a recent splurge, overstuffed and covered in soft velour, and she sighed with pleasure as she curled her legs under a knitted throw and savored this time.

"I love this room," Cormack said, echoing her thoughts. After dinner, he had changed into a green shirt that tapered loosely to his waist and jeans, but she remembered all too well the body those clothes hid. He'd been glorious when he'd stripped by the falls, his stomach kissed by the afternoon sun, his shaft thick and heavy between his thighs. He was comfortable in his human skin.

He filled the room now with the same assurance, relaxed and at ease, while her skin felt tight and antsy, sensitive to touch under a tank top and cotton pajama bottoms over lace panties. She'd left off the bra, too stimulated to deal with the extra friction.

With a glass of red wine balanced in the palm of one hand, he twirled the dark liquid before taking an unhurried sip, closing his eyes as the taste hit his tongue. *I belong here.* That was the message he projected. Her wine, her glasses; it was his as much as hers.

He was home.

And it cast a feeling of rightness in her chest so deep it physically ached. If he'd placed the hilt of his sword on the coals of the fire and then held it on her skin, she'd be no less branded. Some marks remained unseen.

"You've been raiding the wine cellar," she managed to tease without betraying her thoughts.

Grinning without shame, he asked, "Would you like a glass?"

She shook her head. "Maybe later." In her current condition, anything that impeded judgment posed a dangerous prospect.

Walking along the nearest bookshelf, he ran his free hand over the spines, pausing at a tattered volume of *Jane Eyre*—one of her favorites, but not his. As a wolf, he would fall asleep when she read it. His interests leaned toward action and suspense novels. He removed the book and placed the glass on the trunk doubling as a coffee table, sat down beside her and drew her legs up over his lap. An intimate gesture, but comfortable because of the memories formed in this room.

And then he began to read, and she was lost in the deep timbre of his voice. He hesitated at times to decipher certain words, but for the most part recited the verse with steady and determined cadence.

"You've learned so much without me," she whispered as he paused to turn a page. Her interruption ruined the magic of the moment, and she instantly regretted it.

His chest rose and fell with a sigh. He closed the book and set it next to his glass. "Elen—"

"Forgive me," she blurted. "I should never have brought it up again." To reassure him, or perhaps herself, she leaned forward and placed a chaste kiss on his cheek. "Please continue reading. You're very good at it."

His skin was smooth but not soft, she noted during that brief moment of contact, and his scent lingered in the air around them, a meld of midnight breezes through whispering pines. And because it belonged to him, it reminded her of honor, and selflessness, and incredible will. And it would haunt her with hunger for the rest of her days.

She offered a smile, but humor didn't lighten his mood—or hers for that matter. If anything, it became heavier as the questions she'd avoided lodged in her throat, burning for answers.

His hand lifted and covered his cheek where her lips had been. "I haven't learned everything." His voice was quiet, and if she'd been mortal, she might never have heard his confession. "That was the first time I've felt lips on my skin."

There were times in Elen's life where she'd been stunned to silence. Hundreds, she suspected, were she to waste her time counting. A certain moment at the falls came to mind. And had she not been ripped of her spirit less than four days prior? But his admission left her mouth hanging ajar like a child at her first fair—and he was the candied apple waiting to be tasted. "You've never been kissed?"

"No," he stated without apology. "And before you ask, I've never lain with anyone either."

"You're jesting," she challenged, still unbelieving. "I was at Avon, if you don't remember." She refused to bring up the wager. "You had plenty of admirers, and I can't imagine that not one offered—"

"There were offers," he admitted, "and I was tempted."

A log snapped in the hearth, and the flashing flame cast a jagged glow on his profile. As envy burned within her stomach, Elen wondered if she'd somehow caused the flared reaction. "I'm sure you were." It was natural, expected even, for him to have been tempted and curious. In fact, it needn't have been mentioned at all, and definitely not with a sheepish grin that told of flirtations she didn't want to envision.

If his mouth was going to make that wicked turn, then why couldn't it turn for her? It was a sullen thought born of loneliness, but it also gave her courage. More than anything, she wanted to jump over that edge of possibilities. But how? She was hardly an expert on the art of luring a lover. She hadn't flirted in years, decades, really; there hadn't been anyone *to* flirt with who wouldn't have shrunk back in terror.

But this was Cormack. And he wasn't at Avon with those other temptations. He was here, with her, and she wanted him so badly she could barely breathe.

"Tell me what you're thinking." Cormack leaned forward, snagged the wineglass and took several healthy sips before setting it back, as if he needed the extra libation to ready him for her answer.

She looked down at the knitted afghan, worrying her fingers within the knotted holes of the pattern. "I'm not sure you want to know."

"You're wrong. Whatever it is, I want to know." He reached out and covered her hands, turning her wrist to trace a slow circle with his thumb. If his intentions were to drive her mad, he was certainly achieving his goal. "Too much has gone unsaid between us."

"Yes," she agreed. He'd bared his secret, had he not? It felt dishonest, if not cowardly, for her not to do the same. "I'm trying to figure out how to flirt with you."

His eyes widened. "Flirt with me?" A choking sound garbled his voice. "There is"—he coughed twice, and then cleared his throat, shaking his head—"no need."

"I see." The space between them filled with awkward tension, and she cringed at her own desperate foolishness. "Then I'm sorry I brought it up." Mortified, Elen ripped off the blanket and slid her feet onto the floor. "I want some fresh air." Pride kept her from running to the door, but she did make hasty progress, slipping on her garden clogs and favorite knit cardigan before he caught up with her.

A large hand covered hers as she turned the doorknob. "You are not leaving," he said. "Not now."

"This is my house," she reminded him. "I can come and go as I please, so remove your hand and let me be."

"I'm not good with words," he told her.

"I understand you just fine." Wrenching her hand out from under his, she pivoted toward the kitchen and dodged around the central fireplace. There was more than one exit from her cottage, and if she didn't leave soon, he was going to witness her crying. This time she did run, having lost all semblance of pride.

With shifter speed, he made it to the door first, blocking her escape. His legs spread from frame to frame, a dominant stance, as he planted his feet and lowered his chin. "You don't understand a damn thing, but I'm not letting you leave here until you do."

She wove to the side, but he blocked her, and now she was trapped between a muscular arm and the frame of the door, and she suspected the latter might be easier to move. "Let me pass."

"No."

Clenching her hands until her nails bit into her palms, she said, "Don't forget who I am, or what I can do." As long as nature and its elements were near, there was no man, woman, wolf, shifter or sorcerer who could bar her path if she were willing to hurt them to pass.

"As if I could," he taunted, having felt the bite of her gift more than once.

She winced at the unnecessary reminder. Ducking her head under his arm, she wiggled her foot over his knee and succeeded far enough to get his leg wedged between her thighs, which seriously didn't help her cause. Frustrated, she pushed against his chest—and then again because if she didn't do something, she was going to fall apart in his arms.

When the first tingles tightened her spine, Elen realized her recklessness, but it was too late. Emotion was a powerful conduit, especially pain, and her gift surged and expelled before she could stop it. Flames flared in the hearth, then built into a raging chute up the chimney that set the cottage aglow before it settled and died in the grate.

Fire, it seemed, was ready to play. Air responded to procreation, but its cohort fed on all things yearning for resolution, like desperation, anger and suffering. And she presented them all in one bountiful feast. Thankfully, the fiery element calmed as quickly as it flared and hadn't spread beyond the hearth.

"Shit," Cormack hissed between gritted teeth. Two blackened handprints smoldered on the green shirt that covered his chest. "Elen . . . that *hurt*!" But when most men would have run screaming, he pushed her farther into the jamb of the door.

The wooden frame dug into her back. "I'm sorry." And she was. The lingering scent of singed cotton pierced her with guilt. "Let me see your chest," she pleaded while trying to lift his shirt.

He brushed her off. "It's fine."

"If you don't want my help, then go for a run. It will heal after you shift." But she was determined to see what damage she'd caused before he did and continued to tug at the cotton hem.

He snagged her wrists midair, holding her in the vise of his grip. "You can burn me to cinders, drown me, force me to shift a hundred times in a row—but you are not leaving this room until you hear me out."

Ouch. Well deserved, given their history, but words too can burn. "You were nicer to me as a wolf." A petty accusation after what she'd just done, but she was too heartbroken to care. "You would never have treated me this way."

"You're right," he agreed too softly. It was the tone a predator used to taunt its prey, and a warning shiver trickled down her spine. "And I would never have done this either."

His mouth descended to capture hers. She wasn't prepared, hadn't relaxed her lips, and he came in so quickly that their teeth collided. His kiss was untried and stiff, and he tasted of wine, and fury, and carnal needs too long repressed. It was messy and unsophisticated and she had never been so thoroughly undone.

He wrenched himself away with a snarl, but he did not loosen his grip.

No, he used that leverage to push her farther up against the frame of the door, forcing her legs to widen and wrap around his waist. This time there were no layers of skirts to buffer their contact, only his jeans and her thin pajamas over lace undies—and she felt his arousal as surely as she felt her own. She didn't know whether to cry or climax and very well might do both if he didn't stop rocking against her core.

"As I was saying . . ." His lips dropped to the underside of her ear as his breath fanned against her heated skin. "There is no need for you to flirt with me." He thrust against her with the hard evidence of his proclamation. His angle was perfect. Whether by instinct or intuition, she didn't know, but if not for their clothes, he would be inside her. "I'm not sure"—his voice, low and strained, dropped off as a shudder racked his frame—"if I would survive it if you did."

She felt the building of pressure, the tightening of her lower belly that cried for release. Her thin lace panties provided the perfect friction with his thrusts. He *really* needed to stop. "Cormack—"

"Ask me why I haven't lain with a woman." When she remained speechless, he nipped the column of her neck—an act of a wolf to his mate. "Ask me!"

A wave of pleasure shot from the brand of his bite to other, more central nerves that needed no enticements. She was so close. It was cruel of him to play with her this way. "Why?" she asked anyway, because—damn it all—she wanted to know.

A ragged groan concaved his chest as his forehead fell to the painted wood behind her head. After several breaths, he released her arms only for the freedom to cup her face. By then she had no will to fight. His hips and thighs, and other things, kept her wedged on a precipice of pleasure.

Then he lifted his face, and his expression was openly haunted; it bared his soul without caring of its destruction. It was the look of the already damned. "Because I have been waiting for the woman I love."

"Who?" She had to hear him say it, she simply had to. "Who is this woman?"

"Do you really have to ask, Elen?"

"Yes." She nodded as blood pounded against her temples. "Yes, I do."

"You hold my heart in your hands, and even if you don't want it, it won't matter because I am lost either way. I am yours. Do with me as you will."

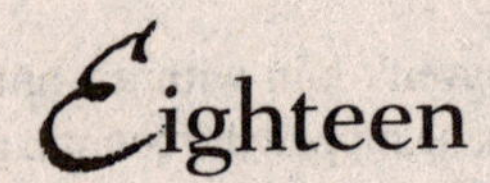

Eighteen

ELEN SWAYED INTO HIM, BECAUSE SOME WISHES WERE too overwhelming when they came true, and she had never wanted one more than this. "If you are lost, then so am I." She grasped his shirt because she needed purchase for her hands as her world filled with glorious colors. "I love you, Cormack."

"I know you do," he said quietly, "but I question in what capacity."

If she weren't on the brink of utter gratification, she may have been more patient in her explanation, but as it was, she could hardly think to form a coherent sentence. "I am about to ease all doubts." She initiated their second kiss and didn't hold back. If he needed proof, then so be it. She ran her tongue along the fullness of his lips until he allowed her entrance with a tortured moan, meeting her tongue with his. His rocking motions became more aggressive; it was a carnal reaction, unpracticed and crude as primal compulsions demanded release. He was unaware, she suspected, of the effect it had on her.

"Elen," he growled into her mouth, concerned—and divinely naïve. "You're shaking."

"I'm not cold," she cried, recalling the last time he'd misunderstood her tremors. "Don't stop." Too desperate to explain, but needing a different angle and harder pressure, she reached back, grabbed the doorframe, digging her fingers around the wood—and arched. "Please don't stop." The friction built, and she was beyond thought, dignity and all reason as her pleasure reached its peak. And then—*finally*—wave after wave washed through her until she was spent and gasping in his arms.

Cormack held her in the vise of his embrace, completely unmoving, a fact she realized as reality returned. And when she opened her eyes, his hungry gaze devoured her, still needy but filled with awe. "That was the most beautiful thing I have ever seen."

"Oh, Cormack . . ." Elen leaned forward and wrapped her arms around his neck. "You haven't seen anything yet. Take me upstairs." She placed a kiss on the corded muscles just under his jaw, reveling in the shudder that racked his body from that simple caress. "We've only just begun."

A muffled ring came from Cormack's back pocket.

He tensed, and then snarled as the sound registered. *"Fuck no!"* If not twisted with need, his scowl might have been comical. *"Fuck,"* he repeated again in contradiction to his gentle motions as he set her on her feet. "It's official," he mumbled under his breath as the ring continued, "I've done something to piss off the Gods." Reaching back, he wrenched the phone from his pocket and brought it to his ear. "What," he answered in a clipped tone that made the harmless word sound more offensive than his previous curse.

She watched with admiration for how well he'd adjusted to his new role as a guard, a position that wasn't easily earned.

"At the clinic?" Annoyance left his voice as he listened, replaced by controlled concern. "Who?" A pause. "Are you sure?"

Then the shrill sound of her clinic alarm echoed from the kitchen. Adrenaline immediately kicked in because nobody sought her help unless all other options were gone.

His lips formed a tight line as he ended the call. "That was Gabriel."

"What's happened?"

"Melissa's hurt. My brother-in-law's waiting with her at the clinic. That's all I know."

The child was Cormack's last surviving relative. Elen didn't make comforting promises but ran upstairs to change. She returned in less than a minute, grabbing her keys. The clinic was within walking distance, but it would be quicker if they drove. "Let's go."

WITH A SWIFT TUG, CORMACK ZIPPERED HIS JACKET closed to hide his singed shirt. Gabriel stood beside the concealed entrance of the clinic and offered a sharp nod at their approach. Of Spanish and Celt decent, he had the golden skin of his mother's people. Eyes so black it was hard to tell where his pupils ended and his irises began. He was a powerful shifter, and he kept the violence of his past untold, but his hatred of the Guardians was as pure as his unnerving gaze.

"How bad?" Cormack asked.

"Not an emergency that belongs here." Gabriel's lips

thinned with annoyance, an odd reaction when his niece may be hurt. "You'll see."

Curiosity cluttered his concern as Cormack followed Elen through the doors of the clinic. Edward, his brother by marriage and now a widower raising a child on his own, sat in a waiting chair, his right arm wrapped in a towel blotched with blood. A large dog carrier made of cream-colored plastic rested by his feet, concealing whatever it held.

"Where's Melissa?" Cormack looked around the room for his niece, and then back at the carrier. His foul mood increased by the second.

A sigh racked Edward's reedy frame as he lifted his hands in apology. "I didn't know what else to do." More human than wolf, the man couldn't shift. He had dark hair and bright eyes, a coloring bolder than his personality; Edward was content to let others protect his family. Cormack didn't dislike him; he just didn't have much in common with him, which had always made their visits awkward, even before the death of his sister.

Walking ahead, Elen crouched in front of the carrier and peeked through the grated door. A jolt of surprise forced her to drop to her knees—and then her gaze lifted to his. "All is well," she reassured him with awe in her voice. "The Goddess has blessed us once again. Melissa isn't hurt, she's whole."

Smiling, she unlatched the metal door of the carrier, and a red wolf pup came waddling out, looked around the room and then launched herself into Cormack's arms with excited yelps. At five years of age, Melissa hadn't been able to shift until now.

Hugging her close, he nuzzled her soft fur. Children were rare gifts among their kind—and new shifters nonexistent until the past few years. Including Melissa, he only knew of two children who could call their wolves. Bittersweet emotions clogged his throat. This had been Taran's greatest wish.

Playful and testing, as all young ones were, Melissa gnawed at Cormack's arm. He growled softly until she calmed, and then he focused on Edward. "You kept her in a dog crate?" Gabriel's earlier displeasure finally made sense.

"I can't control her like this. She doesn't listen." In his own defense, Edward held up his bloodied arm. "And she bites to harm."

"Wolves are guided by authority," Cormack explained as anger turned to frustration. If the man had even an ounce of dominance in his personality, he would not be having this issue. Taran had been the alpha wolf in that relationship, and Melissa obviously took after her mother.

Elen went over to Edward and nodded at his makeshift bandage. "May I take a look?"

He flinched back, shaking his head. "It will heal. I'm here for my daughter because I don't know what else to do. She doesn't listen to me anymore, and I'm afraid she'll run off and get hurt or attack one of the other children."

Shunned yet again, Elen's hands fell to her sides. "If that's your wish, I won't force my help on you."

With controlled motions, Cormack placed his niece on the floor before closing the distance, purposely crowding the man and dominating his space. "Melissa lives because of Elen's care, and you will show her the respect she deserves." He spoke in a tone that dared refusal. "Allow her to look at your arm."

Edward looked both ashamed and lost. He had loved Taran, but she had been beyond help after protecting their child with her own life. Was it his sister's ultimate selflessness that had granted this rare gift? He suspected it was.

Keeping his gaze to the floor, Edward submitted to the command. Cormack gestured for Elen to continue. She hesitated only a moment before unwinding the towel and prodding gently around his torn skin.

"I would like to stitch this up," she said, "if you will let me. Or if you would step outside, I am confident I can heal it with—"

"Needle and thread," Edward interrupted as his legs twitched nervously. "No enchantments. You can do it right here, and then I'll bring Melissa home. I shouldn't have come."

Cormack gritted his teeth when Elen gave a soft sigh, grateful he'd thought to grab a jacket to hide his shirt. She retrieved a small medical kit from a cabinet on the wall, washed the wound, administered a pain reducer and bent her head to the task without complaint or comment as the man flinched at every touch.

"You will visit my brother before you return home," she said while applying a clean bandage. "This news shouldn't have been kept from him. Cormack and I will follow you there."

Cormack's voice dropped low as he pulled her away from curious ears. "Merin will be there. Are you up for this tonight?"

"Not really," she admitted while her gaze dropped to his mouth. "I'd rather go home and be with you."

"Don't," he warned as selfish need pounded blood through his veins, wanting to feel that mouth under his once again. Now that he knew his niece was safe, his former state of frustration quickly rose.

She blinked at him innocently. "Don't what?"

"Flirt." Just because he couldn't resist, he led her around the corner and into a private room, and then pressed her against the closed door. "I've already warned you. I will not be responsible for my actions if you do. I've waited too long."

Damn her if she didn't arch and run her hands down his chest to linger on his waistband. "And I haven't?" Her hand feathered down to rest on the obnoxious bulge that now strained against his pants.

"Elen," he hissed, "*please*." He'd come damn close to spilling his seed at the same time she'd unraveled in his arms—and he would be there again if she continued.

"Please what?" Her lips curled in satisfaction, and he couldn't help but lean down and claim her mouth. So soft, her lips were, parting with a sigh. And she tasted of oranges and sweetness, and if she didn't stop those noises, he was going to take her on a hospital cot.

"Not here," he growled when she playfully nipped his bottom lip. Not with family outside waiting, and more at Rhuddin Hall; he wanted their first time to be without distractions. *Bloody hell*, did they not deserve that at least? Somehow he managed to drag his mouth away. Panting, he rested his forehead against the door above her head. He gave a frustrated sigh and yanked her hand away.

If it didn't involve his family, and hers, Cormack would have sent Gabriel, but his pride refused not to be present where honor dictated he should. Walking a distance away for his own sanity, Cormack held up his hand when she would follow. "Give me a minute." He dialed Porter and provided an update on recent events. After his eager appendage calmed, they returned to the waiting room. He scooped up his niece in one arm and the crate in the other, handing the vile contraption to Gabriel on the way out.

"We're headed to Rhuddin Hall to tell Dylan. Can you burn this?"

"With pleasure." Gabriel ruffled Melissa's ears, and Cormack felt her tail whack against his side. "This is a good day."

"Her father is weak." Cormack didn't care if the man heard. He would raise her himself, but he doubted Edward would relinquish that role. He may be a passive man, but he loved his daughter.

"We'll help him," Gabriel replied, "for Taran."

Nineteen

When they arrived at Rhuddin Hall from the clinic, Merin was still there, lingering after dinner. Elen felt no hatred toward her mother, just an awkwardness that seemed impossible to breach. They were strangers, made so by almost seventeen hundred years of separation, a greater divide than the violence of their past. Thankfully, the distraction of Melissa eased their reunion, since a good portion of the conversation focused on the child, a balm to soothe their painful history.

The whole family gathered in the great room, along with Edward and their new shifter. Merin sat on the sofa, leaving a cushion between them. Cormack stood behind Elen, with his hand on the back of the sofa, grazing her shoulders with his knuckles in silent support. Porter stayed by the hearth in arm's reach of several swords. Dylan and Sophie shared an oversized chair, and Joshua sat on the floor playing with a thrilled child in wolf-pup form.

It would have been a lovely gathering if not for the topic at hand and the woman leading it.

"Edwyn is a traditionalist." Merin offered information on the eight remaining Council members, and she held every person's attention except for Melissa's. "Rhys turned cruel after the death of his mate and cannot be trusted. Neira is a tedious woman with a sadistic nature, but do not let her beauty or childlike voice fool you. She is a powerful wolf without a conscience. Her only weakness is the pleasures of the body and the pain she craves. She keeps flesh-slaves to satisfy her needs. When Pendaran meets his death, I predict Neira and Rhys will be the first to fight for his seat, and they are both strong enough to win."

The flickering glow of the fire outlined Porter's stiff silhouette. Silently listening, he turned to face the hearth, keeping his back to the room, but not before Elen noticed his features pinch at the mention of Neira's name. His Celtic cross tattoo stood out like indigo ink on parchment, stark against his bare cranium that reddened as more Council members were discussed. There was a violent history there, and Elen knew some but not any concerning Neira. However, Porter was a proud man, and if the tortures had been of a sexual nature, he would have kept those stories untold. Perhaps it was that experience that kept his wolf dormant, for the Irishman had the full power of a shifter; she'd felt it once on a cursory contact. Porter was whole, and yet he had never called his wolf.

"Maelor is obsessed with his wife and his castle," Merin continued. "He leaves only if either of those two things is threatened. William was allowed to live after his betrayal, and last I heard he may have earned his position back. He despises humans and would be content to live isolated with his purity and prejudice intact, but he wants an heir. He will return for the child at Avon, and this one here if he knew of her, to raise her under his control until she comes of age to breed."

"And Bran?" Dylan prompted, resting his hand on Sophie's leg—who looked ready to jump up and scoop Melissa into her protective arms.

Without asking her husband, Sophie leveled a look toward the girl's father. Edward remained in the far corner, waiting in timid silence for an appropriate time to leave. "I want you to move into Rhuddin Hall. It will be good for Melissa to be around other shifters, where she's directly protected. Joshua can help her adjust to her change as well."

Edward looked to Dylan for approval, not entirely displeased. It was a great honor to live in the alpha's home.

"There are rooms in the east wing." Dylan supported the decision, and Elen felt Cormack's sigh of relief ruffle her hair. It resolved his worry, she knew, without separating the child from her father.

A calculating smile of approval tugged at Merin's lip before she answered her son's question. "Bran wants to survive like us all. He and Gweir are similar in their opinions, although Gweir hides his better. I don't believe either will initiate an attack. They are comfortable in their territories. If confronted, they will annihilate any threat without mercy."

"We should kill them all." It came as a quiet admonishment from Porter. His shoulders rose and fell on controlled breaths. "Every single one. We should gather our allies together and attack them in their homes—before they come after ours."

"You would lose," Merin said without censure. "You are greater in numbers, but they are far greater in strength. Plus," she offered on a sardonic laugh, "we are wolves, even those of us who are more human than not; we're compelled to fight for our territories. There is no winning this war. Even if you kill every Council member, others of our kind will seek dominion. It is the instinct of the animal that rages in our blood."

Unchallenged because of its truth, her opinion cast a heavy silence in the room.

Elen was the first to speak. "What would you suggest we do?"

Merin's gaze held such sadness. Like rain in winter, it had the power to melt ice. It wreaked havoc on broken trusts. This was the first time Elen had spoken to her directly, and the hesitation in her answer was almost . . . *vulnerable*? "Your territory is rich with power. Cherish it. Protect it. And do what you must to strengthen your children."

"And when they attack us here?" Elen challenged, having been directly involved in all three assaults.

"That is when we kill them," Merin said, "as I would have done if not for Taliesin's interference. I will not grant another mercy. When they come to us, they must die."

His voice thick with frustration, Dylan interjected, "How are we to fight a sorcerer who attacks on grounds that we can't see?"

"I don't have an answer for that." Merin sighed with remorse. "Your safety came at the price of me playing his game, and now my greatest move has been revealed. Moreover, I don't think you have the heart for such deceit, or the guilt that comes of it." She looked away briefly. "I have done things that haunt my dreams so that yours could be free."

"If some of those dreams are of me, then put them to rest." Elen reached over and gently placed her hand on top of her mother's. For a moment, she thought Merin would withdraw, but then she turned her palm up and squeezed. "I know," Elen shared quietly between them. "Pendaran told me it would have been him if not you."

"He would have mutilated you," Merin said on a broken whisper.

"I understand." It was enough, Elen realized, or a precious beginning. Anger poisoned the giver more than the receiver, did it not? And forgiveness unburdened dark emotions. The fire crackled in the hearth in response.

Clearing her throat to announce her presence, Sarah entered the room and whispered something to Dylan. "Excuse me for just a moment," he said, and left with the female guard. He was gone but a minute, leaving the room in curious silence. When he returned, his gaze was guarded. "It's a local incident," he shared. "Nothing concerning the Guardians. But the night is growing older than me. And Elen has had a trying few days. I would like a private word with you both in my office before you leave." He nodded toward Elen and Cormack. "Porter, you as well."

"Indeed." Merin stood with everyone else. Speculation entered her winter gaze, but she accepted her dismissal with grace. "I will return to your lake house and travel in the morning."

"Wait here," Dylan told her. "This will only take a minute, and Sophie and I will drive you there when I'm done."

Merin gave a slight nod. "Then I will wait."

Elen lingered. The words she wanted to say clogged her throat, so she settled for a simple, "Good-bye, Mother. Maybe one day you will come to my cottage for tea."

"Invite me and I will be there."

"Then make sure we know how to find you." It was an offer she hadn't planned to make, but it felt right. As she rounded the corner, Joshua said something that made Merin laugh, and the sound brought memories of her childhood to the surface, earlier ones, when her father still lived. Merin had been happy once, before the Council forced her hand.

Perhaps she could be again, Elen thought as she followed Cormack and Porter to Dylan's office. She waited until Porter closed the door, knowing her brother wouldn't have separated them without a purpose.

"That was Luc on the phone," Dylan said without further delay. "He needs you in Avon." Their youngest brother held no memory of Merin before their father's death. He only knew her as the Guardian who'd shunned him from birth. No doubt he'd asked Dylan to keep his situation between them, which explained this private meeting. "It's urgent, or I wouldn't be relaying the message so soon after your recovery."

"What's happened?"

"Mae's had an accident," Dylan said with measured calm, a tone that indicated trouble. The calmer it became the more she knew to worry. "I know what she means to you, Elen. There was a fire in her bedroom, and she was trapped." He paused. "It's not good." Mae was the first born without the ability to shift, a fact that hung in the room without needing to be said. Worse, human hospitals were out of the question because even non-shifters of their kind healed at a rate that would attract dangerous attention. "Since Mae is their healer, they had no one else to call."

He didn't insult Elen by asking if she was okay to leave. Mae was one of her few friends before Cormack and her teacher before Ms. Hafwen. More than a teacher, really; Mae had comforted her when her own mother had done the Council's biddings. Burns were the worst form of injury, even if Mae healed faster than the human rate. She didn't have the ability to shift the damage away. If conscious, she was in excruciating pain.

There was no question of Elen going. "I'll need to gather a few things from my cottage," she said. *Like a pixie.*

Dylan nodded with understanding. "Porter will drive you."

"I have my license," Cormack mentioned in a defensive tone edged with annoyance.

And Elen was all too aware of why he wanted to be alone.

"All the same," Dylan replied, "I would like Porter to check Avon's equipment and make sure all is working well. According to . . ." He cleared his throat, pausing to amend his instructions. "According to what I know of spirit traveling, we have a few days before Pendaran has fully regained his strength. You will be protected at Avon, but I don't want you traveling after tomorrow. Stay with Luc or come home, but make a decision within the next twenty-four hours. Porter will return either way in the morning."

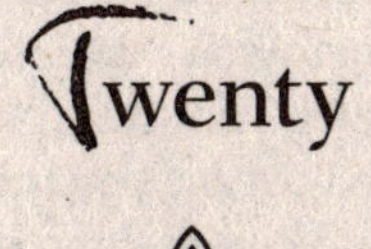

Twenty

THE MEN RODE IN THE FRONT OF PORTER'S SUV, WHILE Elen sat in the back with their bags. Having been in a hurry, they'd grabbed a few changes of clothes and her medical bag. *Plus a pixie.* But Ms. Hafwen seemed content to remain hidden in the tote that rested by Elen's feet while she slept off her earlier indulgence.

The vehicle smelled like leather and man, and a dark scent that was distinctly alpha. Yes, Porter had secrets, but they were not hers to know, so she wouldn't pry.

Making good time, they arrived in Avon well before midnight. A crisp wind traveled off the White Mountains, and the night offered clear skies. A waning moon cast a shimmering glow on jewel-colored woods. Elen couldn't help but admire the lush island as it came into view, with a castle hidden behind a healthy forest. A river acted as a natural moat, and a stone bridge provided the only entrance to the island. Not long ago a battle had raged on that bridge, and the island had been nothing but broken trees and death, once starved and now whole as rightness replaced imbalance.

After parking next to a stone carriage house, Elen snagged the bag at her feet and walked to the back of the SUV. Understanding her intent, Cormack distracted Porter with conversations about Avon's defenses.

Turning her back, Elen said softly, "It's clear."

Ms. Hafwen fluttered out and perched on the back bumper. "I will be leaving you for three days in your moon phase, but I will return."

Elen bent as if to tie her shoe, and whispered, "Where are you going?" Though she had her suspicions. The newest gateway to the Land of Faery was on Avon's island.

"Home," she confirmed. "Something has grown during your sleep, and I need answers that only my brethren can provide."

"Why does that sound ominous?" And why did Elen suspect she had something to do with it?

Ms. Hafwen's hesitation didn't calm her apprehension. "Pendaran's weapon was encased with relics of a once-mighty oak tree," she explained. "It was known in this world as the Druids' Great Oak. For the Fae, it was a Tree of Hope, and our most trusted gateway, before Ceridwen destroyed it."

"I know the history of Cadarn," Elen said. "And Nerth, its twin." The latter weapon was now buried with its dead owner, or should be, if Math's burial had followed the tradition of their kind.

The pixie remained silent for a moment, as if contemplating how much to disclose. "I felt its rebirth when you fought Pendaran. The Great Oak grows again. Soon it may be strong enough for travel."

"I grew a second gateway?" Elen felt a sudden urge to sit

down. "Is that bad?" What if Ceridwen had wanted it to stay destroyed? Or worse, what if it grew into something vile? "It's in Pendaran's territory." That couldn't be good.

A breath of impatience fell from her tutor's mouth. "Your humility is a rare thing indeed, especially among your kind, but there is a place for confidence as well. You have given us a gift. All of Faery will be pleased. But this will turn Pendaran's interest into an obsession. The gateways offer power in its purest form, and untainted immortality; it will drive his madness to control you. While he's still weakened, I'm returning home to discuss plans for your safety."

Honored but justly alarmed, Elen forced her emotions aside for the purpose she'd been called for. "Will you at least stay while I see to Mae?"

"I have full faith that you will do what needs to be done without my assistance. But do not listen to any of that woman's teachings while I'm away. We have made great strides in your learning, and I would hate to have our hard work foiled."

The pixie shifted into her animal form after that final warning, flitting over the river as a winter wren. A farewell song pierced the air as she disappeared into the forest beyond, and Elen couldn't help but feel melancholy over her departure.

Gareth, Avon's porter, waited for them at the entrance of the bridge. A stoic man with dark hair. The patch he once wore no longer necessary now that he was allowed to shift. Like many of Avon's residents, he'd suffered tortures under his former Guardian's leadership and had been forced to bare his scars like a badge of dishonor. Thanks to Rosa and Luc, those times were in the past.

"Cormack," Gareth greeted with a hearty pat on the back, still stern but not entirely humorless as he once was. Not just the island was healing, although hearts took longer than earth. "Good to see you, but I wish it was under better circumstances. Porter," he said next, "I have a list of questions for you when there's time." Then he held out his arm to Elen, a courteous gesture to escort her over the bridge. "And you, Elen, are always welcome."

Gareth had told her once that the people in Avon had lived too long under Guardian rule to fear her. Now that they knew her power, she'd wondered if they would, but his offered arm was a welcomed sign.

Cormack brushed the man away with a scowl, taking her hand in his, and received a chuckle from Gareth in return.

"I'm going to be losing money soon, I think," Gareth said as they crossed the bridge. "Your former rooms have been prepared, but I will show you to Mae first."

"How bad is she?" Elen asked, ignoring his reference to the wager.

Turning serious, he shared, "The worst I've seen."

The walk wasn't long, but Elen increased her strides. Castell Avon soon came into view, with its medieval turrets and outer grounds now covered in lawn instead of dust. Guards nodded as they passed through the bailey, greeting Cormack mostly. He'd made friends during his stay here, and they were happy to see him return.

Luc and Rosa waited inside the entry hall. With ink-black hair and silver eyes, her brother resembled their father. He looked well, Elen noted as he scooped her into his usual gregarious hug.

"Are you okay?" Luc asked, no doubt having been fully informed of both Merin and Pendaran's visit.

"I am," she assured him, turning to Rosa next. Luc's new wife wore a large sweater over loose pants, her makeshift garb while under Guardian control. Her features were strained, as to be expected, but she offered a welcoming smile and opened her arms.

Elen accepted the second hug, and then sucked in her breath as the reason for the loose clothing became apparent, at least to her senses. The power of *two* shifters rose to greet her. She leaned back. "Rosa . . . ?"

Only Luc and Mae know, she mouthed with a secret smile. "And my cousin," Rosa said openly. "We will talk after you see Mae. I have questions."

Luc's beaming expression made Elen suspect that more than just those four knew that Rosa was carrying his child. But children of their kind were so rare and often lost before term, not to mention hunted by the Guardians, so she understood their secrecy. Nonetheless, Elen gave her brother another quick hug before they brought her to Mae's temporary room.

The smell greeted her first, charred hair and flesh that hadn't been washed due to its fragile condition. Blessedly, Mae was unconscious. Elen had brought herbs to make a poultice, and other medications to alleviate some of the pain, but the damage was too great for such minor remedies. She already bore the scars of her years under Guardian rule; this final damage removed any remnants of her former features.

"The fire started from a gas lantern." Luc spoke low from behind her. "It fell and broke by her feet, and the accelerant spread up her clothes. It was instant. We contained the fire to her room . . ." *But it was too late for the woman trapped within.* His lips pressed in a thin line as the result of the accident lay unconscious before them. "We're bringing electricity onto the island." His determined tone suggested there had been a debate on the matter, but his decision was made. "I intend to make use of Porter's contacts while he's here. The construction will begin soon."

Rosa approached the bed to stand beside Elen. "Can you help her?"

"I don't know," she said, but leaving her like this wasn't an option. And Elen's powers weren't viable within the thick mortar and stone of Castell Avon. Understandably, there was no fire burning in the grate or windows open to air. Battery-operated lamps illuminated the room instead of the gas lanterns. Her feet stood on cold tiles, and the river ran a good distance away. There was nothing for her to call because nature was beyond these walls. "Find me a gurney or something that will suffice. I want her carried outside."

"I know where there's one," Gareth supplied without hesitation. "I'll be right back."

A carrier was found; it was old and stained and probably used for unsavory purposes before Luc's time, but it was sufficient. "Do you have a stream close by, or a pool of water?" Elen asked around the room. "The river is too forceful for what I want to try."

"Follow me," Rosa said. Ignoring the residents of Avon who lined the hallways with curiosity and concern, she led the way out of the castle. They traveled on a meandering path lined with moss and leaves shadowed by night. Cormack and Luc carried Mae's unconscious form as reflective eyes of woodland creatures watched their progression through the trees.

The trail curved along a gently flowing stream that dipped to form a pool. On the outskirts grew a tree, a sapling no taller than Cormack, but it shimmered as if golden fireflies danced among its leaves. Its potency was like nothing she'd experienced to date, not even from Ms. Hafwen or Pendaran. It lured her like an enchanted song, offering promises of power and temptation from another world.

It was the Tree of Hope, she understood without question,

and the gateway to Faery. Ms. Hafwen had scolded her for her lack of confidence, but it seemed unbelievable that she had grown a second gateway such as this. Elen wasn't sure if the others recognized what it was, so she forced her gaze away. "Set her down on that bank." She pointed to a flat surface close to the water's edge. Acting on instinct, Elen waded into the pool fully clothed. The water came chest-high, a sufficient depth, as she gestured to Cormack to roll Mae into her arms. When the water covered her body, Mae awakened and thrashed in disorientation—and then screamed.

The sound wrenched the night air with her agony. Leaves rustled as creatures scurried, and the Tree of Hope shuddered as if moved by an unseen wind or responding to a cry too anguished to ignore.

Luc stepped to the edge, ready to jump in, but Rosa held him back with a gentle hand.

"It's only me," Elen soothed in a calm voice removed from what she felt, grasping Mae under her arms in a lock hold around her chest and keeping her head above water. She called to the forest, her element of Earth, and then the Water that surrounded them. Their energies rose, quicker than expected, and stronger too. That alone made her wary, but she had committed to this course and would see it through.

As always, she was merely a conduit, but the force of the power that greeted her almost sucked her under the water. Her feet sunk into the gravel bottom of the pool. As currents traveled over and through nerves, she held her ground and poured everything she received into her patient. Water cleansed and Earth fed broken flesh. Soon screams became disjointed wails, and then panted moans.

Ms. Hafwen had told her she'd know what to do, but this was an enchanted pool, by an otherworldly tree—and far beyond Elen's experience. Or her control. As charred skin knotted into scars, she tried to unravel the joining. She pictured a braid, as her tutor had instructed many times, with her as one of the stands, along with the other two elements, and then attempted to disentangle them in her mind's eye. But the elements would not leave until the healing was good and truly done.

Within minutes, the energy dispersed as quickly as it had come, but not by Elen's doing, and not before Mae was fully healed; even old injuries had been replaced by new skin.

"Elen child." Her former teacher's voice came as a hoarse murmur ragged with exhaustion. "I knew you would come." Her hands lifted from the water to her face, now absent of all scars and baring a mature yet unmarred vestige of her former youth. She frowned. "What have you done?"

Elen shook her head, unwilling to accept credit. "It wasn't me." She had the knowledge to heal some injuries with enchantments, and to heal using human procedures—but not to remove scars, and some of Mae's could very well be more than a thousand years old. "It's this pool."

A magical pool by a blessed tree.

A shiver racked her spine, and not from awe or from the chilled waters that surrounded her. Pendaran would stop at nothing to gain access to such power.

And Elen was that access.

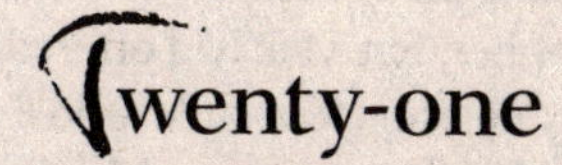

Twenty-one

MAE'S ROOM HAD BEEN STRIPPED AND CLEANED BY THE time they returned. The residents of Avon crowded out of concern and curiosity, their obvious relief making the latter less offensive. Elen sensed her friend's embarrassment, and wasn't surprised when she told everyone to leave. If anything, Mae had no problem speaking her mind.

"You have seen your fill," she scolded, shooing them away. "I have a face, just like all of you, and it is nothing worth gawking at." The understatement made Elen smile. Maelorwen was a handsome woman by any standard in history but obviously uncomfortable with their praise. "I am tired, so let me rest."

"I will check on you in the morning." Elen squeezed her hand, waving everyone out before her.

"They can leave, but you can stay." Mae sat up and fluffed

her pillows. "I will hear how your days have been, and how your garden grows. Will you have a good harvest?"

Mae had taught her all the medicinal uses of plants, her first mentor when she was but a child. Elen had followed her about the old forests of Cymru like a lost pup. At the time, Merin had been called to serve the Council, and Dylan had yet to return for her, but Mae had offered a welcoming hearth and comforting arms to a child who'd needed both.

"I wish you could visit my garden, Mae."

"Perhaps someday," she said with a wistful tone. "We are healers, and we mustn't stray far from the people who need us."

"It is our burden and our blessing." Elen earned a dimpled smile for remembering her mentor's words. "Rest now and we'll visit tomorrow."

"I will make you a spiced potage," Mae informed her. "Like I did for you in Cymru, and we will share recipes."

"Sleep well." Elen smiled, because Mae had always put her to bed with similar words. She repeated them in melancholy affection. "And may you dream of first kisses until the sun chases away the moon."

Mae became quiet, her gaze a thousand years away. "I used to say that to the daughter of my heart."

"You used to say that to me."

"You are one and the same, Elen child."

Leaving her to rest, Elen closed the door and made her way to the Great Hall. Cormack sat at a long table with a bunch of Avon guards, sharing ale and laughing over something Teyrnon had said. Elen knew Teyrnon well from Rhuddin Village before he became Luc's second-in-command. The Norseman was a surly sort but had always treated her with respect.

"Teyrnon," she greeted, extending similar acknowledgments around the gathering. She hadn't seen them since summer, and received welcoming smiles in return. Mae was beloved in Avon, and many gave words of gratitude. Unused to such genuine sentiments, Elen felt her cheeks warm. As always, it felt good to use her gift for the purpose for which it was given.

A woman at the end of the table ignored the exchange, preoccupied with her own pursuits. One of four former Walkers, and the only female, Aeron lounged between two male guards, offering flirtations with a silky laugh and soft brushes of her hand. Having served Ceridwen, she was unnervingly beautiful, and spirited, an enchantress with dark hair that hung in waves to her waist. The thought came without jealousy, just appreciation.

Though perhaps her admiration wasn't as strong as the men by her sides, Elen admitted with a grin. She had met Aeron once before, and chose not to form opinions based on a single encounter during a stressful time. The woman was powerful, and ancient, born shortly after the Guardians had been given the ability to shift. No doubt she had witnessed many sordid acts done by their kind. Aeron's experiences didn't seem to bother her, or more likely, frivolity and earthly pleasures were her ways of coping with them.

The Walkers, or *Beddestyr* in their mother tongue, had once been messengers to Ceridwen in the Otherworld. All four had been relieved of their powers to walk between worlds, fired by a goddess for not controlling her son. Having been trapped in a dreamlike world created by Ceridwen for more than two hundred years, Luc and Rosa now had all four living in Avon until they adjusted to this modern age.

However, a new Walker had been assigned, a dangerous fact they kept secret to all but family. Audrey, a precocious child, now bore the daunting role of Ceridwen's messenger.

Luc and Rosa had adopted the girl as their own. Audrey was, as far as Elen knew, the only Walker with power and therefore the only communication Taliesin had with his mother.

Reminded of the others, she looked about the room for Aeron's former comrades, finding none. When Rosa joined her, she asked, "How are the other Walkers faring?"

Rosa pursed her lips. "Well enough, I suppose." There was a hesitation in her voice, or maybe concern. As their keeper, she was responsible for their welfare. "Aeron is bored with our island, I'm afraid. They're now messengers without a purpose, and it has been an adjustment for them, more so than the century they've awakened in. Gawain, Morwyn and Nesien tend to keep to their rooms, or the library, exploring the Internet behind the safety of these walls. I suspect they'll venture away from Avon soon to experience it in person."

Or so she hoped, according to her wistful tone.

"Join us for a drink," Teyrnon interrupted. Ale sloshed over the rim of his tankard as he gestured toward an empty seat.

"Thank you," Elen said, "but I'm tired." She looked to Cormack, sending him a pointed glare, ensuring he didn't believe her lie. Her gaze fell to his mouth as she imagined all the things she planned to teach him this night. "If you don't mind, I think I'll head off to find my bed."

Ignoring Teyrnon's chuckle, Cormack stood. "I'll get the bags from the car," he announced in a neutral tone as he brushed by—too impersonal for her liking. Had he not understood her intent?

"You can bring Elen's to the green-and-blue room on the family wing," Rosa called after him, pulling Elen away to the center of the hall for more privacy. "I know you must be tired, but can you spare a moment to talk?"

"From what I can sense, the babe's healthy," Elen assured her, frowning at Cormack's retreating back. "We can do a thorough exam tomorrow, if you like."

"Thank you," Rosa said. "I would like that very much."

Nodding an escape, Elen caught up to Cormack just as he descended outside, weaving her fingers through his hand to stop him. "You know I was—"

"I *hurt*, Elen." He spun her about so quickly that she found herself pressed up against a stone wall, surprised speechless. "You can't look at me as you just did." His mouth descended on her neck, trailing kisses up to the tender spot just under her ear. Did he do that by instinct? Because the sensation had her gasping for breath. "You must know what it does to me," he accused, rocking into her so she could feel the hard evidence of his words.

"Bring me somewhere private," she pleaded, clawing at the waist of his shirt and diving her hands underneath. "I can't wait any longer."

"Our room will be private." Removing her hands, he stepped back, but his stiffened stance proved his restraint had worn past thin. "Your clothes are still damp from that pool, and I need a shower—"

"I don't care." She reached for him again.

"*I* care." He halted her with his gaze, simmering with blatant need. "I don't want distractions our first time, and there's something I have to get from the guards' quarters first."

"Okay." She ran her hands over her face. She had no idea what he needed from the guards' quarters, but if it was important to him, then she could wait. "I'll meet you up there."

"Go to the kitchens and order us some food while I shower." Cormack's tone was harsh, daring her to argue.

"If you haven't noticed, I'm not exactly lacking in nutrients," she teased. "Unless you're hungry—"

"We will be. And we're not leaving our room for a while."

THIRTY MINUTES LATER ELEN CLIMBED THE STAIRS TO her chamber. It was well past the midnight hour and the halls were empty. With Cormack waiting in their room, excitement and adrenaline danced through her veins.

Castell Avon had modern amenities, with electricity provided by generators, but it was a limited source. Now that the Walkers were free, and powerless, Luc was right to modernize the island, just for safety alone. Until then, gas sconces provided light in wide hallways as she carried a tray of meats, cheeses, bread and fruit, along with a chilled bottle of white wine produced from grapes grown on the river Rhine.

She'd had to rouse a member of the kitchen staff, only to receive a knowing smile when she'd requested the items, along with two glasses and an opener. Balancing the tray on her hip, she opened her door—and found Cormack asleep on top of the bed. Disappointment surged. If the sisters of fate did indeed exist, then they were having a grand old time twisting her strings.

Placing the items on a butler's server along the side wall, she quietly closed and locked the door. This room had been redecorated over the summer with calming colors of blue and green. A four-poster bed, currently occupied by a rather large man, had new draperies tied to each corner. Two overstuffed chairs and ottomans sat on either side of the hearth where a fire crackled in the grate, casting a soft glow about the room. It was homey in a formal sort of way.

Resigned, Elen spotted her bags through the open door

of the adjoining bathroom. She stripped out of her damp clothes and hung them over the tub before quickly washing and preparing for bed. With none of her nightgowns available, she used one of Cormack's clean T-shirts and a new pair of lace panties, but no bra. It would do.

Too wired to sleep, she opened the wine and poured a glass, sipping quietly as she walked over to the bed. Cormack slept above the coverlet and on his back, with one arm raised over his head, while the other rested by his side. His hair was still damp from his shower, and he wore jeans but no shirt, as if he'd just rested his head and sleep claimed him first.

His chest rose and fell with even breaths. She was not one to marvel over physical attributes, but this was Cormack, and his body was meant for pleasure, like a goddess had molded him for her personal divine gratification. His frame was large and toned, with wide shoulders and a firm chest that tapered down to his hips. His hardened stomach would provide the perfect friction were she to ride him just like this.

And as that image flooded her mind, another, more wicked one, followed. It was greedy and selfish, but all her niceness had been used up for the day. He looked peaceful and innocent, but the man *was* practically immortal after all. Their kind did not die from lack of sleep. They might go mad, of course, but that took a few weeks. And had he not said, *Do with me as you will*?

She needed to touch him. That was all. Well, *no*, she wanted more, but for now that would do. Taking a sip of her wine, she gently set the glass on an end table, and gave in to temptation. Starting by his heart, she brushed lightly across his chest, tracing down the indent between and lingering on the valleys and curves of his muscles. Flattening her hand over his stomach, she felt the soft hair that began just above the waistband of his jeans and disappeared below. She had never seen him in this restful state, at least not in his human form, and took in her ravenous fill.

Her hand lingered over the button of his jeans. She swallowed, wanting . . . Oh, how she wanted. She burned like molten earth, fed by a need that had been denied for too long. Even now she felt her body moisten and swell just from imagining what waited beyond that closure, and how it would feel inside her.

Or how it would taste.

She thumbed the button. A quick flick was all it would take.

A sound made her jolt, an intake of breath perhaps, followed by a sudden rise under her hands. She snapped her eyes to his face.

Cormack was awake.

And watching her.

A fire raged in his gaze. "Kill me now if you stop, Elen, because then I'll know I'm well and truly cursed and I cannot be tortured anymore."

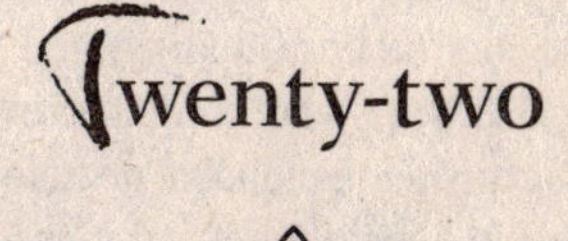

Twenty-two

NEEDING NO FURTHER ENCOURAGEMENT, ELEN RELEASED the closure with a quick tug and the gentle slide of the zipper. He wore no briefs underneath, and his erection sprung forward, thick and begging to be stroked.

"Lift your hips." Elen had no idea how her voice sounded steady, because she was anything but.

He did, allowing her to tug off his jeans, and when they bunched around his thighs, he helped her by kicking them off. Then he lay back down before her in an offering of her most decadent wish come true. His shaft curved in an arc toward his navel, darkening as it swelled even more under her gaze. Abs flexed as he tried to control his rapid breaths.

"Elen . . . *please*." Her name, followed by a desperate plea and a husky growl. His expression was strained and perhaps nervous too. As if he expected pain, or the greatest pleasure known—and not caring either way as long as it was her who gave it.

Ah, this was a heady power indeed—to be desired so completely, and to desire back even more. If she had to choose between this passion and her gift, she would choose passion every time, with him, and for love. And that ultimate selfishness may one day be her undoing, and yet she didn't care. It was no surprise wars were fought, crowns abdicated and countries lost for this unquenchable need to be cherished. Sadly, many scorned its worth, belittled it or worse, made it sordid, but they had never loved as purely as this. If they had, they would know it was a craving more tempting than lands, dominance, hypocrisy or greed. Because none of that offered the same fulfillment, or equaled its reward.

Gently, she placed her hand around the base of his erection.

And he arched off the bed. Both arms fell to his sides as he fisted his hands on the coverlet. *"Fuck!"* He thrashed as she tightened her hand around the base, sliding back to the tip, then repeating the motion.

She moistened her lips. "Tell me what you want."

A sardonic laugh fell from between clenched teeth. "Everything."

"You will have everything" She couldn't help but smile while amending her question, "But what do you want first?"

"I want *you* to come. I want you to come while you're on top of me." His answer, as always, surprised her, when most men would have requested her mouth replace her hands, which she would have gladly done. She was also surprised by the modern term that divulged his knowledge; he had seen sexual acts, no doubt, and heard countless boastings, even if he hadn't been touched until now. "I want you to peak with pleasure as you did in the cottage," he expanded.

Did he not think she understood what he meant the first time? "And I want to be inside you when it happens."

Her toes curled into the thick carpet under her feet. "We can do that."

ALL BLOOD DRAINED FROM HIS HEAD AND DROVE INTO one eager appendage. Every nerve ending was cocked and primed, and her gentle touches were driving him fucking insane. It took a strength of will Cormack didn't realize he possessed to pry her fingers away. He hadn't waited almost four hundred years to have their first time end in three seconds. Swearing, because he needed to, he jerked the corner of the blanket over his lap. Her hungry gaze on his groin didn't help his restraint.

"Open the drawer in the nightstand," he ordered.

She frowned but did as he asked, pulling out the only box within. She looked back with surprise. "You bought condoms."

"The guards keep them in their quarters," he explained. After Avon's battle, Luc had brought them several boxes, declaring they were free to come and go as they pleased, as long as they didn't draw dangerous attention to Avon or endanger the mortals. "Sometimes they visit local towns when off duty."

"I'm sure," she said.

"Certain nightclubs are a popular destination." Their kind was not susceptible to diseases, but they were to pregnancy, and to the mating bond that resulted. Though rare, it was a risk many chose not to take. "The female guards have taken to using them as well." *If not more*. They must answer to certain natures of their wolves, and once mated, a possessive instinct rose, and it was as unforgiving as the wild blood that ran in their veins. Some women, and men, preferred their freedom, as was their right.

She was quiet for a moment. "Do you want to use one with us?"

"I do not," he said without compunction. "But I want you to have the option."

She placed the box back unopened and closed the drawer. "I, like the guards, would have seen to it myself if I had wanted that option, but I appreciate the gesture."

His heart pounded hard against his chest, a bloody miracle in his current state. His beast had been relatively calm until that moment, but unfurled with arrogant interest. "Are you sure?"

What she offered was no small gift.

"More than anything I've ever been sure of in my overly long life." And to prove her point, because he wasn't tortured enough, she pulled the shirt she wore over her head and let it fall to the floor. Her breasts were the perfect size, her nipples tightening in the open air. And as she shimmied out of her final garment, and kicked the scrap of lace to the side, his gaze was drawn to the tawny thatch of hair at the peak of her thighs.

She stood without embarrassment, crawling onto the bed with even less and removing the blanket with an impish grin. Bold she was. Confident too. This was not a side of her he'd ever seen, not with sexual intent in her gaze, a fortunate thing when he couldn't act before now, for it very well might have driven him to self-destruction.

Shoving pillows against the headboard, Cormack sat up because he wanted to see every inch of her flesh, every strand of her hair, every expression on her face as she positioned herself on his lap with one leg on either side. Her skin was warm, smooth, sliding across his thighs. His cock was wedged between her stomach and his, and all she needed to do was lift up, and then down, and then—*finally*, if the Gods were merciful, this incessant ache would ease.

"Wait." He knew his size, and suspected hers to be much less. "I've heard women need to be readied first."

"I am very much ready." A secret smile turned her lips. "But sometimes I'm not. Would you like me to show you how to tell?"

He was nodding before he found his voice. "Show me." Even to his ears it sounded like a snarl.

"Cormack." A soft, all-too-satisfied laugh fell from her mouth. "If you saw the look in your eyes . . ."

Was he supposed to care how he looked? With Elen's ripe softness straddling his thighs and her breasts swaying mere inches from his face? Reaching up, because he was helpless to do anything but, he traced a tender nipple. It *was* soft, yet puckered, and she bit her bottom lip through a feminine moan.

"You like that." He chuckled, because he knew she had, as all lovers must know these things when dealing with the mysterious responses of a woman's pleasure. Men had no comfort of obscurity; their evidence rose quite vigorously for all who cared to see.

"I do." Elen nodded. "Very much. But I would like it even more if you would put it in your mouth." She even arched to give him better access.

A sound rumbled from his throat that he himself did not recognize. He'd seen it done, many times, and dreamt of doing it to her many more. But reality was far more potent than dreams, he realized, as he lowered his mouth on the offered bounty. He suckled the tender peak like a babe. And she tasted of sweetness and forest, and when her thighs began to tremble, it was Elen who pushed him away.

He must have frowned, or given her some questioning sign,

because she answered before he asked. "It felt good," she explained. "Too good, and I'm getting close. So if I am to show you, I must do it now." Reaching for his hand, she unfolded his fingers, placing it palm down on her taut stomach, and then guiding it through her soft curls. "Here." She positioned his fingers over her most private core, lifting up slightly on her knees to help his exploration. Her thighs flexed around his hips. "What do you feel?"

"Heat." He groaned. "Moisture." *And tight slippery softness.* Imagining it around his cock, the needy organ primed and jerked.

"That's because I'm aroused. You will know the difference now when I'm not." She placed her hand over his and moved his finger slightly up. "And here?" Her breath hitched and her words became ragged. "Do you feel that?"

"Yes." It was a nub of flesh, tiny and hidden between her folds, but swollen enough to distinguish what she spoke of. He'd known it existed, had even heard many names for it, but they all seemed too vulgar for something this delicate. Cadan, Rosa's cousin, had once called it a pleasure button. Or rather, he'd told Tesni she'd needed to get hers twisted, and Cormack had overheard.

Assuming that's what it liked, he did just that to Elen's.

"Easy," she hissed. "It is the same there for me as the tip of yours is for you. It likes the same things, responds to the same things."

"Oh." He hadn't touched another person until her, or been touched, but he was a Pagan, not a saint. His exploration of his new form had not been completely ignored. Nor had his eager new appendage allowed it, especially in the mornings. Cormack *had* pleasured himself, as she must have assumed, therefore he changed his caresses. "Like this?"

"Ummm . . ." She nodded, humming an encouraging response.

Inspired, and fascinated, he circled it one way, and then circled back, bending his finger and rubbing it with his knuckle, and then his thumb. It was so small compared to his. Satisfaction curled in his gut, because he was learning her cues, and she was getting close to peaking as she had once before. It was beautiful to watch, now as much as then—if not more so, because he felt and saw different nuances without the restriction of clothes. Both nipples furrowed into hard points and that nub of secret flesh swelled under his thumb.

She liked when he flicked it, he discovered.

She liked it a lot.

"Cormack—" She slapped him away in a sudden, desperate motion. Holding his wrist against her thigh when he tried to return, she rested her forehead against his chest as rapid breaths fanned his skin. Panting, she held her release back to fulfill his initial request.

Moved beyond words, he lowered his lips to the soft silk of her hair. Closing his eyes, he inhaled the scent that had given him the strength to live his cursed existence. He had dwelled in shadows, barely surviving between worlds, and unwanted in both. Elen had shown him kindness, and acceptance, and a home. She had given him a reason to wake each day, and he was as bound to her as the blood of his beast was bound to him.

Her face lifted, openly baring her trust as if she held it up to him in her palms. Trust, he learned in that unequaled moment, was as precious as love. Their history called for no less. He kissed her forehead, then her temples next, cupping her cheeks to lift her mouth to his.

A whimper fell from her parted lips. "I love you so much, Cormack, it almost hurts."

"I know." Because he felt the same glorious pain—*had* for more than three hundred years and knew now it would never end. If anything, it grew worse, like a vise around his heart that constricted by the mere thought of her name.

Her mouth molded to his. Their kiss began gentle but soon turned frenzied, more biting than orchestrated, and far from controlled. Her thighs flexed around his waist, his only warning before she lifted and rocked her pelvis forward. He felt her hand slide downward to the base of his shaft, holding it steady as she aimed it toward her core, and then the most blessed heat.

Tight. So tight. *Fuck.* He couldn't breathe. She moved up and down in increments, taking more of him each time. But it was taking too long. Shaking, and driven by a reflex more primal than honor, he grasped her hips and shoved her down, would have apologized if he had a voice, but that was swallowed by a growl that rolled up from his gut to his throat as his shaft embedded fully into her core.

"Yes," she cried as her body began to shudder, letting him know that she was riding the same carnal wave.

Planting his face in the crook of her neck, he grasped her hips as she rocked; blinded by a pleasure he'd never known, and a hostage to its mounting promise.

Dear Gods . . . He was lost.

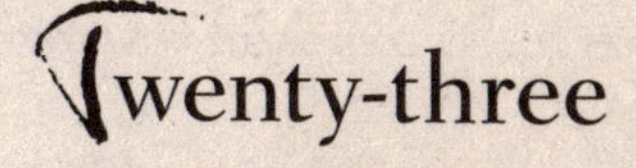

Twenty-three

ELEN HEARD THE WHIMPERS FALLING FROM HER MOUTH and tried to bite them back but it was no use. She'd never been with a man of her kind, or one who possessed her heart as completely as he possessed her body. She was filled with him—and she had never felt so whole. Cormack rested his face in the crook of her neck. Not to kiss her, she knew, or to give her pleasure, but for succor when the edge of absolute surrender burned their blood and raged fire through their veins.

A deep rumble vibrated next to her ear, a continuous growl that didn't relent, dominant and yet needy; a wolf at his utmost vulnerable point who sang his most primal song.

An awakening occurred from that sound. Something hidden in the deepest recesses of her spirit swayed to the same melody; it had been dormant for all of her life; not even torture had coaxed it to rise. If only the Guardians knew it was security, comfort and wholeness that roused its beastly head.

This joining of flesh promised a binding more powerful than her gift. She felt it, and yet she could not stop it—nor did she want to. Even if the castle walls tumbled around them, her will was not her own as the wildness unfurled and another half rose.

A darker half.

And it had nothing to do with elements or plants. No, this unfurling tasted of recklessness and domination. It was the creature that had been melded into the blood of her ancestors on a broken night by a desperate goddess. And while Elen might not be able to shift, and her wolf might forever remain dormant, she felt the instincts of her own beast in that moment as surely as Cormack felt his. And if she was willing to steal another's power as she did for him, she could shift. She realized that possibility now more than ever, but she would never take another's life for herself. *Never.*

The selfishness of the act would only bring darkness and death to everything and everyone she loved.

"I can feel her." Cormack's lips moved against her skin, stirred to speak. "I can feel your wolf." Confusion muddled his voice, pleasure too, possession and elation; it was all there, rumbling up with the undercurrent of the creature that wanted to meet hers.

"As can I," she gasped, throwing back her head as her pleasure mounted toward that shining peak, and she knew this fall would be the most fulfilling of her life. "I'm not stopping." Desperate, so desperate now, she rode him hard.

Cormack bit her neck; and none too gently if she felt it through her furious haze. *"Elen . . . !"* He shouted her name.

And it resonated off the stone walls, loud enough that the whole castle must have heard. And then she knew why, glorified in its source. His shaft jerked, thickening even more within her, and then pulsated to expend his seed.

And she could do naught but follow. They fell together; two enchanted souls tumbled down that most ancient cliff as wave after wave racked her body around his. The convulsions kept coming, and she wasn't sure if she could withstand the onslaught, but her body thought she could and continued with more.

In the aftermath, when the pleasure eased to echoes of small twitches and raw nerves, she collapsed across his chest, utterly spent.

Cormack's hand brushed her hair back from her neck. He inhaled; his bite must have left a mark. He didn't apologize. Indeed not. There was an arrogant twist to his lips when he cupped her face between his palms and rested his forehead against hers. "I am yours and you are mine."

"I am yours and you are mine," she repeated back as their breaths mingled with their vows.

There would be no pretty ceremonies for them. Their wolves had already chosen this union. Like a Celtic braid, their souls were knotted and they loved too deeply for this to unravel with anything less than death. This was no fleeting encounter to be ended after one night, or ten, or even a thousand. Their kind were tied by the instinct of their beasts, and until one died, it would be a permanent joining.

Cormack was her mate—and she was his.

LUC HAD JUST BEEN ABOUT TO DRIFT OFF TO SLEEP WHEN he heard Elen's name travel through the hidden passageways that meandered behind the walls. He relaxed, knowing it came from Cormack, and then burrowed back under blankets next to the softness of his wife. There would be many in Avon seeking partners after that carnal wail.

"Well," Rosa giggled, "that explains why Elen was in such a hurry to get to bed."

Luc treasured the sound of her laughter—because her past had offered her so little joy. Moving his palm to cover the growing bulge of her stomach, he nuzzled the exposed skin at her neck. Five months along now and soon it would be impossible to hide. His heart beat against his chest as her hands covered his. He had known love once before and had found it again. He was blessed and his sister deserved no less. "It's been long in coming."

"It sounds like it is." She giggled again, and he realized his innuendo, marveled that she'd made the playful twist to tease. "I'm not sure if I've ever had one that long."

A bark of laughter erupted from his throat. "Liar." Flipping on his back, he rolled her until she rested on his chest. Rosa wiggled, finding purchase, and sucked in her breath when she realized his need had risen to her challenge alone. His amusement dissolved, replaced by his intent. "Should I remind you, Rosa?"

"Yes, I think you should." A gleam entered her eye, but there was heaviness in her gaze as well. He knew her mind wandered to other worries. And when a woman worried, there would be no pleasures until the talking was done.

Brushing her hair over her shoulder, he asked, "What troubles you? Is it Mae?"

"No." A gentle mirth returned to her voice, but it was fleeting. "Mae is doing just fine, thanks to Elen. Her life with the Guardians has been crueler than most, and it is a blessing to see those scars removed."

"Then what is it?" He knew she fretted about the babe, and their Wulfling.

"Danger is close, Luc. I can feel it." She paused. "Everyone in Castell Avon has been with me from the beginning. Everyone but—"

"The Walkers," he finished for her. Their bodies may have been here, but their spirits had been in the Vale, a dreamlike world Ceridwen created to meet with her son.

"Ex-Walkers," she amended. "Audrey doesn't count. She's ours."

Yes, the little Wulfling was now theirs, and the only messenger Ceridwen now employed. Even Pendaran didn't know of her assignment; not yet at least. Luc did wonder why the Goddess would put such a responsibility on a child. Taliesin, no doubt, responded better to innocence, and the other four were anything but.

"I don't trust them," Rosa said. "They once answered to the Council. As did I, I know," she added in a defensive tone before he could correct her. "But they . . ." Her voice trailed off. "They were Guardians before they were chosen as messengers. I just don't know them enough to trust them. Their histories began long before my time, and you were never allowed in their guild. How do we know where their loyalties lie?"

"We don't." But he believed they feared Ceridwen's displeasure more.

They had been in a coma-like state for almost three centuries, kept on this very island and released from their imprisonment because of a meeting Taliesin refused to speak of. Having nowhere else to go, the Walkers had stayed, because they clearly had little respect for the Council, and because they were unaccustomed to this century. He allowed them to for the same reasons.

But he'd also learned to heed his wife's intuition. "What would you have me do?"

"It's time for them to leave." Her voice reflected the weight of her decision. "They have learned the ways of this time and have means to provide for themselves." She had been their keeper, but now that they have returned to full form, they could also betray. "Soon. Before I can no longer hide that I'm with child."

"It will be done." Luc circled his thumb inside her thigh until her worries drifted away, waiting until her eyes grew heavy and her breaths increased. "Now, I do believe my skill has been challenged, and it would be wrong of me to let that rest uncorrected."

"Ummm," Rosa agreed. "You must thoroughly correct it."

BLACK CLAWS EMERGED AS PENDARAN GRIPPED THE EDGE of his desk. Elen's name, shouted from across an ocean, wove its lust across his skin. A binding had occurred. Even Pendaran's wolf rose to its cry. *Stupid Bleidd.* Names held power and should never be professed with such reverence. It turned whispers into matter that carried on the wind for those who knew how to listen.

Mated wolves were such a bloody nuisance. Merin was the perfect example, having carried her bond beyond death and willing to betray him for her broods. How many times had he heard Merin's excuses for letting her children live? What were her words? She'd said them often enough over the years. Ah, yes . . . *I have found their penchant for survival interesting enough to see where it might lead.*

Admittedly, he could not fault her insight, considering what her daughter had brought to life in his woods. Because of that alone, he *would* have Elen; or rather, he would have her gift under his command. She held no other allure for him, and she certainly wasn't worthy enough to carry his heir. He was intrigued by her—*not* tempted. His nostrils flared with the mere thought. Rosa, on the other hand, would have been fun; still might be, given time—but not Elen. She was too soft for his tastes, and too human. While offensive, her binding to a Bleidd did not change his goals, but it called for an alteration of his plan.

But what?

An idea formed. An attack not linked to him. He'd done it before and could do it again. It must be forged with her blood. She lived with wolves, after all, and they knew her scent. The cowardice of it was distasteful but the strategy sufficient enough that he did not care.

More important, Pendaran had not forgotten Taliesin's threat on Avon's bridge. Ceridwen's son must be pacified, and Taliesin had made it foolishly clear that he wanted Merin's children to live. Pendaran had no intentions of harming Elen, but her protectors mustn't know, Merin especially, at least until he had answers.

Weaving plans, Pendaran weighed his options against potential outcomes. Should he kill the former Bleidd? Cormack; was that not its name? More important, how would Taliesin react? The boy's penchant for noninterference was as predictable as his addiction. Unsure, he let out a long sigh. Taliesin's actions at Avon were disconcerting. Indeed, his volatile compunctions warranted caution.

Let them all wonder, he decided. Let them plot a course of revenge instead of a rescue; the former will add doubt and make them complacent with time. If they were stupid enough to have forgotten his dominion, then let them come. By then his power will have returned in full.

Not even Taliesin would fault him for defending his own territory.

As a Seer, the boy would know everything, of course. Perhaps he might even visit. Pendaran's lips twitched in a knowing smile. Yes, perhaps he might.

Relaxed now, his claws receded. He would convene a Council meeting soon, but not yet. Sitting down at his desk, he phoned the airport to prepare his private jet. He'd bring servants to carry Saran there and Elen upon their return, and perhaps two other Council members. He was not stupid enough to enter his enemy's woods to meet his favorite adversary without at least two more powerful wolves by his side. But who? His power had returned enough so that he no longer appeared ill, but they must be ones he could control in his current state.

William and Neira, perhaps? They had been to Avon when Math had reigned, several times, and knew the area. More important, they held no affection for Merin and would not spill his secrets for her. William's betrayal had been allowed but not yet forgiven. His harboring the Wulfling without reporting her was a disappointment. Unmated female shifters were too rare for such deceit. It was a conundrum, really. He admired the man's gumption. *Alas,* Pendaran thought on a sigh, *if I killed all my Council members for stupidity over seeking a mate, I'd have none left.*

Was it a wonder he'd grown bored? The thought of listening to Neira's nefarious voice for six hours without relent held little appeal, but her weakness was one he could control, so he would resign himself to the trial ahead.

He removed a sheet of parchment from his drawer, dipped his quill and penned a letter to travel across an ocean. This one included a map. Little did the dissenters realize that he owned land next to every one of their territories. The letter would arrive before him. He looked at the clock, calculating his time with theirs. Yes, it was enough to travel while they slept. What form should he give its delivery this time? *A black wolf,* he thought. That would remind the enchantress to behave.

If not, she knew the penalty for not heeding his demands.

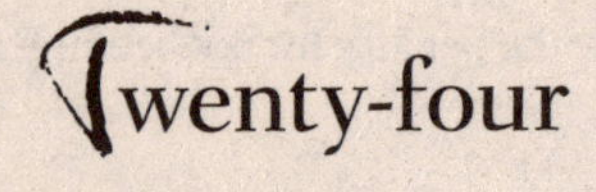

Twenty-four

The following morning, Cormack stepped into the shower without waiting for the water to warm, knowing the heater ran on propane and generators. All the staff would have showered before beginning their day, draining the hot water for at least the next hour. Lathering quickly, he scrubbed his chest, gritting his teeth under the frigid spray. Cold as a mountain stream in spring, and still it didn't cool his happy appendage. The damn thing was more eager now that it knew the pleasures it had missed.

Cormack grinned, too grateful to care.

"I'm heading down to check on Mac." Elen's voice grew louder until she leaned into the open door, then her eyes heated as they landed on him through the glass partition.

Immediately his wolf rose—among other things, but he squelched his instincts to order her to stay. Having been raised by his sisters, two formidable women who had demanded their independence, he knew to respect Elen's. Men who smothered were never tolerated for long. He needed to give her breathing room, but not without reminding her of important limits.

As her assigned guard, he had that right. As her mate, he demanded it.

"Don't leave the castle until I'm with you," he pressed. "You are not to be alone with anyone we don't know, do you understand? I don't care if someone's drowning in the river and only you can save them. Find me first. Pendaran may be weak but he's getting stronger by the day—and I don't trust his reach."

Not a foolish woman, she didn't argue. "I promise not to leave the building without you," she repeated with diligence. "And I won't be alone with anyone I don't know or trust."

"Thank you." Feeling eased, he waited for her to leave, but when she lingered, he asked, "What are you thinking?"

A slow smile turned her lips. "I'm thinking I'm jealous of those bubbles."

Chuckling, he slid the door open to flick cold spray at her. "Want to join me?"

"Stop," she yelped. If she were a cat, she might have hissed. "It's freezing." Jumping out of his range, she announced with playful impudence, "I'm leaving now, just in case you're wondering. I shouldn't be long, and when I return, I'll replace those bubbles with my mouth."

Her parting words took a moment to register, along with how far down the lathered soap had slid, but when they did . . .

"Elen . . ." He jumped out of the stall, suds and all, lunging for the outer chamber door, and then craned his head out into the hall. Her impish laughter trailed around the corner. Bare-assed and besotted, he growled, "I warned you not to flirt."

"That wasn't flirting," she called back just before she disappeared. "That was another promise."

UNABLE TO STOP SMILING, ELEN MADE HER WAY TO THE first floor, uncaring of the knowing grins she received in return. Never had she been this happy, and she marveled in the day, of life and joy—and a love that swelled her heart to bursting.

The halls of Castell Avon filled with the disjointed sounds of stringed instruments being tuned. Since it was still morning, she wondered at the sound, and then became more curious as she walked through the great hall. A long table made of oak had been pushed against the far wall, freshly polished while the floors were swept.

Audrey, the Wulfling, came dashing around the corner, her face aglow with excitement, while Tesni chased behind. Both came to a halt when they noticed her. Elen cleared her expression, knowing that Tesni had pursued Cormack but failed. The child, thankfully, removed the awkwardness.

"Elen," Audrey cried, and then launched herself into her arms. "We are having a dance. For Mae. And I get to go. You get to go too. Unlike last time, when we weren't allowed." Eyes the color of russet leaves sparked with annoyance over the memory.

"Do I?" Elen adjusted the excited bundle in her arms. The power that rose from her equaled this island and came close to Ms. Hafwen's. Without doubt, this child was connected to the Otherworld, and Luc and Rosa had a precocious handful to protect.

"Maybe," Tesni insisted, her face flushed but lovely, "if you behave." She offered Elen a polite nod before holding out her arms to retrieve the child.

"No maybe." Audrey gave her caretaker an adamant frown as she switched holders. "Mama Rosa said I could." Her bottom lip protruded in an impressive pout. "And Walter is making me chocolate cake with orange frosting."

The cake was probably for Mae, considering the woman loved chocolate and oranges. And she was the very person Elen had left Cormack to see, a true test of how much she cared, remembering his image in the shower with slippery suds sliding down his stomach as he lathered his chest. Despite the water's temperature, it was a true sacrifice to leave him there and not follow those bubbles with her parting promise.

Wanting to return without delay, Elen asked, "Have you seen Mae?"

"She is in her kitchen," Tesni offered. "It is good to see her whole again. We are grateful."

"As am I." Elen ruffled Audrey's hair in passing, smiling because she felt comfortable doing so. At home she would have withheld the gesture, having seen more than one parent's eyes filled with fear. Yes, she loved this place, and their people, for the simple fact that they trusted her, or rather, recognized that she meant no harm. "I'm sure I'll see you tonight," Elen said to Audrey. "Will you save me a dance?"

"If you want me to, I will." Her chest rose and fell with a dramatic sigh. "But only after I dance with Papa, Cadan, Gareth, Teyrnon and Cormack." Her fingers counted off her potential partners with innocent yet eerie insight, for she had chosen the most powerful ones. "And Porter."

A grin turned Tesni's lips. "Well, we can't fault her for taste."

Elen couldn't help but agree. "No, we cannot."

The castle had two kitchens, one added later on with modern amenities and gas appliances, now bustling with activity as scents rose to tease her stomach, and an original one toward the back of the main building, built with a central kiln for bread baking and a hearth along the outer wall. The original kitchen was now Mae's domain. Shelves lined the walls filled with herbs and powders kept in glass jars. Boughs of sage, hawthorn and willow lay strewn across a long wooden table, tied with twine to dry. A jar for payments rested on a smaller table by the door.

Mae offered her healing services for free but never her special tonics.

Currently she stirred a concoction in a kettle that hung from the hearth, much like the one Elen kept in her cottage, but larger. Only Mae would return so soon to fire without fear. The scent of ginger rose from the stew, along with mint and a few other herbs she couldn't quite distinguish because of the ginger, but the combination had a soothing effect.

Elen loved Mae's kitchen. It reminded her of childhood, of many afternoons spent learning healing properties of herbs, how to prepare them, and how to apply them. More than a mentor, Mae had been her substitute mother when her own had been consumed by sorrow over losing her mate.

"Elen child, I am surprised to see you this early." She gestured toward an empty seat by the hearth.

"You cut your hair." Elen hugged her first, and then brushed her fingertips over the blunt ends, dark but soft, like the pelt of a mink. "I like it." There was a bald patch behind her ear and above her temple where scars had once been. The style would help it look less patchy while the rest grew in.

"Sit," Mae ordered as dimples overcame her cheeks, adding softness to her formidable features. "Rest. After the caterwauls we all heard from your room last night, it is a surprise you can walk. I made you a tea to soothe your aches." She grabbed a mug from a line of hooks and ladled in a portion. "Drink."

Accepting the mug, she sipped the tonic. Her aches reminded her of the most beautiful night of her life, but she also wanted to enjoy this night just as fully. "What's in this?" It tasted pungent but not unpleasant.

"Ginger, mint, feverfew and juniper," Mae recited with impatience. "You have the recipe." A twinkle entered her gaze. "I omitted the black cohosh root."

Remembering the recipe, Elen looked down at her hands, knowing why Mae had omitted that one herb. "I can't think about that," she whispered. "I want it too much." Black cohosh root was good for menstrual cramps and inducing labor, but not good during the early stages of pregnancy.

"Time will tell." Mae patted her shoulder. "If ever there was a binding, it happened last night. Your mating braid has woven its strings, and it is strong. I can feel it even without your Cormack in the room."

"Enough about me." Her oldest friend had just suffered an ordeal and she had come to check on her, not revel in her own joy and selfish wants. "How do you feel?"

"Ah, my apprentice still wants to check on me, does she? And here I thought this was to be a friendly visit. Well, rest your fears. I am ready to have some of what you had last night . . . That is how I feel."

A light knock sounded. Peeking her head around the corner, Bethan placed rolled bills in the payment jar. When the visitor would linger, Mae shooed her away. "You have grown strong, Elen child. To make these old bones feel whole."

"It wasn't me," she professed once again, pausing when another person came to place money in Mae's jar, gold coins this time, offering a grudging nod before leaving. "It's that pool." A magical pool by a magical tree. "Did you not see—"

"Hold your tongue," Mae hissed. "Of course I know," she chastised in a hushed voice, "but do not say its name aloud.

Whispers carry from these walls." Her hand lifted, no longer gnarled. She held Elen's chin and pinned her with a stern gaze. "Have you forgotten what I taught you? We keep care of our secrets. It is how we survive. Never forget."

Mae released her when another person came with an offering for the jar.

Unsettled by the warning, Elen changed the subject while visitors came and went. "Your kitchen is busy today. What concoction have you brewed that has caused such high demand?" Last visit she'd learned how to mix poison ivy in soap, an unpleasant contraceptive for female shifters, and one that had the same effect on males in a different manner. Mae titled it: Soft As Worms.

Mirth entered golden eyes. "It was not me doing the brewing last night."

Cadan, Rosa's cousin, turned the corner next, adding to the tally; a powerful shifter, more graceful than ruthless. With red hair and green eyes, he walked like a wolf who knew others couldn't help but watch. His beauty made him a pawn for Guardian attentions, a bane he used to his advantage if necessary—to protect Rosa. Their bond was as close as siblings', unbreakable even by Math, Rosa's first husband.

"Elen," Cadan greeted with a grin. "You made our Mae a very wealthy woman last night." He yawned, not looking too put out, and then winked a farewell before returning to the main hall.

Understanding dawned. "This is about that ridiculous wager, isn't it?"

"You cannot expect me to refuse easy pickings," Mae cackled. "I knew you would be the first to dip that boy's stick."

"You bet on *me* winning? For money?" Flustered, Elen shook her head, fanning her face because it suddenly felt hot. Sweat broke out across her brow. An odd reaction because she held no embarrassment, nor should she; in Mae and Merin's time, friends and family would have been invited to witness their ceremony of love's most divine act. But that was before wolves were melded into their veins and the beast's possessive nature took hold.

Once alone, Mae closed the oaken door, lowering the iron latch that served as a lock. "Elen child," she said in a tone that turned heavy with torment, "I will wager the blood of my own heart on you winning."

Elen's flush increased. Her gaze fell to her half-consumed tonic. No, Mae would not do such a vile thing. Almost two thousand years they had known each another, years kindled with memories that had earned her trust. Long before Cormack, Mae had been her only friend when all others had shunned her; more than a friend, a mother, a teacher and a consoler in times of loneliness. It was Mae who'd held her when she wept after her own mother had shoved rods into her spine.

The room suddenly shifted and morphed. Colors blended into an obsidian pool. Suspicion turned to shock. And when her pulse began to race, she knew . . .

"Why?" It fell from her lips as a slur as betrayal wrenched her heart, and then anguish. From a distance she felt her muscles release and the mug fall from her hands; it shattered on the stones of the floor.

Air, she called, and then, *Fire*. Neither element came to her aid, because her self-will had been drugged and her mind imprisoned. Elements only responded to conviction—not intoxicated entrapment. She tried to scream but knew her desperation went unheard. *No! Please no. Not now! Cormack . . .*

Familiar arms encircled her, lowered her gently to the floor. Wetness coated Elen's face, drops, not trails, falling from above like hot rain.

"You are the daughter of my heart." Clogged with tears, Mae's voice wove around her like a dark dream. "But you are stronger than the daughter of my blood. You have everything where Saran has nothing. You will survive where she cannot. Someday you will understand. Someday you will find forgiveness for what I have done. You will dance under the stars and whisper my name, and when you do"—her voice broke on a sob—"know that I will hear, know that I will be watching and dancing with you."

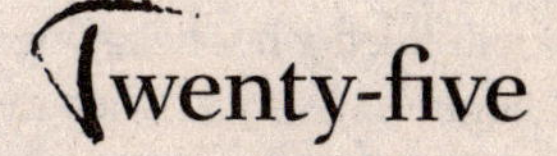

Twenty-five

A SMALL FIRE BLAZED WITHIN A CIRCLE OF STONES, crude but sufficient for the caldron that bubbled above, hung from cast-iron rods. For all appearances, it resembled any modern campsite—except for the enchantress who stood behind the fire stirring her brew. The first born without the ability to shift, but like the ruby-throated hummingbird, she had proven her worth and flown the distance on the wings of another power. Enchantress, sorceress, healer, midwife—*witch*; no matter the title, Maelorwen owned them all.

And yet with all that potency she had not been able to cure her own curse, or her daughter's—divine proof that their wolves came from a power beyond her reach.

Maelorwen's healed visage surprised Pendaran. Not because of her inability to call her wolf—she could have healed her skin with magic at any point—but because she held her secrets close and her power unknown . . . *unless crossed.* She reveled in anonymity, welcomed the scars that hid her identity. Indeed, her healing held a signature of a sweeter gift from a kinder, less secretive heart.

Obviously not Mae's; no doubt she had *not* been pleased.

Pendaran chuckled. Seeing her beauty restored brought forth memories of beginning times, when they had walked free among mortals, worshiped and feared. A melancholy sigh fell from his mouth. Science and machinery reigned in this modern day, owning the loyalty of humans as completely as his kind once had—if not more. It seemed every mortal these days held a gadget in their hands, unable to live without their new god of technology.

It saddened him. The reason why, he admitted, that Elen, with all her otherworldly gifts, held such an allure, even in all her sweetness. She reminded him that there was a higher place beyond this realm. That reassurance had become as important to him as the answers he sought.

Scents of licorice root and lungwort rose from the cauldron: a blood-growing potion. He had demanded it made in his last correspondence, an added insurance for Maelorwen's cooperation. She needn't know he intended to use Elen's own blood. To her right, a woman lay on a bed of autumn leaves—but *not* the woman he sought. Aeron's hair spread in a dark blanket across the earth, her mouth lax in drugged rest.

Pendaran knew the Walker well and therefore scowled, ignoring the power that coated his throat when he stepped into the clearing. "What is this? I told you to bring me Merin's daughter."

"Elen is near, Daran," Maelorwen scolded without looking up from her task, using his common name as only his family had done before their deaths. "First you will seal your penned promises with a spoken oath, and then I will reveal her location as you have revealed this place to me."

"You dare issue demands," Neira hissed, stepping next to Pendaran, her breaths sharp whistles in his ear. Familiar with Maelorwen as the witch from old, as all Guardians were, but not aware, he suspected, that she spoke to the very same woman who'd felt her whip six months prior.

Maelorwen hid in Avon as a mutilated *Hen Was*, her features concealed under scars. He'd known she was there, skulking in shadows after the death of her mate and daughter, unaware the latter still lived. He also suspected that she had provided Dylan with access to Math, Rosa's first husband, while the Guardian had been preoccupied, just one of many men foiled by her deceitful ways.

Dear Gods, he had missed her about to keep him entertained.

More astute than his comrade, William frowned in recognition, but kept his observations silent, as did Pendaran's own two servants. The beasts contained within iron crates, however, did not. Their howls wrenched through the clearing like broken screams from madhouse dungeons, muffled by the blankets that covered their cages, off-putting nonetheless.

With patience worn thin, Pendaran rested his hand around his sword, now held by a leather scabbard. A replica of his old one was in the process of being cast from iron. "Why is the Walker here?" He had been specific in his demands that only Maelorwen knew his plans.

"It is not easy to carry a grown woman," Mae complained. "I had my Elen in the wheelbarrow I use to gather herbs, but I was noticed by the Walker after crossing the bridge, and Aeron is bored, so she says she wants to come."

An impatient sigh expelled from her lungs. "So then I had to carry two."

"Do not act feeble with me, Maelorwen," he warned. "I have seen you bring an entire village to their knees." In fact, Pendaran had never questioned why Llassar had fallen under her spell.

"Would you have me kill her?" she asked in a knowing tone. "They have lost Ceridwen's favor, but they are shifters of pure blood, and females are few."

With false disdain, he said, "The Walkers' loyalty was cast when they stayed with the rebels upon awakening." But, no, he did not want Aeron to die, as the witch well knew. Perhaps he should give her to William. That might be the perfect comeuppance the man deserved.

"Leave her or take her, it does not matter to me." She gave an absent wave. "Aeron is your problem now and not mine."

Neira left his side to circle the unconscious form. Next to the rich darkness of Maelorwen and the slumbering Aeron, the Guardian appeared tiny and pale. If it suited her, Neira could assume the role of an ashen child, a ruse that had lured many men to her aid, and then imprisonment in her playroom soon after.

"Neira," Pendaran ordered, removing Cadarn, "return to me." Sulky eyes lifted, and then fell to his sword, called by a tone he used when causing pain. Preferring to be the giver, not the receiver, she submitted to his command.

Maelorwen smirked, mocking him for the company he kept. "I will not tell you where Elen is until you speak the words aloud. You know what I say is true, because we have been here before, have we not? Torture me, burn me, rape me or kill me . . . but I will *never* yield to you. You will not find her," she challenged. "The others will come before you do."

Yes, they had been here before. No greater advisory had he yet to meet, the very reason he'd kept her only weakness alive and hidden under his personal care. "It is the Bleidd I would use to make your secrets spill."

"My tongue will tie even more if you do," she warned softly, "for then I will know you intend to kill her after all."

"The Bleidd will be free." He clipped the words she wanted to hear, waving for the servant to remove the blanket from her cage.

Maelorwen's gaze fell and faltered. "And Elen," she pressed. "I will have your vow to keep her unharmed."

Pendaran ignored William's snicker. Unlike Neira, the witch would never submit, a lesson learned a long time ago at the cost of his brother's life. Moreover, Maelorwen was skilled, but her skills did not equal his, and whatever she was about, he would break it once his strength returned and he had Elen under his control. Plus, he did not want to be here all day for an oath he already planned to keep—*to some degree.* "Elen will remain unharmed." And because he knew Maelorwen, he added, "But confined within my care and under my control." And then another, "And our agreement is void if you do not reveal to me where she is."

A satisfied smile spread across her lips as dimples concaved her cheeks. A warning tightened his spine; Maelorwen's true smiles never boded well for him. "Proclaimed twice in ink, and now in voice, I ensure your pledge." Uncaring of self-harm, she cupped her hands into the boiling brew, and then threw it in his face, repeating her incantation in their mother tongue. "May it keep your word true and your honor bound."

In reflex, he turned his head and closed his mouth—but not in time. *Damn this lingering weakness.* Did she know?

Gritting his teeth, the liquid burned and tasted sour on his tongue, and it was not the potion he assumed. A small fizzle heated his veins. He forced a laugh, a charade for others to hear and not question his delay. "An oath-binding spell? Really, Mae? You disappoint me. Have you forgotten who I am?"

"It is you who forgets." A fire lit within her golden eyes, twirling like mists of Summerland dreams. "All harm done to my Saran and Elen will return to you in thrice."

"What folly is this?" Frozen until then, William stepped forward. "You will allow this insult?"

"The insult comes from you." Pendaran kept his tone low in warning. "*Never* question me. I will finish the task I have come to do." His gaze remained fixed on Maelorwen, drawn by an enchantress riding her power. "Where is Elen?"

"Release Saran, and then I will tell you where she is."

Pendaran flicked his hand for it to be done. "She refers to the Bleidd," he told the servants when they hesitated. "Release it."

The mother watched in grave silence as the black wolf struggled to walk and collapsed twice. Maelorwen's gaze lifted to him, filled with the same wounded confusion he'd once seen from another set of eyes. "You would do this to your brother's daughter, Daran?"

"If Llassar had done what I asked," he snapped, "then she would not have lived to suffer." His Council members knew their history, but it needn't be bared for retrospection. It brought shame to his lineage when his own brother had left his Council seat to live in hiding with a witch and their get. Pendaran had, of course, found them.

When the wolf stood, unsteady but proud, Maelorwen found her voice. "I would hold you in my arms once again,

Saran, but our time will come in a different place. Go south. Follow the river to an island. You will find help there."

Saran turned to Pendaran, too weak to lunge, but her lips peeled back to reveal canines as a growl vibrated low in her throat.

"Go," Maelorwen ordered, stern with desperation, "unless you prefer to be back in his cell." Saran looked to her mother, made a step toward her, only to receive gravel thrown in her face. "Go!"

The black wolf staggered and disappeared into the trees.

"Like wounded prey," he warned. Rustled leaves and snapped branches told of the wolf's direction as she faltered from fatigue. "Our agreement is void if you do not give me what I seek."

"After the pines there are two oak trees intertwined as one." Her shoulders slumped and her voice deadened. "You will see a boulder beside their roots." She paused. "It is not what it seems."

He inclined his head to William. "Go where she's instructed. If it's Elen, bring her here."

The woods remained quiet where the Guardian searched; a skilled wolf in a warrior's skin eager to make amends. William returned with Elen lax in his arms and a sneer on his face as if what he held had a stench. He lowered her next to Aeron and returned to Pendaran's side.

"You have dwelled among the weak for too long." Triumphant, Pendaran smiled at his adversary. "It has made you complacent. You should have included your name in your oath spell." Not that he wouldn't break the other names once he regained full strength. Closing the distance between them, he stated, "I cannot let you leave to tell our tales and bring the dissenters directly to my gates."

"My daughter lives and she is free." Her chin lifted, exposing her neck without resistance. "That is all that matters to me."

Pendaran readied his sword—but then hesitated before the final strike. She accepted death without fear, reminding him once again of his brother, who had done the same for her. Regrettably, the recollections of his youth were dying with each betrayer, and it made him feel oddly depressed—*and old.* If she hadn't challenged him in front of other Council members, he might have let her live.

"I take no pleasure in your fall, Maelorwen." However, it must be done.

The slightest of smiles turned her lips. "But I will take pleasure in yours."

He thrust his sword through her heart. As soon as iron pierced her beating organ he realized his grave error. Black fire burned through his veins as her spell kindled and took hold, dormant until his potent binding act. His breaths faltered, and in his weakened state he almost buckled from its force. She had ensured his vow with her own life's blood, and a death binding could not be undone.

Not even by him.

"Well done, Mae," Pendaran whispered, because worthy adversaries were so few. Buckling forward, he used her body as a shield for his limitations, pretending to sneer in disgust, not agony, as he lowered her to the ground and removed Cadarn.

Under watchful eyes, he straightened out of sheer pride and walked over to Elen's lifeless form. Unconscious and malleable, she appeared even softer than he remembered, almost sickly sweet. With the tip of his sword, he sliced a vertical path down the inside of her arm, letting her blood drain and pool among amber-colored leaves.

Because of the oath bind, with each drop spilled he felt the effects of three. Ensnared by enchantment, but not weak of will, he waited until a quarter of her blood drained before removing his necktie and wrapping it around her wound. He was a shifter and sorcerer—not a healer—but since she was immortal, he need not be. Like autumn, it was a temporary death, a slumber, and soon a reawakening.

"Gut the witch," he ordered his comrades. Twisting Elen's waist-length hair until it formed a thick rope; he made a quick slice by her shoulder, smirking as a branding bite was revealed on her tender flesh. Her silken tresses fell like golden serpents to coil within a burgundy pool. When all was done, Elen's scent mingled with Maelorwen's; it appeared as if a massacre had occurred.

It would do. The rebels would not call in human authorities with their scientific tests, knowing what the danger of discovery would bring upon them all. Their theories would come from scent and the instinct of their wolves.

Pendaran gestured to the *Hen Was* standing beside the second carrier containing a healthier beast than the first. A feline creature hissed within, chosen because it was native to this land, aggressive because it sensed their wolves and hungry because it smelled blood. "Unleash the lynx."

Even a rabbit eater would not resist a fresh kill. When the creature was done dragging entrails and consuming flesh, luring other natural predators to do the same, no one would assume Elen still lived. Not even her mate.

Pendaran intended to continue sending gifts, perhaps even a summons to her brother, forcing them to question his involvement. The Guardians' strongholds were spread wide and far across countries. The rebels did not have enough shifters to attack everyone at once. They would argue, send scouts and find no evidence of Elen, and then argue some more. They would question who—or what—had caused her death. Uncertainty would fuel doubt, and with doubt their campaign would fail before it even started.

Pleased with the results of his plan, Pendaran turned to his fellow Guardians. "Doubt is such an efficient tool for dissension. Do you not agree?"

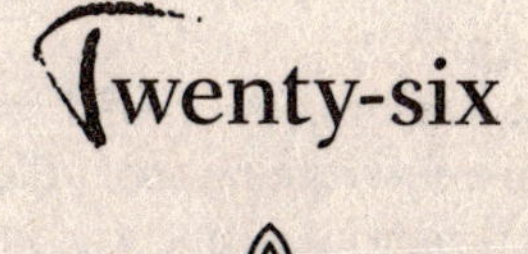

Twenty-six

BY EVENING CORMACK SUCCUMBED TO THE BLINDING panic that gripped his gut. They'd searched the castle, the island and even the local town—but he knew, from the acid that lodged in his throat and the fear that seized his heart, that she'd been taken. "Elen promised not to leave, and she wouldn't have done so without a fight."

Unless she'd been incapacitated at the time, but he could not think of that possibility and still breathe.

Decorated tables remained untouched as Avon guards and family assembled in the great hall. After combing the area until nightfall, they all returned to share information and regroup for another search.

"Mae took one of our service trucks from the carriage house." Fear thickened Rosa's voice, woven with disbelief. "She does this often enough to gather materials off the island that it didn't warrant the guard's concern. Aeron is missing as well."

"Mae is one of us," Tesni argued as doubts poisoned the air.

Angered by their protective assertions, Cormack snapped, "It was Mae." It had to be. "Elen would not have relaxed her guard around Aeron."

"They might still return." A hopeful comment from an asinine guard who knew nothing about Elen.

"No. Cormack is right." Luc understood Elen's practical mind. His features were strained with that knowledge. "She wouldn't have left willingly without telling anyone her plans."

"I was assigned to guard her." Cormack paced as fear and guilt roiled into words. "I should have been with her. I should—"

"My sister was taken from *my* territory," Luc cut him off, growling low under his breath. "From *my* home. And by someone we all trusted. If you must blame someone, then blame me."

"We've expanded our search to a wider radius." Porter placed his hand on Cormack's shoulder.

"Leave off!" Cormack shrugged away the man's condolences. "I'm not in fucking mourning." He shook from sheer rage fueled by shock and wanted no touch but hers. He didn't know whether to collapse or rip out someone's throat. "I'm going for another run," he growled. "I'll circle the river again and see if I can pick up her scent." He reached the top landing when Gareth filled the door, blocking his path.

The anguish on the guard's face tore a hole in Cormack's chest. Gareth gave a slight shake of his head, a gesture that expressed horror without words. "We . . ." His voice clogged as he looked away. "I am sorry. We found Mae outside of Avon. What is left of her," he added quietly, "and Elen . . ." He gave another sorrowful shake of his head.

"Fuck you!" Staggering back, Cormack stormed, "It's not Elen. It's *not* her! It can't be her."

Silence filled the great hall, silence and downcast eyes—and then growls as their beasts unleashed.

"Come." It was Luc's voice, cold, still in control, but deadly. "Let us go see what's been found."

"Shouldn't he stay here?" Gareth looked to Luc as he spoke.

Lucky for the man, Luc said, "No. He is my sister's mate. He'll hurt anyone who tries to stop him."

ELEN AWAKENED TO DARKNESS, A SPACE SO BLACK THAT not even shadows moved. Her head hurt and her body ached. A soft mattress held her weight. Woozy and gripped by thirst, she tried to sit up, flinching from the pain of her efforts. Her right arm throbbed. Terror gripped her chest and stole her breath. Her ankles were weighted, and the clang of metal echoed in the black space as she tried to move her arms and legs. Shackles bound her to the metal frame.

Stay calm, she thought. *Stay calm and feel.* The air was dank and absent of life, she forced herself to inhale nonetheless. Reaching out her senses, she found nothing that answered her call. She was enclosed by stone and surrounded by metal. Even the blankets smelled of chemicals and polyester woven by machines. Nothing in this room lived, nothing but her. Wherever she was, nature was far beyond her reach.

Calm be damned. She screamed.

* * *

WITH HIS EYES CLOSED, TALIESIN LAY NAKED WITHIN wild blackberry brambles, allowing their sharp thorns to slash his flesh. He must feel pain to bear his life for those who hurt because of him. If not physical pain, he would only turn to drink. Still might before the end of this wretched night. As the son of an earth goddess, he was not limited to one animal's form and had flown to Avon as a golden hawk, then farther north to the land Pendaran owned, where he shifted and waited in the shadows of the storm he created. The thorns did not drain enough blood for what he had done.

Even knowing what was to come, he jerked when he heard Cormack's disjointed bellow pierce the night; half sobs, half snarls, and then the screeching of a wounded wolf. Animals fled in a thunder of scurrying feet because of that sound. Like a torture that never ended, Taliesin had heard the man's desolate cry repeated again and again in his dreams over the last six months, a vision foreseen that couldn't be unseen. And all because of his interference at Avon's battle. He listened now because he deserved to suffer its sound.

In cruel clarity, his Sight forced more predictions into his memory. The past, present and future collided in a personal mind-fuck. He saw Luc grip Cormack around his chest as they collapsed together in a heap of shared torment. In Castell Avon, Rosa escorted three former Walkers across a bridge and banished them from her home. In the deep bowels of a dungeon that had once held a witch's daughter, he heard Elen's screams, felt her fear, her heartbreak. And Merin—he shook his head and scrunched his eyes, for what good it did—he couldn't watch Merin's reaction, so he moved on to lands more west, where Dylan met with Isabeau and other leaders. But as Pendaran predicted, dissension and doubts infested their decisions, and they chose to keep to their own territories.

Council members grew bolder and chaos ensued.

Because of him.

Taliesin wept.

Storm clouds erupted in the sky. Fat drops of icy rain fell on his face. They tasted of elements and power. His mother wept too, and her tears had the ability to cause far more devastation than his.

Hours passed. Voices raged. Cries resonated through the forest, both human and beast. He'd chosen a spot he knew wouldn't be found, but Taliesin was forced to visit his mother when the rain turned to acid on his skin. Her sorrow destroyed the world and sickened mortals in its path; it required action before more deaths were caused because of him. Rising from the brambles, he shifted and flew to Castell Avon. He didn't hide his approach, nor was he denied access. He kept spare clothing in the former tombs of the Walkers, now empty of bodies. Returning back to his human form, he dressed before visiting the child.

Rosa was with Audrey when he knocked on her chamber door. They sat together on a bed covered with stuffed animals and soft blankets, the child's face hiding within her adoptive mother's arms.

"I knew you would come." Rosa's mouth thinned, and those damning violet eyes lifted to him. Her animosity toward him never wavered, proof of her sharp perception.

Accepting her judgment, he said quietly, "I need to speak with Ceridwen." As the keeper of the Walkers, Rosa wouldn't deny his request.

Audrey snuggled closer to her new mother, her big eyes

shiny with tears. When he'd first learned a child had been assigned as his new messenger, he'd wanted to care for her himself, a selfish thought soon discarded. Everyone he cared for ended up dead, and he did not want her on his conscience with the rest.

"Hello, Audrey." Crossing the room, he sat next to her on the bed.

"Hi." Her voice was small, unlike her normal vivacity. Perceptive creatures, children absorbed the emotions of those around them, especially this one. "The lady is sad."

"I know." He placed his hand next to hers, turning it palm up. "I would like to see her if I could."

Nodding, she curled her hand inside of his. As soon as they touched he was awakened in the Vale, a world of dreams created by his mother. The trees that lined her imaginary path darkened with gloom. Gray leaves withered and hung from stems. This was not the spirit world of earth. No elements danced in this place of imaginings, just emptiness and glances without touch.

His mother stood on the path with arms crossed around her stomach. Long golden hair fell to her waist. Her eyes shadowed as she turned to face him. "I would take this pain from you if I could."

Expecting anger, her words surprised him, as did her reddened appearance that hadn't come from tears, at least not hers. "What happened to your face?"

She sighed, and the Vale sighed with her, dropping dead leaves on an empty ground. Her attention turned to the child. His messenger heard their thoughts as well. Handled with care and lectured about secrecy, but still a child—and his nightmares did not belong in her mind.

"Audrey, I will speak with Taliesin alone. Do you understand?"

An impertinent voice returned, "I won't be able to hear you anymore, but I can't let go of his hand."

"Very good," Ceridwen returned with praise. Audrey didn't like to be excluded. "We will visit together afterward." Then she waved her arm and blunted the child from the dream.

Satisfied their young messenger could no longer hear their conversation, she turned back to Taliesin. "I am not immune to the powers of my brethren. Hafwen has been barred from returning. She is not pleased." Welts pocked Ceridwen's face and arms with evidence of the pixie's displeasure. "I have let Hafwen help as much as I dare. Elen must face the rest of this battle on her own."

"Pendaran will destroy her gentle heart."

"Do not be so sure. You may see some of their futures, but not all, and you do not see their souls." A spark lit within his mother's gaze. "Her spirit is strong enough to change her fate. The Great Oak grows again because of her."

"Is it large enough for travel?"

"The trial has begun." Her cold response evaded a subject that caused her shame. "No travel is allowed between worlds until the worst of it ends."

"And yet I must live among them and do nothing to help," he spat. "I hide in shadows like a coward when I would lead their army—"

"You are *no* coward!" Ceridwen interrupted with harsh reprimand. "But you *are* my son and your help will unbalance their world. You must learn to accept who you are or more harm will be done."

"The harm has already been done." A bitter laugh fell from his mouth. "And now another field will fill with blood because of me."

"Taliesin . . ." A shadowy hand lifted across his face, a

mirage of a caress, since he felt no touch in this place of dreams, only the warmth of a small palm that covered his in reality. "That is my bane to bear as much as yours. I am not faultless, nor am I unmoved. Humans are curious creatures. Even in all their weakness I have witnessed the greatest acts of courage. Valor transcends our worlds, and we are all powerless to its call."

"And then more shifters are born," Taliesin taunted. And the cycle of his cursed life continued. His mother meddled where she shouldn't, and then lectured him for doing the same.

Her absent shrug carried no shame. "Some of them have proven worthy of my gift, others have not. I have been tempted many times to end them all, but as long as you live among them, I will continue to reward the ones who have earned the right to walk by your side."

"Merin said as much." He didn't miss the underlying warning in his mother's message—as if he needed more weight on his conscience. Her reaction came from fear, he knew, because of his actions on Avon's bridge. Her threat, however, was clear: If he died, so too would they.

"I do have a particular fondness for that warrior," she admitted. "As do you, but they must fight the rest of this battle on their own—"

"Or more warriors will fall," he finished.

"There are dark times ahead, Taliesin." Her voice softened with concern. "Promise me you will not find solace in drink."

"I can't make that promise." As she well knew. "But I will try."

"That is all I ask."

"I won't be returning for a while," he told her.

"I understand."

Animosity usually preceded their farewells, but this one

was oddly calm for what was to come. Focusing on the small hand that covered his, Taliesin returned to the reality of his life, where Rosa glared at him with violet eyes and tucked Audrey under blankets, as if to buffer her from his touch.

"Will you help us?" Rosa asked, her voice daring him to prove her hatred of him false.

"You don't want my help." He offered only truth. "What has happened this night is a result of the last time I tried."

That thought made her frown. "Where will you go?"

"I don't know," he said, and walked into the night to disappear into the mortal world.

As always, the siren's song of fermented spirits called—but there were other ways to find oblivion. A willing woman's flesh was a good start. Opening his mind's eye, he searched for one who could handle a vigorous session. Music immediately wove about his senses, his vision lured to the nightclubs nearby, where bodies danced and writhed.

The women are too thin in this modern day. He shook his head, searching further through the crowds. He preferred well-rounded curves over jutting bones. Ah, there she was, sitting against the wall, sipping her blue drink. *Jenna.* Her name whispered through his thoughts as her sensuality hit him in waves, neglected by the blinded men of this century. She watched with brown eyes feigning boredom while her friends danced on the floor. Her skin glowed, not deprived of nutrients. A slow smile of anticipation curved his lips. He would be tasting every inch. But first, Jenna deserved to dance.

And the hunt for oblivion began.

I shall cause a field of blood, on it a hundred warriors . . .

—Taliesin
From *The Mabinogi*
Patrick K. Ford translation

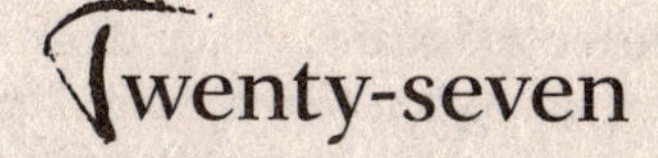

Twenty-seven

HER MONTHLY FLOW HAD COME AND GONE TWICE. THAT was how Elen kept her time, for there were no suns or moons that shined in her cell. Her and Cormack's child, if there'd been one, had never implanted into her drugged and blood-drained body. She mourned, because their mating had been too climactic a binding for there not to have been a conception, and in her heart she knew it to be true.

Pendaran sat in the corner on a metal stool, always keeping his distance away from her touch. He wore a modern suit this visit, with his sword encased in a new scabbard that resembled a cane, honed of iron instead of wood. It lacked the power of the Great Oak. He appeared the dapper lord, with dark hair and pale green eyes—almost handsome, if not for the cruel slant of his mouth and the venom that leeched from his spirit.

The manacles remained about her ankles and wrists, but

more chain had been added to move about the stone room when the servant came to clean. Her hair grew to brush against her shoulders and curl under her chin, but there was no mirror to see, just a bed and a metal bucket for relieving her needs. She wore a plain shift that tied around her neck and back like an apron, or hospital garment without sleeves to maneuver around the chains. Made of plastic fibers, a ridiculous precaution to her powers when she was in the bowels of a dungeon so deep not even Air responded to her call. Even beyond the stone walls, she felt the emptiness of the earth around her, the clay that held no life, deep below the roots of trees.

The servant who washed and fed her was always the same woman. She never spoke, nor had Elen ever addressed her. The *Hen Was* in Pendaran's keeping began as slaves, and while their shackles were invisible and honed of fear, they held just as strong as hers. Scarred beyond recognition, with fair hair growing in clumps, this servant reminded Elen of a pale Maelorwen. The reason, perhaps, for her prejudice. Or perhaps not.

If Elen were to harm her, she wondered if the woman would care. She had been tempted nonetheless. Hatred was an infections shadow that bred its deeds.

An aggravated sigh fell from Pendaran's lips. "I suspect your Bleidd is planning another scouting of our territories." A battery-powered lantern provided weak light in the dank room. "It is time to rid you of that bind." Impatience filled his tone. "Mated wolves are such a nuisance. He should have accepted your death by now. All the others have."

"Fuck off." Yes, Elen had learned to appreciate that word. Cormack, along with her brothers, had come to their homeland, hunting the grounds of known Guardians, only to leave with no evidence of her being held directly under their feet.

Her family still lived, according to Pendaran. All reports had been given by him in great detail; therefore she didn't know what to believe. She suspected this place was Hochmead, but she wasn't sure.

Standing before him, she was forced to listen yet again as the mute servant washed her back. A daily ritual, as if Pendaran needed assurances that she remained clean and well fed. Elen received a warning pinch where it wouldn't be seen. It was the first covert interaction in two months, and she barely managed not to jump.

Pendaran, however, did. He stood to inspect the stone wall behind the stool. Holding the lamp high, he searched for crawling creatures that knew not to enter her domain. A rainbow sheen of wax colored the wall under a ledge, scraped to the stone, but residue remained. Turning back, his eyes narrowed on the woman.

"I am at a crossroads, Elen." He sat in a manner that concluded his suspicion false. "I am in a conundrum I did not foresee. If you had but cooperated with me, we would not be here now." He waved his hand about the room. "I would have dressed you in silk and jewels, and your apartments would have been filled with books and entertainments."

Like a silken creance used for birds of prey, tethered to his will in an illusion of freedom. "I'd rather know the true nature of the chains around my feet."

"You are prone to dramatics, my dear. It is not an attractive quality. I brought you here because of what has grown in my forest, but I am not a stupid man. You would use your gifts against me, would you not? So here you remain, and I am once again bored." The last was given in a sharp tone that warned she'd pushed too far. He never named what she had grown, as if doing so would validate that her power was greater than his. "I would have answers from you, but you will not give them. And I am stuck with you now. I cannot let you free. What am I to do?"

She didn't repeat her earlier words, just raised her eyebrow instead, sending them with her eyes. He ignored her insult like all the others. Every night he wanted answers about her gift and how she'd gained Otherworld knowledge. Every night she refused. Why hadn't he tortured her yet? His earlier reaction made her curious, and she bit her lip hard enough to draw blood.

He scowled as his lower lip twitched.

Her chest tightened with suspicion. "What did Mae do to you?" If anyone had the skill to bind a dark curse, it was Maelorwen.

"Nothing." Standing abruptly, he raised the key and gestured to the servant, who tied the garment at Elen's back, gathered her cloths and scurried out the open door without a parting glance. "Maelorwen is dead, as your mate and family will be if you do not heed my warning. I have been patient until now, but as I have said, I am growing bored."

Metal chains scraped over stone as she returned to the bed. Once again in darkness, she waited until all sounds disappeared to ponder that information. *Maelorwen is dead.* Did she believe him? Moreover, did she care? The tears that gathered proved she did. But Elen had already mourned that betrayal. She was tired of sorrow and incapacity. She must find a way to fight back.

Elen's heart began to race with ideas, always tainted with his threats. He *would* use her family if she pushed too far; of this she had no doubt. Her new suspicion required patience and testing. But she had other gifts that had abandoned her in this place. Or perhaps she had abandoned them. How many times had she called to the elements, begging them to answer? Thousands maybe, in desperation and prayer, but they thrived above, beyond her reach. They never responded to her call.

But she breathed, did she not? Even if the oxygen tasted of residue and stale leavings, like dead molecules sloughed off to sink into the crevasses of the earth. Could it be enough to carry a dream?

"Carry my fantasy," she whispered in conviction. No pathetic prayers or desperate wishes, but an offering given on a playful challenge. "Carry my fantasy to the one who is pictured in my thoughts."

Needing serenity for conjuring happy memories, she let her eyes flutter closed; it didn't change the absence of light but helped relax her mind for pleasant thoughts. She recalled Cormack's face after her last parting promise. The memory hurt, and that was not what Air, the element of procreation, would carry. So she imagined the bubbles sliding down his stomach. Instead of walking down that hall, she twirled and returned, as she should have done.

Laughing deep, he caught her in his arms as she jumped, kissing her with a mouth that was meant for pleasure—*her* pleasure. His stomach flexed as she traced circles in the contours of his abs, massaging the suds into his quickly rising flesh. The door slammed shut. She imagined that too, so she could sink to her knees inside their room without distractions. Cormack devoured her with his gaze; his lips peeled back into a feral growl as she grabbed the base of his shaft.

In the pit of her reality, the barest of tingles brushed her skin. She smiled her first smile in two months. Air liked this fantasy.

"Thank you," she whispered into the chilled room, reminding her of the unforgiving iron that bound her down and the constant cold that seeped into her bones despite the blankets provided. No, she brushed that image aside. She was *not* in this place but back at Avon, where Cormack's hand rested on her head, twisting her hair about his arm. It was still long enough to wrap around his wrist to steady her mouth before his jutting erection. She ran her tongue along the underside, and then up, wrapping her lips around the tip, reveling in his tortured growls.

Take it all in, Cormack ordered.

The crudeness jarred her. It was not a command that came from *her* mind. It was too forceful, too masculine, and undeniably dominant. It was a man's fantasy—not hers. Had Air carried her dream? Had a connection been made? Was Cormack sharing this too, unknowing of her current state?

She could only hope. *I'm alive, Cormack. I'm alive and I love you. I'm being kept by Pendaran below one of his homes. I think Hochmead. Come find me.*

Empowered, she took him in as far as he would go, and then tightened her lips as she dragged her mouth up, swirling her tongue. Again and again, she repeated the motion until he stiffened, shouting her name . . .

"*ELEN* . . . *!*" CORMACK SHOT AWAKE, SPILLING HIS SEED in the damn sheets. He slept in the barracks of Avon, with guards snoring in bunks beside and above him. And still he came, gritting his teeth to quiet his sounds. Worse, so much worse . . . his pleasure turned to sobs as reality intruded and the dream faded—and he knew it was just a mirage sent by sadistic Gods to rip out what was left of his heart.

He had gone to his homeland twice with her brothers, a place he vowed never to return to; they searched and questioned on desperation alone. Merin hunted for answers and reported her findings to Dylan, or rather lack thereof. She had gone and stayed, moving like a nomad in private meetings with Council members who, in her words, had secrets they didn't want revealed. None had information about Elen, or so she'd said; her ragged appearance made him believe her words true. He'd returned to Rhuddin Village to hear her report, otherwise he stayed in Avon where Elen had last been seen.

Everyone suspected Pendaran's hand in her death, but without proof, no other leaders would commit to a full assault that required a gathering of the Council to achieve success. Isabeau, their closest ally, was dealing with her own Guardian issue. Edwyn, a Council member, has begun to visit her. He had yet to attack, but his threats had become less veiled. Their allied leaders agreed to help during assaults but were not leaving their territories unprotected on suspicions alone.

Doubts had caused dissension.

Cormack had gone a third time on his own to search the other Guardians' holdings, only to return with no evidence of Elen. Everyone believed her dead. Was his uncertainty another mirage of misery? The doubts ate at his soul. If she were alive, Elen *would* have found a way home.

But—*bloody hell*—why did her scent linger? Was he not tortured enough? He stayed in the barracks because reminders of her were too painful. Crueler still, he *felt* her. The heat of her mouth, and the drag of her tongue. And her voice . . .

I'm alive, Cormack. I'm alive and I love you. I'm being kept by Pendaran below one of his homes. I think Hochmead. Come find me.

"Cormack?" A feminine voice encroached—but not Elen's. A shadow moved, followed by the yield of his mattress as she sat. Tesni or Bethan? He didn't know, didn't care. Had she been sleeping in another guard's bunk to be so near? "I will ease you," she offered, "if you need."

"No." His voice was hoarse, gruff—*angry* that she would

disturb him when he could still feel the one he wanted but lost. "Leave me, and don't ask again. My answer will always be the same."

Shoving the blankets aside, he yanked on his jeans and made his way out of the castle. He needed to run. More often than not, he stayed in the form of his wolf. Why live as a man if Elen wasn't here? Why suffer a longing so acute he couldn't breathe for want of her scent and presence around him, laughing with him, loving him?

His wolf only knew hunger, hunt, survival and sleep—basic instincts that blunted his rage.

It was safer for those around him if he returned to the beast he was meant to be.

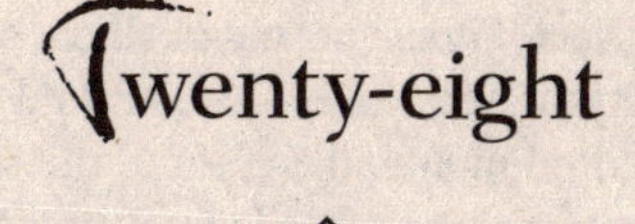

Twenty-eight

HIS COUNCIL WAS MOLDERING LIKE RABID WOLVES. Without his leadership to keep them in line, they would ravage each other for dominance. Pendaran saw it in their eyes, their greed, their suspicions and their scheming. They needed a reminder of his authority, the very reason he held this meeting in his forest.

The Great Oak had grown to almost two times his height, but it was still young. Its leaves had yet to fall, surrounded by earthly trees with skeletal branches readied for winter, an emerald gift under a new moon, and a beacon of hope in the dark night. Roots gnarled into moss-covered grounds, and the air sang with its power that shimmered like midnight stars.

Every Council member paused in silence, and perhaps shock, but with reverence nonetheless. They had not forgotten their beginnings, thank the Gods.

"It is growing strong." Even Maelor seemed impressed enough to open conversation. A giant of a man, the width of his forearm matched the trunk of the Oak and was just as solid. His wife stood next to him, by order, not by choice. Briallen pretended to be a tepid creature, but Pendaran knew her ruse, and that her true mate resided in Avon as a member of their guard. Maelor managed her obedience with his pets.

"How long has it been here?" Bran asked with a frown. Resentment swirled in eyes the color of old seas, the same look Taliesin held many times. They were similar in their opinions, Pendaran knew, only Bran did not have the luxury of security: the Goddess would not care if he died.

"Two months," Neira twittered. She wore a sheer dress of shimmering silk for the occasion, her breasts tiny but taut under the translucent material. It gave her a faery-like appearance, both delicate and sensual; a sadistic little creature who understood her allure.

Even Pendaran had been tempted to her playroom on occasion. "Neira," he warned softly. Only she and William knew whose hand had seeded its growth and that Elen was in his keeping. Merin still had a reach, and he wanted no other members involved. They might unknowingly dribble secrets if she skulked back into their midst.

Curiosity sparked in the expressions of his Council, forcing him to offer one truth. "It grew from Cadarn's scabbard." Their eyes dropped to his weapon. A replica of the old staff protected Cadarn, molded from gilded iron instead of wood; it did not hold the power of the original sheath. Nerth, its twin, was buried with Math, but the thought of desecration left a vile taste on his tongue.

It would be done, however, because he was in need of breaking a witch's curse.

The silence provided an opening for Rhys's entertainments.

He glared at William with a calculating gleam. "You have been forgiven, I see." He pestered out of boredom, but his insolence had grown tiresome. "Our accountant is back in full form, suit and all."

"Rhys," Pendaran said with a sigh, "if I killed all my Council members for seeking a mate, I would have none left. If the child had been abused, then William would be dead, but I am confident she remained unharmed and unmolested."

Pendaran did not tolerate perversion with children. It was the purest sign of a weak mind, and the one rule they all knew to abide or die.

"I was fostering Audrey," William defended. "I would like to retrieve her from Avon and raise her properly before they taint her loyalty."

"We will," Pendaran promised, only because he shared the man's concern. "Be patient. She is not as easily retrieved as Aeron." He rested his hand on Cadarn. The man looked down, understanding the consequence if he chose to reveal his knowledge. "I had Aeron removed from Avon," he announced to the other members, "but I have yet to believe her loyalty to us, so William is keeping her entertained until I do."

"How's that going?" Rhys taunted.

William scowled.

"I will take her from you," Neira chimed in. Women were not her temptation, he knew, but using powerful creatures to manipulate others was.

"Aeron will stay with William," he ordered. "The Walkers have awakened, as you all know, but apparently they have been abandoned by Ceridwen. Taliesin will not seek them out to carry messages any longer." The male Walkers were passive enough, their connection to the boy their only worth, but Aeron was a different matter. Unmated female shifters were too rare. "She is of pure blood and belongs with us."

Edwyn cleared his throat, always a drawn-out process when the man chose to speak. "What are our plans? Cormack, the former Bleidd, has visited my territory. I learned of this while I was overseas," he added, "but they are getting bold. Their holdings are scattered. If we plan simultaneous attacks—they will fall."

"Will you drag us all into your obsession, Edwyn?" Briallen spoke up, receiving a glower from her husband. "Isabeau is mated. She will never want you. Your plan will only earn you more of her hatred." It was a direct insult to Maelor, who bent down and growled something in her ear. She stiffened, but the fire remained in her gaze. Ah, her ruse was crumbling, but her husband would right that soon enough.

"The rebels are all over the globe," Gweir added with little enthusiasm. A stout man, he scarcely stood above Neira in height but compensated with mass. Boorishly content ruling his territory, Gweir resolved turmoil with brutal efficiency but didn't seek it or thrive on it. "Some as far as Russia and the Himalayas."

Rhys sneered. "Have you all lost your bullocks?"

"I understand your frustration," Pendaran interceded, "but we must tread carefully. Taliesin is going through a troubled time and has taken up their cause. You will remember the oath we all gave to keep him unharmed, unless you wish to risk the wrath of Ceridwen on us all."

Edwyn winced, turning toward the Great Oak, divine proof of the threat. "I have not forgotten."

"Let us give our gateway time to grow," Pendaran said. "Our reign will be validated once again, and Taliesin will return to our fold."

* * *

ANTICIPATION HELPED ELEN ENDURE THE SILENCE OF her days, waiting for the dull sounds of steps and turning doors that alerted her of each visit. She counted six creaks as each door opened, louder as the visitors drew near, but suspected there may be more she couldn't hear. The servant woman scurried in with Pendaran at her back. Accustomed to absolute blackness, the weak lantern glowed bright, its light almost harsh. His expression warned of a violent mood as he sat in his corner and watched in cold silence.

It was the same routine every night; the servant handed her a goblet of water and waited while Elen drank it in full, then handed her bread and protein of some sort while she replaced the old bucket with a clean one, leaving the other in the hall. After the food was consumed, she motioned for Elen to stand.

Elen obliged, only this time she pretended to trip over the chains that entangled her feet, Pendaran's vicious mood be damned. She wanted out of this place. To test her theory, she purposely crumbled to the ground. Her right knee took the brunt of the fall, slamming hard against cold stone, sending shards of pain up her leg and forcing air out of her lungs.

Pendaran's sucked in a breath, fisting his hand by his right leg. A mottled flush began to crawl up his neck in florid rage. She sensed he was too pained for words.

Hiding her satisfaction was a difficult task, confident now that he was somehow connected to her pain. *Mae, what did you do?* A dark binding, to be sure—perhaps even the darkest if she were dead and it held Pendaran captive.

As the servant helped her rise, Elen asked her, "What is your name?" It was the first time she had addressed her directly. "Am I in Hochmead?" The woman looked away, but not before a slight shake of her head. *Be careful*, that gesture said.

"She knows not to speak to you," Pendaran snarled through gritted teeth. "I will cut out her tongue if she does. And if you continue with your clumsiness, I will drug you unconscious."

Threats, she now knew—but not without consequences, especially for the woman not protected by a curse. And he would keep her here just to ensure her safety.

The servant motioned for Elen to face Pendaran, always cleaning her from behind where the johnny untied, allotting a simple privacy. *An act of mercy?* Not even a bucket of water was brought within her reach, just damp cloths and disposable plastic toothbrushes to clean her teeth, but the woman had always handled her with care.

"I was told that you were once an honorable man," Elen said softly, "but I find that hard to believe. Truly, you are—" A pinch on the soft flesh behind her arms stopped her words.

"What are you doing over there?" Pendaran accused with a scowl.

To cover, she gave the smarting area a vigorous scratch. "There are bugs in this place."

His mouth tightened in response. "Finish quickly," he ordered the servant, standing to leave. "I don't wish to be here all night."

The woman gathered the empty trays and cloths and scurried for the door, but not before briefly lifting her gaze. This *Hen Was* wasn't completely broken. Clear eyes peered through her scars, blue as forget-me-nots in spring, and they sent a message just as promising: *I will help you . . . if you help me.* And then a slight but distinct nod: *Yes, you are in Hochmead.*

* * *

A PRIVATE TUNNEL RAN UNDERGROUND FROM HOCHMEAD to its forest, a necessary addition for secrecy from mechanical eyes in the sky. Rage clouded his vision as Pendaran hobbled the narrow passageway to the concealed opening beyond. *Clumsy twit . . .* She had crippled him with a simple fall. Shards of pain sliced his knee to the point of nausea.

He must find a way to break Maelorwen's spell. His powers had returned in full, and still he couldn't reverse her curse—because of the death bind. Never had he expected her to forfeit her own life willingly, not only willingly but with calculating intent, and for *them.* Its absurdity went beyond all comprehension. Truly, it defied sound reason—but its grip was irrefutable.

The pain increased each day he kept Elen in her chains. He had vowed to keep her unharmed, and therefore all harm she suffered, he suffered it in thrice. From lack of sleep, his head pounded with a stabbing assault that didn't relent. When Elen scraped her arm, he bled. When she slept three hours, he only slept one. His wrists and ankles throbbed because of shackles he dared not loosen. His bones ached from cold.

Torture, obviously, wasn't an option. He'd shifted five times yesterday to heal his aches, and still they returned.

Despite his threat, he could not drug her. Her last poisoned unconsciousness had come from Maelorwen's potion—not his. If he harmed Elen's family, or worse, her mate, would she refuse to eat as Saran had done? Even now he worried if his threat to drug her might scare her into not taking food. *Worried.* He spat with disgust at the thought, an emotion he hadn't felt since childhood. If he set her free, she would only fuel the dissenters' cause.

Conundrum indeed.

"Maelorwen," Pendaran sneered as he pushed his way through the concealed opening, greeted by brambles and crisp air, "have your laugh, wherever you are, but I will break your curse."

Once under the canopy of manicured evergreens, he stripped and shifted, welcoming a punishment that came from his power and not hers. The elements tasted pure on his tongue as he fed their power to his wolf.

Bones snapped and reformed in a rush of pain followed by pure freedom. And he took his first breath of air without agony. The night air brushed his fur with a cool kiss, carrying the scent of winter's approach. He explored his forest, watched his guards circle his grounds, and checked entrances for encroachment. All was secure. The Bleidd would not find a way inside his manor without facing his death.

He traveled to a carved stone that marked the entrance to the graveyard reserved for the *Gwarchodwyr UnFed*. Thirty-nine Original Guardians rotted under this earth, all buried with their weapons out of tradition. Modern scientists had unearthed too many of their secrets because of such graves. Celts once believed afterlife journeys included physical matter. Only the gateways offered that journey intact, the reason this new one was such a precious gift. Regardless, the customs of their ancestors deserved respect.

He waited in the shadows until assured no one had followed. Shame forced him to complete this mission alone. Not even the dead eyes of his slaves would know this desecration.

It was time to dig up an old friend's grave.

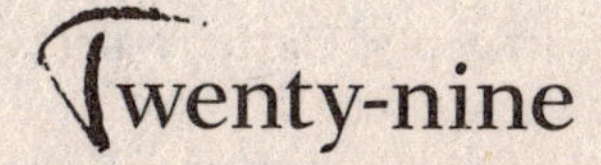

Twenty-nine

THE DESOLATE HOURS WITHIN HER OBSIDIAN CAVE CONsumed Elen's spirit as surely as a dozen demons sucking her soul. Worse, the constant cold and never-ending darkness fed her insecurity. Questions flooded her consciousness and nightmares haunted her dreams, but the questions were worse. Had she made assumptions about the curse? What if the bind was all in her imagination? Had her mind procured hope in desolation?

Had madness begun its encroachment?

No! Elen shook her head and squeezed her eyes tight. Doubts were no longer allowed. To keep her mind from succumbing to this weakness that wanted to claim her, Elen imagined another illusion. Her fantasies were a balm that kept her sanity intact. This time she pictured her cottage, their home and their bed with soft blankets. Heat rose through grates in the floor from a fire that crackled in the hearth below. She wanted comfort, and more than anything, she wanted to be held. Air brushed across her skin in a fleeting caress, unsure but willing to console.

Love me, Cormack, she whispered in her dream.

She received a growl in return—and then pain as bones broke and stretched to his human form. *Always,* he whispered then. The scent of pine carried with his voice. Not in her cottage, somewhere else.

Warm arms encircled her, stark against the cold. He had just shifted, gloriously nude, and he rolled on top of her. This was not what she had come for. *Was it his dream?* If so, she refused to deny his need or his love. They had never done a traditional mating, and she wanted it then more than any other.

I am yours and you are mine, he growled into the night. Parting her legs with his thighs, he entered her in one long stroke, filling her—moving within her.

I am yours and you are mine. She arched as his weight pushed her into frozen ground and not the softness of her mattress. Their desperation raged in their mating. She clawed at his back as she rocked into each stroke. But her pleasure came too soon, claiming her body in violent waves.

"I'm in Hochmead, Cormack." Her cry echoed off the dank stone walls of her cell as her release carried her back to the bleakness of reality. "Come find me . . ."

CORMACK BRACED HIS ELBOWS AGAINST THE FROZEN ground, panting fogs of breath into the frigid November air. His shift had been brutal. When he'd first sensed her presence, he forced the change in frantic haste to feel her again, if only by a dream. And then he'd been sucked under by a different need. His body still pulsed with pleasure and pain from both.

Her hair had been short, her arms bound, her scent coated by darkness and death. And she was cold, so damn cold. Like a corpse.

Fuck! Was he going mad? Had her spirit come to console him from the grave?

He didn't know, but if anyone could find a way to visit his dreams, it was Elen.

A dark shadow crossed his vision. Sitting up, he watched the wolf slowly encroach. The black Bleidd had begun to follow him several weeks earlier, perhaps sensing a kindred spirit. He had lived with her curse long enough to know what she was, if not where she'd come from.

Rising up from his makeshift den where he slept, he snagged his clothes kept in a pile under pine boughs and then shrugged them on. "I'm headed back to the island." They'd had this conversation before. "There's food there if you follow." He always spoke to her with respect because she understood every word.

Skittish, she shook her head and then disappeared back into the woods. He remembered being that wolf, visiting Elen in much the same manner. The memory haunted him as he returned to Avon. He never veered far, checking in daily for news, so the journey didn't take him long.

"Cormack," Gareth greeted at the entrance of the carriage house, offering a pained smile. Like all of Avon's residents, his interactions were awkward and forced, as if he didn't know how to react around him.

"I've come to speak with Luc."

"He's in the library." Gareth's gaze lifted to the lines of trees where the forest began. "Your black shadow has braved further this time," he commented with a frown. "She needs food. I've left her offerings—"

"She doesn't want to be fed like a dog," Cormack said.

She had hunted, though; he'd seen the remains, but she had much to make up for to fill those starved bones. "Give her a portion of your meal and she might accept." *Treat her like the human she is inside the wolf, as Elen did for me.*

"I have a sandwich in the carriage house." Gareth left and returned with a cloth-covered bundle.

"Be careful," Cormack called after the man in warning, "she will follow you forever if you do." *And you will own her heart beyond death.*

He ignored the awkward nods as he made his way to the library. Luc sat behind a large desk, combing through accounts with his wife. They both looked up when he entered.

"I have to go back," Cormack said before they asked. He rested his fist against his heart. "I still feel her."

After a pause, Luc nodded without argument and then looked to his wife.

"You can go," Rosa said, without needing words to know his question, instinctively resting her hand on her stomach. Her clothes no longer hid her increasing size.

"No." Cormack shook his head. She was too close to term, and taking the second alpha put all of Avon at risk. "Luc is needed here until the babe arrives. I wanted to let you know my plans, no more. I don't know what I'll find, if anything. I just know I have to do something, or I'll go insane."

Luc's gaze reflected his torn decision. "I will secure the plane and car, but you're not going alone this time. You will bring Teyrnon and Cadan with you. I'll let them know while you shower and change." His hand gestured toward Cormack's disheveled appearance with a concerned frown. "You won't pass security like that. I'll call Dylan as well."

Which meant more guards would meet him at the airport, if not Dylan himself. Gratitude would be taken as an insult. Instead, he shared, "I dream of her with shortened hair in a dark room surrounded by stone and metal. She is bound by chains on her wrists and ankles, and still she carries messages to me. She tells me she's below Hochmead. I don't know if my mind is playing tricks, or—"

"If anyone can send a message in dreams," Luc interrupted, echoing Cormack's desperate hope, "it's my sister." Once again he looked to his wife.

Rosa's eyes bled to burgundy as her wolf rose. "You're going. I will maintain Avon while you're gone."

IN THE FORM OF HIS WOLF, PENDARAN CURLED UNDER the branches of the Great Oak. Nerth lay in the grass inches from his paws. Dead like its former master, its bleached vines held no power. The curse was unbreakable, and now it consumed his beast as well. Regardless of how many times he shifted, the pain returned.

Struggling to stand, he lifted his face to the waxing moon and howled his frustration. A movement in the branches drew his gaze and halted his cries. Had travel begun? Please let it be true. A tiny bird flitted about, screeching a harpy's song. He snarled and turned away.

Alas, no . . . It was just a common winter wren.

ELEN SENSED IMMEDIATELY NOT TO PUSH PENDARAN during this visit. His volatile mood roiled off him in waves as he leaned against the iron door. She squinted against the light of his battery-powered lantern. Like a creature of night, her eyes had begun to reject even its meager light.

The servant woman rushed over with a chunk of buttered bread and a goblet of water, motioning for Elen to stand with a sharp shake of her head. *Behave*, that gesture said. The routine now included changed bedding, thanks to her incessant scratching done purely out of spite. There were no bugs, but Pendaran took precautions regardless, and if her eyes weren't playing tricks on her, he had welts on his skin.

"I have grown tired of looking at you, Elen." His voice filled with resentment, and something other. Desperation, perhaps, anger too, but the former was just as threatening.

"Why don't you set me free?" she asked without insult, and then added in quiet respect, "Please."

Unappeased, his nostrils flared. "You know I cannot!"

"I know no such thing. Your prejudice infects you. How can you not see that? There is no reason we can't live in peace."

"Spoken like a true Evil Bringer who has never ridden the power of her beast." Pendaran laughed softly as if mocking her ignorance. "We are not pacifists, Elen. We are wolves. The strongest leads, and the weak submit. Or they die."

"I will never submit," she returned. *And if I die, you die with me.*

Again, the servant warned her with a slight shake of her head as she retrieved the empty goblet. She changed the bedding, washed Elen quickly, gathered the old items, and stood silently by the door. Her head bent to the floor, waiting for his instructions.

Doubts crept in. Had Elen imagined her earlier gestures? Had this empty shell of a scarred woman once held a spark of fire in her gaze?

"Yes, you will," Pendaran goaded, gesturing toward the woman in passive repose. "You see how she bows to me. If I keep you in this room long enough, you will do the same. You will begin to look forward to my visits, count every second until I arrive. You will begin to love me. We are immortal, so it may take some time, but it will happen."

Fear gnawed at her gut, because she felt its possibility. She *had* begun to look forward to his visits, just for relief of basic needs and to see light once a day instead of the black obsidian of her cave. Was it a hard stretch to think the mind would one day associate him as that light?

No. And for that alone, she said, "Bite me!"

Pendaran's lips peeled back, revealing canines as he leaned forward, leaving just enough space beyond her reach. "Be careful what you wish for."

"Touch me." She offered him her sweetest smile. "I dare you. Unless you've forgotten what happened to the last Guardian who tried. You seem partial to your wolf, but I can take him from you if you wish."

Even as the words fell from her mouth, she realized she'd pushed too far. Pendaran grabbed the metal stool and brought it down on the back of his slave. The woman buckled to her knees.

"Stop!" Horrified that she'd caused this, Elen lunged, only to be pulled back by her chains. She struggled against them, welcoming the bite of metal into her flesh.

Wincing from her efforts, Pendaran threw the stool against the wall. Metal clashed against stone. Like standing within a bell tower at noon, her ears rung with its echoes, but the whisper of metal sliding over metal made the hairs rise on her arms.

As he removed his sword from its sheath, Pendaran said, "There are other ways to make you behave where I don't have to touch *you* at all." His eyes reflected green fire, wild and uncontrolled, as he lifted his weapon to strike the woman at his feet.

Elen bit down on her tongue so hard she almost choked on her own blood. Cadarn fell from Pendaran's grasp as he buckled and vomited on the floor.

The woman looked up in confusion. Forget-me-not eyes blinked, focused on Pendaran as he continued to heave.

"Run!" Elen garbled a scream.

Scrambling to her feet, the woman paused long enough to point to the mattress, and then ran out the door without a second glance. Her retreat proved her not completely owned. Freedom will always bring courage to even the most trodden hearts.

A foreboding silence filled the room in the aftermath of her actions. Pendaran rose, unfolding with the grace of a serpent. With silent dignity, he sheathed his sword and retrieved the lantern. His lips drew tight but blood trickled from his nose as he breathed. The unnatural light shone bright in his gaze, and she knew beyond all doubt that he meant to keep her in darkness for the rest of her days.

Or at least until she bowed to his will.

Rendered speechless, he issued no insults or threats as he closed the door. Even so, her hope closed with it. The scent of iron clogged her throat, from her blood and his. She had not separated her tongue, but it swelled from the force of her bite. Tears threatened to spill as she dragged herself toward the bed.

As she scooted to the center and reclined, a hard object pressed into her side. Was this the reason the woman had pointed to the mattress? Had she hidden something under the sheets? Ripping the material away, she felt for it with her hands, blinded now and unable to see. More metal touched her skin, but this item filled her with excitement as she clutched the rounded stem with a jagged edge.

Victory bloomed within her chest. It was a key. But to what?

Elen immediately tried her shackles.

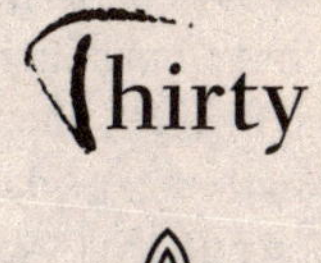

Thirty

THE NIGHT AIR CARRIED THE SCENT OF OLD POWER AND winter-cold earth. There was no snow on the ground as there was back home, but the dampness in the air penetrated worse. Surrounded by a stone wall, Hochmead Manor sat nestled within mountains. For a country flocked with sheep, none of them roamed the open field outside the gates, knowing to stay clear of humans saturated with the scent of wolves. Cormack watched from the forest beyond the field. He counted thirty guards or more positioned behind the gated stone wall, and suspected twice that within.

Luc stepped beside him, followed by Dylan, then Teyrnon, Cadan—and Merin too. Elen's mother had been with Dylan and refused to stay behind. They made a formidable line in the shadows of the forest, including a former Council member, but not as daunting as the guards who scanned the area from behind the stone wall.

Shifters all, he knew, and Guardians by choice. Allegiance to the Council. They followed the orders of the most dominant wolf.

"We can't cross the field without being seen," Teyrnon spat. The Norseman had readily agreed to return with Cormack, his hatred of the Guardians as pure as his. The man's mate was married to a Council member whose castle resided not far from these lands. Briallen chose to remain with her Guardian husband instead of her mate. There was a vile history there that Teyrnon refused to speak of. How the man tolerated the separation, or the betrayal, Cormack didn't know.

"There is a door that leads here from Hochmead," Merin offered. She wore snug brown pants and a matching top, with her blond hair tucked under a brown cap. The only bright object she carried was her sword. He saw Elen in her features, and it made his heart ache every time. "The tunnel runs under the field, but Pendaran keeps its location unknown to everyone except a select few. I am not one of them; I only know it exists. But it is our best chance for entry around the guards. If there are floors below, the tunnel will lead us there quicker than storming the gates."

A sharp sound pierced the night, one he hadn't heard since leaving Elen's cottage. He frowned in the direction from which it had come. "Let us search. If nothing is found in one hour, I will go straight to the front gates."

"That isn't wise," she returned with a heated glare. "I will not have my daughter's mate dead before we get her out. We will search, and we will find the entrance. Let's separate to cover more ground and circle back in fifteen."

"Agreed." Her willingness to believe that Elen was within Hochmead and not dead kept him silent. Once he was alone, a winter wren flitted to a nearby branch. His suspicion proved true when a cloud shimmered and Ms. Hafwen emerged.

She made a sharp squeak as wet frigid air coated tender dragonfly wings. "Let me speak, Cormack. I don't have much time here. I was forbidden from returning."

"I'm grateful you found a way," he said.

"Well," she clipped. "It took me telling the high courts to kiss my feathered arse. There is a reason I should not be involved. I will help you find Elen, no more, and then I must return."

He didn't waste time. "Do you know of a passage from this forest to the manor?"

"Yes. I will—" Her voice broke as shivers dislodged her from the branch. He caught her in his hands as she fell. "I will show you the way." She returned to her winter form in his cupped palms and flitted from branch to branch as he followed her trail.

The forest was different here, tilted at a different angle from the sun, and it grew less wild. A sharp song pierced the air at the end of a trodden trail. He expected a statue, or marker formed of rocks, but was led to a flat surface covered by brambles. Kicking the earth with his boot returned a hollow sound.

Ms. Hafwen shifted back to issue terse instructions. "This is it. I have learned this passage leads to six doors made of iron. The servants whisper of a dragon at the bottom, but I know it is our Elen."

"I can find her from here," he told her then. "You should leave." Black had begun to edge around her wings. "Do you have far to travel?"

"Another gateway has grown nearby." Her voice echoed the sad song of a lute. "It was a gift from a pure heart who is drowning in darkness. Bring her home, Cormack. This is not your greatest battle to come, nor is Pendaran your only enemy. Remember that and prepare."

"Until next spring." He placed a fist over his heart in both farewell and promise. "When we meet again."

"Make it so." A parting chirp followed her words as she returned to the gateway between their worlds, wherever that may be.

A thud warned of a traveler in the tunnel. Cormack crouched in the shadows, watching the earth rise and a small form surface. A blond woman scanned the area. Her scars marked her as a slave, but her fear marked her as a potential guide. He waited until she closed the door before lunging from his hidden position.

"Make one noise and you will die." He had his sword at her throat before she could scream. "I am mate to Elen, daughter of Merin. I know she is in Hochmead. Bring me to her and I will let you live."

Pale in the cold night, her chin lifted as blue eyes met his. Fear bled to courage as she found her voice. "Will you kill Pendaran if I do?"

"Without question," he growled.

THE KEY OPENED HER SHACKLES BUT NOT THE DOOR. Elen leaned her forehead against the cold iron as shudders racked her body in frustration and fear. When the sounds of visitors began, she rushed back to the bed and replaced the shackles, keeping them unlocked and hiding the key within reach. What punishment did Pendaran have planned for him to return so soon? Knowing the first moments of light blinded her, she would wait and let her eyes adjust until he drew near—and then lunge without restraints. Her heart raced as she prepared to fulfill her earlier threat. Never had she thought to use her gift with malevolent intent, but she knew then she would, as she had once for her nephew. To be free, she must.

Fire was the first thing she saw when the door opened. It flashed like a match set to fuel when it entered her room. Someone screamed and dropped the torch, but it blazed high from the floor. The servant woman who had escaped held her arm against her chest as dark silhouettes skirted around the flames.

"Sweet Mother," someone whispered as they drew closer to her. Was that Teyrnon's voice? She couldn't see features; all she could do was squint against the light.

And then a growl came, and it was so pained and familiar she collapsed as tremors became uncontrollable shakes, rendering her hands useless as she tried to claw at her restraints. "Cormack," she cried, but her voice was hoarse and her swollen tongue garbled the words. The tears were uncontainable. "They're unlocked. Help me. *Please . . .*"

His hands shook as well, gentle until the iron was cast aside. With a sob, warm arms enclosed around her, dragging her from the bed as his face buried into her neck. "Elen . . ." His throat was clogged as if it pained him to speak. "I thought I lost you." He repeated the words again and again as he rocked her in his arms. "I thought I lost you."

She felt wetness on her neck. "Never," she whispered as he lifted her. Cradled in his embrace, he carried her past Dylan, Luc and then her mother. She had to blink against the light but knew it was them. Cadan was there as well, his eyes wide in horror as they traveled the state of her condition, lingering on the black bruises that circled her wrists.

Her brothers crowded her and Cormack, wrapping their arms around anywhere they could. Merin even found her hand. It was a group embrace of consoling relief, and she knew she was blessed beyond measure. Her family was her greatest gift. When their gazes lifted, they exchanged similar looks filled with deadly purpose.

"He's dead," Cormack vowed as he carried her out of a hell now kindled with fire. As the final door was breached, she tucked her face into his chest. Still inside the manor but lit by electric lamps and sconces. Like she was looking directly into the sun, the light burned her eyes.

Another tunnel followed, this one rich with life and close to nature. Elen breathed in its richness and savored the taste of pure air. They entered a forest cast in shadows, kinder on her eyes than the other fake light.

"I'm going back in," Cormack told her. "Luc and Cadan are staying here with you until we return."

Denial gripped her chest. She just wanted to go home. "Cormack—"

"It ends tonight," he said, handing her over to Luc's open arms. Before he parted, Cormack cupped her face in his palms. "This is *not* happening again. I'll never survive it a second time. That monster needs to die."

"Then let me come with you," she pleaded.

"No." The finality of his tone defied argument. "You can barely talk, and you couldn't even look into the light of electric lamps. You're not going back to entrapment behind stone walls. Stay here, where I know you're protected and where I know you can defend yourself if necessary."

His logic forced her to accept his decision. "He's weakened," she managed around the thickness of her tongue. "Mae cursed him. He feels my pain."

"Good." A slow smile spread across Merin's face. "We will use that to our advantage."

"Return to us," Luc ordered, settling them both against a tree and not releasing his hold. Cadan removed his jacket and tucked it around her bare legs. She could sense their wolves wanted to return with the others, but they were not willing to leave her alone.

"Lead the way," Cormack said to the servant woman.

She turned toward Elen first, blue eyes shining. "My name," she said, "is Leri."

"Leri," Elen whispered, remembering a childhood friend with the same name and coloring. "Thank you for . . . for everything." They had shared a chamber as children when Merin had been called to serve the Council. Leri had been abused even then. "I remember you. I thought you had been killed."

"The whispers say the same about you," Leri returned. "But I remember you as well." She shook her head. "You never listened even then, always sneaking to the witch's cottage."

The memory that came to mind was not of Mae, but was sad nonetheless. Taliesin had come to their bedchamber to execute the man responsible for Leri's abuse. He'd told them stories as they waited. Leri had huddled on the bed, hiding her face in blankets, while Elen had watched. It had been the first time she'd seen the Serpent of Cernunnos used against a Guardian. Sophie now wielded the weapon with the same precision.

"We are all grateful for your help, Leri." Dylan broke their reunion by waving her forward. "You're welcome to return with us to Rhuddin Village when this is over. But before we can leave, I need you to show us to Pendaran's chamber, if that is indeed where he is."

"I accept your offer, but I will only give you directions," Leri said, gesturing toward the manor flanked with guards. "You are less vulnerable to their swords. If you lose and I'm left within"—she paused to shiver—"it will not be a kind death for me. I am staying here with Elen."

"Come," Merin said, walking ahead. "I know where his

chambers are." No one asked her how, because some answers need not be known.

Elen waited until they disappeared back into the tunnel before crawling out of Luc's lap. "Pendaran not only feels my pain," she said to their questioning looks, "but if affects him much worse." She removed Cadan's jacket and handed it to him. Her hands shook as she tried to untie her covering. Leri helped her remove it, as she'd done many times over the last few weeks.

Luc was already shaking his head; his silver eyes were sharp in the night. "What are you doing?"

"Getting cold. Trust me. I will stay like this as long as I can stand without causing myself true damage." Nature supported her plan, dropping below normal temperature for this time of year. Elen lay nude on the frozen ground, letting the frost coat her skin and seep into her bones. "I can't help them inside the stone walls, but I can help them another way from here." Soon the burning began. Frostbite became dangerous when there was no pain, when blood left extremities to protect central organs. When that happened, she would return to the warmth of her brother's arms and Cadan's coat, but not before.

As the burning became sharp tingles, she looked up to the sky. It was a clear night filled with stars. She could not move to dance, nor was she ready to forgive until Cormack was safe, but Maelorwen's last words wove a path around her heart nonetheless.

And not for the first time, she wondered who Mae's daughter was, and where she might be.

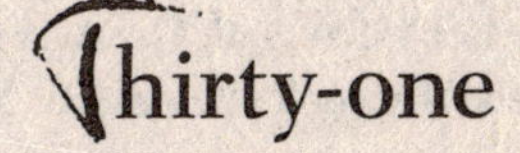

Thirty-one

Cormack had never removed a person's head. He had trained for it, of course, but never executed it in reality. He removed eight on his way to Pendaran's chambers without regret. The first one was a clumsy ordeal, the second one better, and the ones that followed swift and sure. The image of Elen in that stone cell fueled his purpose. Forever imprinted in his mind, with her body tangled in chains, pale and hiding her face from light. Anyone who willingly followed the man responsible deserved to die.

They made it to the top floor without detection, but once the clang of swords echoed through the halls, the guards swarmed to their leader's defense. Dylan fought at the end of the corridor; none had yet to breach his area.

Teyrnon did the same at the top of the stairs. "Get it done," he called. "They've sounded an alarm."

Blood coated his clothes, some of it his, but most of it

theirs, as Cormack approached the guard posted by the door to Pendaran's chambers. The man raised his weapon, readied his stance, leering at Cormack, only to lose his head by Merin's sword. A brown blur and a circular glint marked her strike.

The chamber door opened without resistance, its occupant too arrogant to keep it locked. Or so he'd thought, until Cormack halted in the threshold, pausing to fully grasp what he saw.

The leader of all Guardians lay on his back within the canopy of his ornate bed. Like a fallen monarch in his final hour, he gasped for air. Black rings circled his wrists and bled to violet bruises beyond his elbows. His hands formed disjointed claws like a corpse in ice. Convulsions shook his body. Blood trickled from his mouth, turning his teeth red as he snarled at Merin's approach.

"Did you think you could meddle with a witch's daughter without consequences?" Merin asked. "Or mine?" Her tone lowered with menacing intent. "That is what you did, is it not? Saran never died. You kept her. You kept her until you had a use for her. I can think of no other reason for Mae's betrayal."

She spoke of events that came from a shared history that obviously included Maelorwen's daughter. Dear Gods, was Saran the black Bleidd?

Pendaran kicked out and arched, a wail of rage sending pink spittle into the air.

Undaunted, Merin leaned over him. "True strength comes from what we are willing to sacrifice for the ones we love. You have forgotten our ways, twisted them for your own gains. I always knew it would be your downfall in the end."

A gurgle rose from Pendaran's throat as he fought to

speak. "Not just *my* downfall," he rasped. "Not just *my* end." His body clenched, contorted by chills and fragmented laughter. "Who will control the Guardians? *You?*" Even when facing death, he mocked. "You will make this war unstoppable. There will be no sides, only wolves seeking dominance. The end of our kind has begun."

Cormack had not come here to talk, or to gloat, but to do a job and leave. Pushing Merin aside, he reared his sword high and removed Pendaran's head in one firm stroke. Enforced by adrenaline and resolve, his weapon embedded into the mattress, passing through flesh and bone, and sending up a cloud of feathers coated in blood.

"It's done," he said to her raised eyebrow. Floating feathers gently landed on Pendaran's dislodged head and torso like snow. Finished without preamble, Cormack nodded to the door. "Let's get back to Elen."

"My daughter has chosen well," was all she said. An ancient weapon covered in bleached vines woven into Celtic knots rested beside Pendaran's torso on the bed, along with Cadarn encased in a similar sheath, only formed of metal.

Merin took both from her dead enemy's side.

ELEN FELT THE MOMENT OF PENDARAN'S DEATH LIKE an easing of an unseen weight as the curse unraveled. "He's passed over." His malevolence hovered above, watching her from the spirit world, and then nothing.

"We're not out of here yet." Luc crouched just behind the buffer of trees, pointing toward the horizon. "The guards are blocking the exits, more have flanked the side."

Cadan wrapped his coat around Elen and began to lift her from the ground, but she pushed him away. "Stand back," she warned. "I am about to call my weapon." Now that

Pendaran was dead, there was no reason for her not to heal herself and fight the guards outside the stone walls. Having seen her in action, Cadan didn't argue, nor did her brother.

The forest was strong here, and it knew her from childhood, when she played and laughed and gathered herbs with Mae. She reached out as a woman grown, feeling the old roots gnarled underground, dormant for winter but not dead. Air brushed through their hidden spot, excited to join, sending a sharp wind that whistled through bared branches, waiting patiently to learn her new game.

She called Earth first, the element that had accompanied her from the beginning. The ground began to melt and turn soft as its energy hummed along her skin. Her muscles relaxed and warmed as she thawed along with the grounds around her. It fed her body and began to heal her injuries. Her tongue burned as skin knitted and reformed, and wrists and ankles healed as well. Restored and vibrating from energy, she stood.

Leri tilted her head in curiosity but didn't run, perhaps sensing her best chance of survival was with them.

"Here," Cadan insisted this time, helping her with his jacket and zippering it up the front. "I have a feeling this is going to be a wild ride." The jacket smelled like leather and the musk of a powerful wolf; it fell to mid-thigh.

"I'm going to step out of the forest," she told them. "Stay back or stay close."

Leri stayed back, while Luc and Cadan flanked her sides. They walked in plain view, crossing the field. A guard shouted, and others followed; a few spilled from the gates and began to approach.

"Pendaran is dead. Let our comrades pass or you will follow his fate," she called across the field. "Back away from the doors and let the others leave."

She heard voices rise in argument and dissension, and then several growls as guards shifted. Once in the center of the field, Elen opened her arms wide and raised her face to the sky, offering every emotion she felt for her family inside. Air and Earth gathered in a furious joining much like the one at her cottage, and she let the vortex surge uncontained. In her mind's eye, she pictured it circling the manor. It spread wide, sucking up rocks and debris from the field in its path, encroaching past the gates.

"Remind me never to piss you off," Cadan muttered by her side.

One guard held a torch that blazed high into the wind, fed by its sibling elements. Wind and flames became a destructive shield. Screams followed; shouts and cries of wounded wolves. Finally they withdrew, accosted with a power greater than theirs. Without Pendaran leading his guards, chaos erupted. Many ran, others shouted for everyone to clear out. Servants and guards poured from windows and doors, escaping behind the manor.

Elen held her stance but almost faltered when Cormack staggered through the gate, followed by Dylan. Teyrnon carried Merin in his arms. The unraveling could have gone smoother, she admitted, but it didn't cause the damage she feared. The forest shook as the tumult spread wide.

She held her ground until the wind lessened to a gentle breeze and the fires reduced to smoldering smoke in the dry field. The manor remained standing but scorched black with dust and soot. Earth settled back into its winter slumber. A hundred warriors, maybe less, watched from a distance. Their wounds bled into the field as they headed toward the forest to shift. She sensed that others had fallen to their deaths within and watched as they began to fight each other.

It was time to leave.

A breath rushed out of Luc as if he'd been holding it the whole time. "Where the hell did you learn how to do that?"

"A very dear friend." Elen looked to the manor. "I hope the servants escaped unharmed."

Luc turned her toward the woods. "I would say they knew a better exit." A line of *Hen Was* formed along the trees, drawn together as they watched the fall of their imprisonment.

Teyrnon placed Merin on the ground. Blood ran down her side, and a long slash crossed her face where a guard had tried to remove her head but failed. "This is only the beginning," she warned. "Maelor lives but an hour north. He will be here soon, and then the others will be informed. Pendaran controlled the Council. Even with his twisted ambitions, he always remained loyal to Taliesin. The others will not, and they will ravage each other for control. Without Pendaran's intervention . . ." Her voice trailed off.

"Dark will always balance light," Elen said. "One does not exist without the other."

"You are the balance, my daughter." Merin handed her swords to Elen, lifting her hand to the cropped ends of her hair with thinned lips.

The ancient weapons hummed in Elen's grasp, and she felt the Great Oak answer from the forest, sending temptation down her spine in a whispering caress of otherworldly energy. Nerth and Cadarn; with both their masters departed, they sought another to wield their power. Buds formed on the bleached vines of Nerth, opening like spring's first leaves. Dead wood sloughed off like a serpent's skin as green shoots emerged. Vines wove into a new scabbard made of a living braid. Cadarn, even while encased in iron, reacted to the rebirth of its twin; jewels on its hilt glowed like rainbow embers kissed by the wind.

Elen hadn't orchestrated this healing. No, this power

came from a world beyond her grasp. It arose as a request, not a gift. She was not meant to be the master of these ancient weapons, but perhaps their keeper—and their protector. For a while, at least, until their rightful owners claimed them.

Merin smirked as if witnessing divine proof of her earlier proclamation. She turned to Luc and Dylan. "Protect your territories. I fear there are more dark times ahead." The bleak warning cast a silence among her family. She stripped and shifted in the open field as the men formed a shield. It was a graceful dance of human flesh to golden fur. Soon her howl pierced through the night sky; it was a cry of both victory and sadness.

"We will worry about that another day." Cormack gathered Elen in his arms. "For now, I'm taking you home."

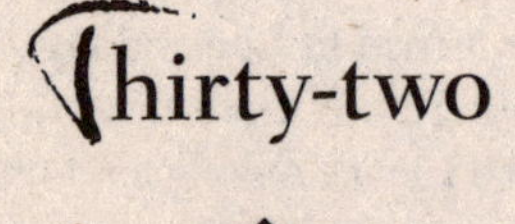

Thirty-two

Every home had a scent, and Elen closed her eyes to savor the dried herbs and pine that marked her cottage. A fire blazed in the central hearth and soup simmered on the stove. More than anything, she needed to be here, with Cormack. It was this image that had sustained her through eight weeks of darkness, and it had come true. There was no greater homecoming than this. Sophie hugged her as soon as she walked through the door, followed by Joshua.

"I need a shower," Elen warned. They had stopped briefly in a hotel before their flight to change and clean up, but she was eight weeks due for a full soaking. Even with Merin's private plane, interactions with the mortal world were necessary. Her mother had stayed behind in their homeland to spread word of Pendaran's fall to the other Council members, and try to ally Bran on her side, along with Maelor—to Teyrnon's raging displeasure. Luc, Cadan and Teyrnon had returned to Avon once they landed. The farewells were a blur, the journey back even more. A part of Elen still felt numb, as if her soul hid in the shadows, unsure if this was just another fantasy.

"Do you think we care?" Sophie shook her head, wiped at her face. Tear-kissed hands lifted to the chopped ends of Elen's hair. Turning, she grabbed a chair from the kitchen table and placed it in the center of the floor. "Sit. I will be right back." She returned with a spray bottle, scissors and a comb.

Such a simple gesture, and Elen felt her throat clog in gratitude. Layers framed her face when Sophie had finished, curling just above her shoulders. It felt light and done by caring hands.

She reached up and tested the feathered ends. "Thank you."

Sophie gave her a tight hug that lingered before letting her go. "We'll leave now and let you have some rest."

Dylan took his wife's cue, nodding to Cormack and then Elen. "I'm holding a meeting on Arwel Passage once the sun sets. All of Rhuddin Village has been ordered to come. I want you both there."

The passage ran from the village to Rhuddin Hall, and was the place where their first battle began this looming war, where Sophie had lost her mother and Elen removed a Guardian's power and gave it to Cormack. Malsum, one of their most loyal guards, had also fallen.

She didn't know what her brother had planned, but she sensed it was a pivotal change in the future of their territory. "We'll be there."

Joshua was the last to leave. "Are you okay, Aunt Elen?"

She would never tire of hearing him call her that. "I will be," she promised. And to ease his concern, she added, "I heard you took care of my animals while I was gone."

"Chickens like spaghetti." He grinned, but it was forced, a buffer for the concern in his dark eyes that had aged more since she'd been gone. "They fight over it like it's a pile of worms."

"He spoiled them," Sophie warned, gesturing her son to the door. "They may never eat feed again."

Once alone, Cormack scooped her in his arms and carried her to the second floor. Needing tactile reassurances, Elen ran her hand over the wooden slats of her walls on her way up the stairs. He set her down in the bathroom and turned on the shower.

"You can stay." She stopped him with her hands on his forearms as he turned to leave.

"I can't." He rested his forehead against hers. "I want you, Elen. I want you more than you can possibly imagine, and I know you need this time—"

"I don't."

"You do." He stepped back. "I'll be waiting for you right here in the hallway."

In the end, she was glad he gave her this privacy without an audience to use facilities and wash private areas with her own hands for the first time in two months. When the warm water beat against her back, she let the tears flow as the events of the day unfolded and she realized she was free, and home, and with the man she loved, and who loved her in return.

She had survived. And Pendaran was dead. She didn't know what the future held, but for today they were safe.

Her fingers were pruny by the time she turned the water off. Everything remained in its place, her moonflower cream, toothbrush and floss. She used them all, then wrapped a soft towel around her torso and opened the door.

Cormack kissed her temple and led her to their bed.

"Dress while I shower," he told her. "Afterward we'll talk, read, sleep . . . or do whatever you want."

"I need you," she whispered. "That's what I want."

His breath hitched. "Elen—"

She sensed his hesitation, *hated* that Pendaran continued to disturb them, even in death. "He didn't touch me."

Guilt caved his shoulders like a physical force. "He imprisoned you in a cave below earth, below nature and everything you need to thrive." Tears welled in his eyes before he looked away to hide them. "He kept you . . ." He shook his head, unable to continue.

"Hush," she soothed. "You will not mention that again. It is done and we will move on." She began to unravel the towel.

He cupped her face in his hands and gave her a lingering kiss that promised security more than seduction. "It is done, but we won't bury our hurts either to fester later. Rest now. I won't be long."

While Cormack showered, Elen dried and brushed her hair, taking note of her pale appearance in the vanity mirror. She was thin but not gaunt, nothing that sun and home wouldn't cure in time. Her eyes and wounds had healed, and so too would her soul.

Heat rose from the first floor through the cast-iron grates, warming her room. Crawling into bed, she waited for her fantasy to be complete and proven true.

ELEN WAS ASLEEP WHEN CORMACK RETURNED. He closed the curtains to block out the day before joining her in their bed. This evening's meeting would come soon enough, and until then he would hold her in whatever capacity she required, even if it was just rest.

Sliding next to her, he wrapped his arm around her waist and snuggled her close. He had cursed the Gods countless times over the last few weeks, and offered his first prayer for her safe return. His heart beat in a rhythm next to hers and lulled him to peace.

He awoke with a start as Elen began to thrash. Her eyes were open but unfocused, back in the nightmare of that cell. "It's me," he said in a calm but firm voice. "You're home, Elen."

"Cormack?" A breath fell from her lungs as her eyes focused. "I thought—"

"I know." He nuzzled his face into the crook of her neck, inhaling the bitter scent of her panic. "You're home," he repeated, "with me."

Her body began to relax back into the mattress. "Love me," she whispered. "*Please.* I need to feel you."

"Always." He wrapped her tight in his arms, resting his chin above her head. "Let me just hold you for now."

"I want more."

"You are so fragile, Elen. I fear—"

"I am immortal," she argued, "and you will not break me."

Need rode him hard. He was but a man, and his mate was asking for the very thing he wanted to give, and still . . .

He found her hand, kissed her palm. "I love you, Elen. I love you more than the air that I breathe." He had professed these same words to her in his mind as a wolf many times over the years, and did so now for her to know how much she meant to him. "If I had to choose between the two, I would choose you."

He took her hand and placed it on his chest, palm down, running it down his stomach, and then lower, letting her feel the evidence of how difficult it was for him to deny such a request. She needed security. He showed her this wasn't a rejection. "But I think we should wait until you've had time to heal and absorb what you've been through."

"I am healed."

"Not here." He placed his palm over her heart. "Not where it matters most. But you will be."

She shuddered, then relaxed, curling deeper into his warmth. "I love you just as much, Cormack, if not more." Whispered words filled with exhaustion. Even breaths fell from her lips seconds later as she fell back to sleep, secure in his love.

Thirty-three

Winter's first snow covered Arwel Passage as every occupant of Rhuddin Village gathered to hear their leader's speech and learn of yesterday's events. The trees in this section grew tall without allowing light to reach the forest floor. It was a canopy of pines that spread to the rivers beyond. Hundreds of faces watched through their vertical trunks, wary and yet curious.

The fact that meetings were usually held in their local church only added to their trepidation.

Elen knew each and every one of them by name, even though they avoided her gaze. Cormack held her hand within his. Porter stood by her other side, and Joshua after him.

Sophie marched with Dylan along the trail, wearing black pants tucked into knee-high boots, a fitted jacket and the serpent whip wrapped around her waist. Dylan wore warrior gear, staking his claim as alpha and Penteulu of this territory.

"I settled into this land before it was proclaimed as the New World," Dylan began with a booming voice to silence the whispers. "I did this for my siblings—and for freedom from the Guardians' leadership. As the years passed, more of you came for sanctuary." He paused, turned toward the right of the trail, and then the left, scanning all the silent faces. "You came to me for protection. I granted it because of my sister's tender heart. Make no mistake . . ." He paused only to look at her. "You are here because of Elen."

A murmur began to spread across the crowd.

"Pendaran is dead," Dylan continued. Ignoring the cheers that were raised, he went on. "He was killed by two hands, one a former Bleidd." He raised his arm toward Cormack. "The other a mother's desperate act to free her daughter." He watched Sophie as he asserted his next words. "Not unlike my mate, who did the same to protect our son from you."

Silence descended in the forest.

"I was reminded recently that power does not make a warrior's heart, that it is what a person is willing to sacrifice to protect their family that proves true strength." He lifted his wife's hand and placed a kiss inside her palm.

Letting her hand drop, Dylan scanned the forest, his stance grave. "You shunned my sister, and I allowed it because of what you all suffered under Guardian rule. I understood you acted on the nature of your wolves. And then you shunned my mate, and still I defended you for the same reason."

"What is he doing?" Elen took a step forward, but Porter and Cormack stopped her with raised arms across her chest.

"It ends today." Dylan waved Alise onto the trail. She

was Rhuddin Village's town secretary, but her official job was to create new identities every eighty years or so, over a normal human life span. Elen helped with fake birth and death records. "Any person who shuns my family from this day forth is not welcome in my territory.

"A war has begun," he continued in the shaken silence. "I heard an hour ago that Rhys has claimed leadership of the Council. Edwyn has mounted a campaign against Isabeau in Minnesota. Our allies are scattered and under the same threat. We don't have enough guards to leave our territories unprotected." Dylan let the gravity of that news trickle among the crowd. "Guardians will come to claim our lands, and we will fight for our territories. No one is safe."

"What about the children?" The shout came from a female voice as other opinions united to be heard.

"We will protect the children as best we can," Dylan proclaimed, "as we always have. If you have no wish to fight—that is okay. There is no shame in survival or wanting peace. But you must leave, because you will not find that here in the days to come. Alise will create new identities for you and provide sufficient funds to live in the mortal world."

"What if we choose to stay," another voice called out. The person who spoke was new, a man with a long scar that ran from his left eye across his nose. Fourteen of Pendaran's former servants had requested sanctuary, including Leri. Sadly, the rest had refused and traveled to Maelor's.

"Then you will be trained to fight," Dylan returned. "You will be given a home and weapons, and you will learn to defend your families from anyone who means you harm." Taking his wife's hand in his, he walked to where Elen and Cormack stood. "Alise's office will be open all week. You have seven days to decide."

At the end of the week, Alise issued eighty-four new

identities to descendants of an immortal race beginning a life hidden among humans, and they were sent away with genuine salutes for success and peace on their new journeys.

Four hundred thirty-seven remained to defend a territory rich with life and freedom, for a leader who demanded only what he and his family had already given.

THE BABY CREATURE WAS NOT HAPPY TO BE TUCKED inside Cormack's jacket. "Be patient, little one, you will like where you're going."

He received a whispered hiss in response as tiny claws punctured his chest. The kitten had come from a litter in the village that needed homes now that their providers had left to start a new life. Born in October, it was eight weeks old, with yellow tiger stripes and golden eyes. Its mother had grown accustomed to the scent of wolves, or perhaps the scent of their kind that didn't hunt felines.

The cottage was dark when he entered, the fire in the grate the only source of light. The kettle that Elen used for mixing tonics rested on the floor, cold and empty. No herbs had bubbled over that fire since she returned. Mae's betrayal continued to poison her joy, and might be the hardest for Elen to overcome. Common activities brought sadness with memories. She tried to bury them and move on, he knew, but this pain bled from the heart and needed time. She had called Avon to make sure Gareth continued to look after Saran, but she wasn't ready to return.

At the moment, she sat in the gathering room with a blanket over her lap. A book rested on the arm of her chair as if she'd been trying to read but couldn't concentrate.

"Hi," Elen said, offering a smile. "Did you get what you needed from the village?"

"I did." Placing his hands on the arms of the chair, he leaned forward and captured her mouth. She sighed into his embrace, her lips parting to deepen the kiss, reaching her arms around his neck to pull him down farther.

The kitten issued an outraged meow.

And Elen froze, her gaze snapping up to his. A spark of wonder entered winter blue eyes and a few shadows were chased away. "What have you done?"

Reaching inside his jacket, he retrieved the bundle of yellow fur and placed it on her lap. "There are other homes she can go to if you don't think she'll fit well with us."

"Oh, Cormack . . ." She scooped the kitten up. It blinked at her with curiosity, turned and settled into the crook of her arm, batting at the strings of the knitted blanket that dangled like potential prey. The kitten pounced a second later, and then rolled back into Elen's lap. Soft laughter filled the air. "I think she'll fit perfectly."

Cormack closed his eyes to that sound, savoring it for the gift it was. "Ms. Hafwen might pox me when she returns."

"I'm not sure if she will return," Elen said.

"I am," he told her, lifting her chin. "She came in winter to help me find you, and she will come again this spring."

And before then he planned to chase away more shadows.

A white blanket of snow covered Emerald Moss Trail. The hound barked with excitement, sensing his presence. Taliesin sat with his back against a birch tree bowing with the weight of winter. The tree reminded him of Elen, who lived at the end of this trail. Ice coated her soul as it did her forest. In time they would thaw and reach for the sun.

"Tucker," Sophie called, chasing the hound that refused to keep her pace.

The crunching snow warned of her and Dylan's approach. He stayed, waiting for the moment they saw him.

"Taliesin?" Dylan offered a hand for him to stand. "Bloody hell, where have you been?"

He shrugged. "Around."

"Are you okay?" Sophie hugged him, as he knew she would. "I've been worried about you." She leaned back, searching his face with welcoming brown eyes. "Are you staying?"

"I can't." He stepped back because her offer was too tempting.

Dylan's chest fell with a weary sigh. "Then why are you here, Taliesin?"

He shrugged. "I'm enjoying the quiet between storms." Taliesin ruffled Tucker's ear and turned to leave. "I'm glad you won this battle, warrior," he called over his shoulder.

"But how many others will we have to fight?" Dylan challenged back.

More than you want to know. But Taliesin kept that premonition to himself. There were other visions of their future that offered a balance to the dark times ahead. One in particular would arrive soon. A babe conceived under summer's first moon would take her first breath in the arms of her aunt.

Not all his predictions ended in darkness.

But they all must be allowed to unfold without his interference. Taliesin needed that reminder now more than ever, and he combed his mind's eye for a diversion before his yearning for family and companionship lured him to stay. Fleeting nights with strangers made his loneliness more acute. As he disappeared into the forest, a vision came, one from the not-so-distant past, oddly enough.

Leri was not the only thief of keys.

With bloodlust and revenge driving his beast, Dylan had crouched along the dark hallways of Castell Avon, unaware of the true identity of the scared *Hen Was* who'd addressed him from the shadows . . .

"YOU ARE DYLAN AP MERIN," MAELORWEN SAID.

"Yes."

A curious glint sharpened her glare. "I see death in your eyes, warrior, but also honor. Is it Math you've come to claim, or our Rosa?"

"Math." Denial, he sensed, would only delay his intent.

A contorted smile turned the unscarred side of her mouth. "Then you are correct . . . this single slave and a locked door won't keep you from your task. But I will have your word you'll not harm our mistress."

"Or what?" he challenged.

"For *what," she corrected, holding up a stainless steel key, an oddity amongst a manufactured illusion of medieval grandeur. "Take who you've come for, warrior, and leave the others be."*

"Agreed."

THE VISION LEFT AS QUICKLY AS IT HAD COME. TALIESIN inhaled a deep breath of crisp air to clear the images that followed. Dylan had learned Maelorwen's identity after Luc had claimed Avon and its recently widowed queen.

When Maelorwen had given Dylan a key, she'd allowed him entrance to Math's private chambers without detection, and in that singular act, she had set the course for their future.

If Dylan or even Mae had known what their actions would bring about, it might have influenced their decisions and caused other outcomes. Rosa would never have sought Luc for help, a vision too clear and unclouded *not* to be a potential reality. Their child would never have been conceived.

No, Taliesin thought with bitterness coating his throat, *I cannot interfere.*

He couldn't be a part of their lives, or anyone else's. Not truly. He couldn't love or be loved, for he would destroy this world to have such a precious thing.

After all, he was the son of the Crone.

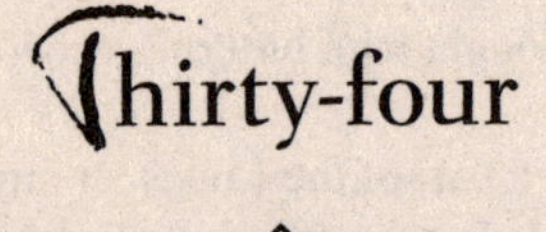

Thirty-four

CORMACK KNEW THE VERY MOMENT WHEN THE MAGIC returned to their cottage and Elen's spirit gleamed with happiness once again. The scent of cinnamon, nutmeg and cider simmered from the iron crock in the hearth. It was the season for holidays and wishes and for yuletide cookies by crackling fires. And his wish came true with the healing of her soul.

She held an armful of fresh holly boughs, and her cheeks glowed from being outdoors. Holding the door wide, she ducked under his arm and he snuck a kiss on her frosty lips. Golden curls framed her face as she laughed, and winter remained outside instead of in her gaze.

Closing the door, he waited while she dumped her holiday greenery on the counter, kicked off her boots and hung her coat and gloves in the entryway. Their baby tiger, officially named Greta, immediately pounced on the shoelaces and tried to climb into the nearest empty boot, her tail slashing as her head disappeared.

"Cormack," Elen gasped in surprise as he scooped her up in his arms, and then just as quickly her body melted into his. "Please tell me you're *finally* taking me to bed."

The emphasis on the *finally* made him chuckle. "I've taken you to bed every night."

"You know what I mean."

"I do," he whispered against her lips, "and I am, because you're ready now."

"I've been ready," she teased, wrapping her arms around his neck. "Now I'm neglected and you're going to have to work for it."

"That sounds like more of a reward than a challenge," he warned. As he walked her up the stairs, her mouth played havoc with his balance, nipping along his chest. Letting her slide down his length, he ordered, "Arms up."

Heat sparked in her gaze as she complied, helping him with her pants and under things until she stood before him nude. Her curves had filled back in, and her breasts tightened under his gaze.

A slow grin tugged at his lips. "Beautiful."

"Arms up," she challenged in return, only she lingered with her mouth on the areas she unclothed. Her breath hitched as he shrugged off his pants, his desire for her revealed in eager lengths. They tumbled together onto the bed, and he rolled so she was on her back.

"Now, I believe you said I needed to work for this." He claimed her mouth, absorbing her soft sighs, and then ran his lips down her neck and to her breasts, taking the tender peaks into his mouth.

"I lied," she gasped, writhing under him. "I'm ready now, Cormack." Her legs opened wider, and she arched up to take him inside her. "I need you."

He slid down, nipping kisses over her stomach. "I'm not sure."

"I'm sure." Her hands clawed at his hair, trying to pull him back up.

He kissed the inside of her knee first, and she stilled. Then he kissed her inner thigh, and a shudder followed.

"Cormack?" Suspicion hung in her voice, but also excitement.

"I want to kiss you here." He ran his fingers along her core, finding the nub of flesh she taught him how to pleasure, circling gently. "May I?"

A whimper fell from her mouth. "Yes." Her legs opened wider to give him better access.

So sweet she was, and soft under his tongue. He repeated the motion he'd learned she liked best, over and over without relent. Her legs began to tremble a moment before she arched, and he felt her release as her body convulsed and she collapsed, sated.

He placed his arms on either side of her and rose, keeping his full weight off of her body. Her eyes fluttered open, filled with contentment, and love, and trust. She was everything to him, his heart and his happiness.

"I am yours and you are mine." He entered slowly, gritting his teeth against the heat that threatened his control.

As always, she enflamed his beast, rocking up when he would be gentle. "I am yours and you are mine."

Her pleasure rose a second time, he felt it with the gripping of her sheath, and like once before, he sensed the rising of her wolf. His beast unfurled, wanting to tie their spirits as he joined their bodies. She felt it too, or he knew she must, because her teeth grazed his neck, nipped once and then sunk into his flesh.

The claiming triggered his release. A growl rumbled from his throat as he arched, spilling his seed in a wave of pleasure so deep his spine ached from its force. Her cries echoed his as she unraveled a second time beneath him.

Afterward he collapsed on his back, dragging her against his side.

Her cheek rested against his heart. "I hope . . ." The wish fell unfinished from her lips.

But he knew what it was, because he knew her. "As do I, but even if we are not blessed with a child, I have you."

And Elen was more than enough to make his life complete.

A WINTER BABE CHOSE TO ARRIVE A WEEK EARLY, IN A blizzard. Cormack drove Elen as soon as they received the call, but traffic moved slowly due to whiteout conditions, and it took almost seven hours to reach New Hampshire. Elen's last memory of Avon had been in Mae's kitchen, but her heart clenched in remembrance instead of pain as she crossed Avon's bridge. Anger poisoned the giver more than the receiver, and she'd finally come to that place of peace.

Almost everyone had gathered in the great hall, offering genuine welcomes. Many of the guards sat on the long table, sipping tankards of ale as they waited for news.

Gareth greeted her with a smile, folding her into a tight hug that lifted her off her feet, a gregarious gesture from a once stoic man. "You have no idea how good it is to see you again."

"The feeling is mutual," she said. "Is Rosa in her chambers?"

When Gareth nodded and set her down, Cormack wove his fingers within hers, claiming a kiss. "I'll walk you up and then wait it out down here with the rest."

He had lingering memories, she realized, and wasn't ready to let her walk about the halls alone. "I would like that."

The door to Rosa's chamber was closed. She knocked before entering, and Cormack nodded a hasty farewell as soon as he glimpsed the scene within. Cadan, Rosa's cousin, sat on the floor with his legs spread wide as Rosa used his chest as a backrest. Her mead-colored hair had been braided back. Sweat-soaked tendrils had escaped and matted to her forehead. Luc crouched between her bent thighs, whispering soothing words as a contraction gripped her stomach. Rosa wasn't a screamer, but her face mottled bright red and a moan fell from her lips as she rode the wave.

Luc's relief when he saw Elen was palpable. Cadan's even more.

"The last hour has been the worst," both men shared at once.

"She won't stay on the bed." Cadan's steady gaze beseeched Elen for help. "Said it's too soft."

Bethan had made a makeshift pallet with blankets and towels over the rug, or Elen assumed it was her because she hovered by the door with more towels in her arms.

"That's fine." Elen spoke to Rosa as she opened her medical bag, which held the items she needed. "I'm going to check where the baby's head is positioned."

Luc scooted back for her to take his place. Children were so rare among their kind. Almost all of Elen's experience came from delivering human babes while in school. Rosa was fully dilated and the baby's head had begun to descend. This was clearly a human birth; a Bleidd was born in a membrane sac like pups.

"Rosa," Elen ordered in a firm but gentle voice, "next contraction I want you to push as hard as you can."

With eyes squeezed shut, she nodded. Luc moved to take his mate's hand, whispering encouragements through her labors. Five contractions later, the head crowned, and Elen shifted the shoulders to ease the babe out on an angle. "More towels," she ordered Bethan, who immediately slipped them under the babe as Elen quickly removed the placenta and cord.

A healthy wail filled the halls of Castell Avon, followed by distant cheers. Her niece's first breath of life resonated with strength and power. Elen placed the babe, her ink-black hair curled around scrunched features, in her parents' arms, and then rested her hand on Luc's shoulder. "She's beautiful."

The two men nodded in agreement. Tears fell without shame.

It was customary for mothers to shift after birth to heal, those who could, but Rosa turned to smile at her cousin instead. "Will you get Audrey so she can meet her new sister?"

There was no shadow dark enough to steal the light of this day.

AT THE END OF THE STORM CAME A QUIET NIGHT IN A white-cloaked valley. Glints of moonlight sparkled on the snow-covered trees as Elen followed two wolves, one brown and the other red. Gareth and Cormack had shifted to run, while she required snowshoes for the journey. She carried a basket of food and woolen blankets. Cormack rarely took the form of his wolf, having been trapped for so long, and she enjoyed watching him run through the snow.

They traveled through a private reserve the residents of Castell Avon had purchased, a secret haven during the time of their former Guardian's reign. It was an hour's hike from the road to reach the makeshift homes built in hills and behind trees. Soon the hidden nook came into view, and Gareth broke away to issue a howl to warn of his approach.

A black wolf padded onto the trail, her legs sinking into the snow; she halted once she noticed Gareth wasn't alone. Her lips peeled back to reveal canines as a low growl emerged.

"Hello," Elen said, making a clumsy approach with the wooden webbed shoes. Her legs burned with exhaustion from the hike. "I believe your name is Saran."

The wolf quieted but watched with wary golden eyes.

"My name is Elen." Gareth and Cormack flanked Elen's sides, sending a message without words that she was a friend. "I was taken by Pendaran and placed in a stone cell below Hochmead." She shared this only to let the Bleidd know she understood her plight. "I believe you know of this place."

The black wolf sat, tilted her head. Her fur glinted like the coat of a mink under shimmering stars. According to Gareth, she refused to be near confined spaces, so he'd showed her this reserve, where she could easily escape but also seek shelter from the cold. He had earned her trust.

Stamping her shoes to pat the snow, Elen unbuckled them from her boots and made her way toward a rock. Clearing off the snow, she sat down and opened the basket. She removed a sandwich filled with roasted beef and gravy and tore it in half. Elen didn't eat much meat, but she took a bite then for Saran's benefit, offering her the other half. "My brother and his mate live on an island not far from here. I believe you know where it is."

Saran snagged the sandwich and chewed while she listened.

"You are welcome in their home." The wolf prepared to bolt; Elen could see it in her stance and the way her eyes shifted to the shadows within the trees. "My brother was once a Bleidd, like you. His name is Luc, but the Guardians call him the Beast of Merin."

A glint of recognition entered her gaze. Malicious rumors always skulked among their kind, and it seemed even into crevices far below the earth.

"Luc will be kind to you. He will welcome you into his home, as will his mate. And I can assure you they don't judge children by the actions of their parents." It had been some time since Elen called her gift, but she did so then. Reaching her senses into the dormant forest, she felt for life under the snow. It began to melt, and Saran backed away but didn't run. Soon moss appeared, yellow and bleached until Elen fed it with life. A daisy seed took root, a green stem emerged and unfurled, followed by a bud and white petals.

Plucking the flower, Elen held it out to Saran. "Your mother loved you very much. She would want you to go."

The wolf paused, her gaze searching. She wanted to trust, but she had more years of shadows to chase away. However, she was Maelorwen's daughter and proved it by stepping forward to nuzzle Elen's hand.

The air between them shimmered with energy as soon as they touched. Elen sucked in her breath. The power that rose from the black wolf held two signatures, one of an enchantress and the other of a shifter. Elen curled her hands into the dark fur and tested the dormant energy underneath. This needed no taking of a life but a trigger to ignite what was already there.

Saran blinked with surprise but not fear, and a knowing that came from her mother's bloodline.

"Do you want this?" Elen asked to be sure.

Fire blazed in golden eyes, followed by a sharp nod.

Elen fed her a single spark of energy and an enchantress emerged. Dark mahogany hair fell down pale shoulders after her shift. She remained on all fours, her face forward with an expression of awe and uncertainty.

Gareth shifted as well. For what purpose, Elen wasn't sure. Nude, and obviously besotted, he reached into the basket and grabbed a wool blanket he had packed earlier. Wrapping it around Saran's form, he lifted her in his arms. His possessive stance removed all doubts of his intentions.

Having already earned her trust, Saran frowned as if trying to find a place for unfamiliar limbs, giving them more attention than the man holding her. Like Cormack, she seemed fascinated with her hands.

"Are you planning to carry her out like that, Gareth?" Elen couldn't help but tease.

Silver eyes narrowed. "If I have to. She's not staying here." He looked down at Saran's upturned face in an expression similar to Cormack's when Ms. Hafwen had revealed herself. Gobsmacked, to be sure. So much so, that he leaned down and placed a tender kiss on her lips.

And received a slap across his face. Well, it was more of a swat from a clawed hand, and an affronted snarl.

Elen laughed at Gareth's bemused expression. "May you dream of first kisses until the sun chases away the moon."

Saran stilled when she heard the words, looking to Elen with wide eyes. Yes, her mother had said them to her too.

Curling her hand in Cormack's fur, Elen lifted her face to the sky and hoped that Maelorwen was watching. In the summer, she would dance under the stars, but for now she whispered her name . . .

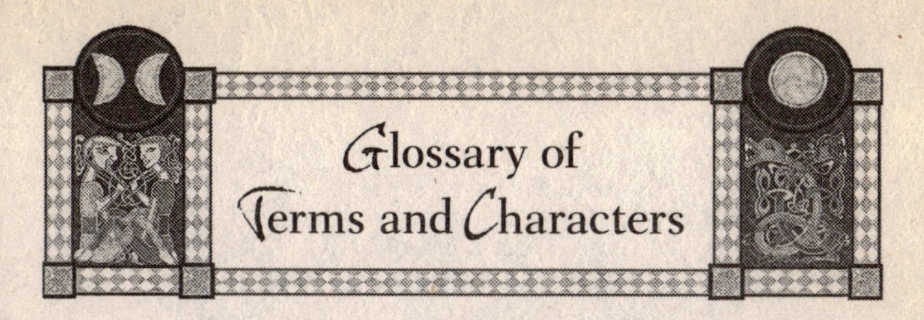

Glossary of Terms and Characters

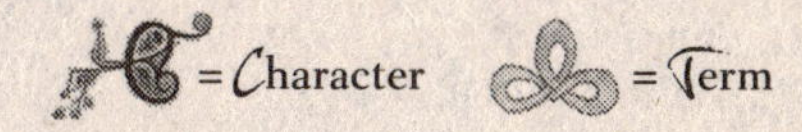

AERON

Former Walker; once a messenger to Ceridwen in the Otherworld; has lost the ability to walk between worlds.

ANNWFN; OTHERWORLD; LAND OF FAERY

Homeland of the Welsh Celtic deities, similar to *sídh* of Irish mythology; where the *Tuatha Dé Danann* reside; the Land of Faery and magical beings.

AUDREY (AD 2009–)

Child who can shift into a wolf; parents were killed while in hiding to protect her from the Guardians; assigned as Taliesin's only Walker.

***BEDDESTYR*; WALKER**

Messenger to Ceridwen in the Otherworld.

BLEIDD; WOLF

A Guardian descendant born or trapped in wolf form who cannot change to human; human intelligence exists within the wolf.

BRAN

Original Guardian; member of the Council of Ceridwen.

BRIALLEN

Guardian who resides in Wales with her husband; wife of Maelor; mate of Teyrnon.

CADAN

Son of Neira; cousin of Rosa; Math's former lover.

CASTELL AVON; RIVER CASTLE

A castle on the island of Avon; located in the White Mountains of New Hampshire; home of Luc and Rosa.

Ceridwen; Celtic Goddess

Welsh Celtic goddess, worshiped by ancient Celts as the great sow goddess; though less recognized, Ceridwen was also revered as the goddess of wolves; known to brew potions of transformation and knowledge; Earth Mother of Darkness and Light; master of animal transformation; birth mother of Taliesin.

Cernunnos; Celtic God

Welsh Celtic Lord of Animals; worshiped by ancient Celts as the Great Hunter; commonly depicted in Celtic artifacts with horned animals, such as the horned snake of Celtic tradition, and the stag; honored by ancient Celts as the leader of the Wild Hunt, where spirits of the dead were carried to the Otherworld.

Cormack

Brother of Siân and Taran; born in wolf form without the ability to transform to human; human intelligence exists within the wolf; given the power to shift by Elen in the first battle of the Dissenters' War against the Guardians.

Council of Ceridwen; governing assembly of Original Guardians

A self-proclaimed governing body compiled of eight surviving Original Guardians.

Council members in alphabetical order: Bran, Edwyn, Gweir, Maelor, Neira, Pendaran, Rhys, William.

Cymru; Wales

Homeland of the Original Guardians.

Daron

Leader of the Ontario territory; views the Original Guardians with disdain.

Dewisedig; chosen human

A human mate of a Guardian or Guardian descendant whose offspring can transform into a wolf.

***Drwgddyddwg*; Evil Bringer**

A derogatory description of Guardian descendants born in human form without the ability to transform into a wolf. The name was created by Original Guardians, fearful of their loss of power.

DRYSTAN

Leader of the Blue Ridge Highland territory of Virginia; views the Original Guardians with disdain.

DYLAN (AD 329–)

The alpha wolf and leader of the Katahdin territory; husband and mate of Sophie; father of Joshua; eldest brother of Luc and Elen; son of Merin.

EDWYN

Original Guardian; member of the Council of Ceridwen.

ELEN (AD 331–)

The healer of the Katahdin territory; sister of Dylan and Luc; daughter of Merin; cannot shift into a wolf but can manipulate nature.

FINNBARR (AD 1682–)

Also known as Porter; head of home security of Rhuddin Hall of the Katahdin territory; has a tattoo of a Celtic cross in honor of his Irish mother; cannot transform into a wolf.

GARETH

Porter of Castell Avon.

GAWAIN

Former Walker; once a messenger to Ceridwen in the Otherworld; has lost the ability to walk between worlds.

***GWARCHODWYR*; GUARDIAN**

Descendants of Original Guardians who follow the command of the Council of Ceridwen.

***GWARCHODWYR UNFED*; GUARDIAN, FIRST IN ORDER; THE ORIGINALS**

An Original Celtic warrior appointed by Ceridwen to protect her son Taliesin; taught how to draw energy from the earth to transform into wolves; served Taliesin as a child; ages at a very slow rate. The oldest surviving Original Guardian was born 95 BC. There were forty-eight Original Guardians; only nine remain.

GWEIR

Original Guardian; member of the Council of Ceridwen.

Hafwen; Ms. Hafwen

A pixie sent to earth to teach Elen how to use her gift; until trust is granted, the viewer will see her only as a winter wren.

***Hen Was*; old servant**

Slaves to the Original Guardians and the Council; Guardian descendants born without the ability to transform into a wolf; age at the same slow rate of an Original Guardian.

Isabeau

Leader of the forest region of Minnesota; family was tortured and killed in the house of Rhun while serving the Original Guardians.

Joshua (AD 1995–)

Son of Dylan and Sophie.

Kalem

Leader of Alaskan territory; views the Original Guardians with disdain.

Koko (AD 1868–AD 1946)

Luc's deceased wife.

LLARA

One of four leaders who occupy the territories of Russia; views the Original Guardians with disdain.

LUC (AD 342–)

Youngest brother of Dylan and Elen; son of Merin; husband of Rosa; banished at birth by his mother for being born in wolf form; raised by Dylan; known as the Beast of Merin.

LYDIA

Daughter of Enid; sister of Sulwen; works in the kitchens of Rhuddin Hall; cannot transform into a wolf.

THE MABINOGION

Also referred to as *The Mabinogi*; a collection of Celtic folklore from medieval Welsh manuscripts, including *The White Book of Rhydderch* and *The Red Book of Hergest*. The first translation of *The Mabinogion* into English was by Lady Charlotte Guest in the mid-nineteenth century.

Madoc

Leader of the mountain regions of Montana; captained the ship that brought Luc, Elen and Dylan to the New World; views the Original Guardians with disdain.

Maelor

Original Guardian; member of the Council of Ceridwen; husband of Briallen.

Maelorwen

Also known as Mae; healer who lived in the hills when Dylan and Elen were children; taught Elen the medicinal uses of plants; the first Guardian descendant born without the ability to shift; tortured by the Guardians; currently resides in Castell Avon.

Math (62 BC–AD 2013)

An Original Guardian; former leader of the White Mountains territory of New Hampshire; former husband of Rosa; loyal to the Council of Ceridwen; executed by Dylan.

MELISSA

Niece of Cormack; daughter of Taran and Edward; mother was killed in the first battle of the Dissenters' War against the Guardians; five years old.

MERIN

An Original Guardian; mother of Dylan, Elen and Luc.

MORWYN

Former Walker; once a messenger to Ceridwen in the Otherworld; has lost the ability to walk between worlds.

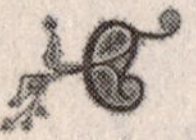

NEIRA

Original Guardian; member of the Council of Ceridwen; mother of Cadan; aunt of Rosa.

NESIEN

Former Walker; once a messenger to Ceridwen in the Otherworld; has lost the ability to walk between worlds.

Nia

Leader of the northern New York territory; views the Original Guardians with disdain.

Pendaran

Original Guardian; head of the Council of Ceridwen.

***Penteulu*; head of family**

Leader of a territory; alpha wolf.

Porter; respected servant

Head of home security.

Rhuddin; heart of timber

The name Dylan chose for his territory, located around Katahdin, the highest mountain peak in Maine; the northern end of the Appalachian Trail.

Rhun (58 BC–AD 2013)

An Original Guardian; killed by Sophie in the first battle of the Dissenters' War against the Guardians.

RHYS

Original Guardian; member of the Council of Ceridwen.

ROSA (AD 1702–)

Widow of Math; wife of Luc; leader of the White Mountains territory of New Hampshire; parents were killed while protecting Rosa from the Council of Ceridwen.

SERPENT OF CERNUNNOS

A flexible sword in the shape of Cernunnos's horned snake, forged in the Otherworld as a gift for Taliesin. The wearer of the Serpent is given a heightened perception of their surroundings and a connection to beings of the Otherworld.

SIÂN

Dylan's ex-lover; eldest sister of Taran and Cormack; threatened a pregnant Sophie in the woods the night Sophie left Dylan; the woman who gave Sophie her scars; killed by Math.

SIN

See Taliesin.

SOPHIE (AD 1975–)

Wife and mate of Dylan; mother of Joshua; daughter of Francine; the first human to give birth to a shifter in more than three hundred years; her aging process has slowed since carrying Dylan's child.

SULWEN

Daughter of Enid; sister of Lydia; works in the kitchens of Rhuddin Hall; cannot transform into a wolf.

TALIESIN; "SIN" (42 BC–)

Son of Ceridwen; possesses powers of transformation and prophecy; Sophie's former employer. Taliesin spent much of the medieval ages intoxicated; therefore, it was during this time that many stories of his antics were documented by humans. Though the Original Guardians were assigned by his birth mother as protectors, Taliesin views most of them with disdain.

TARAN

Deceased sister of Siân and Cormack; mother of Melissa; killed by Rhun in the first battle of the Dissenters' War against the Guardians.

TEYRNON

First-in-command of Luc's guard; mate of Briallen; Guardian descendant with the ability to shift; father was human of Norse descent; homestead destroyed by the Guardians in the late 1600s for daring to live outside their rules.

TREE OF HOPE

A gateway between earth and the Otherworld.

VALE

Also called Glowing Vale and *Ystrad Gloyw*; an ethereal dreamlike world between earth and the Otherworld.

WILLIAM; GWILYM

Original Guardian; member of the Council of Ceridwen.

WULFLING

Wulflings begin as infant shifters, often deserted by the death of their parents while in hiding; left to fend for themselves; without the company of humans, they are unable to learn by example; instincts of their wolves often become more dominant than their humanity.